# THE BILLIONAIRE'S SECRET CRUSH

## BILLIONAIRE NEXT DOOR

### ELIZABETH MADDREY

# 1

## CODY

"You're sure you don't mind taking this on?"

I sat behind my desk at the Ballentine Coalition and stared at my boss. Jackson Trent wasn't known for double-checking that someone was okay with a project he was handing out.

I cleared my throat. "I guess. I mean, I've never been in charge of something like this before, but I think I can handle it."

"I wouldn't have asked you to do it if I didn't believe that was the case." Jackson grinned as he stood. "And you never know, you might get something unexpected out of it. I certainly did."

My eyebrows lifted. "I don't follow?"

"Oh. I thought everyone knew I met my wife when I hired her to cater a fundraiser. We did not exactly hit it off right away." He shrugged, and a smile played at the corners of his lips. "Worked out in the end."

"Yes, sir."

I wasn't sure exactly what other reply was appropriate. Jackson was my boss. He'd given me a task. Sure, it sounded like I could have objected—maybe—but then what? It wasn't as if the fundraiser didn't need to happen.

"All right. Good luck. If you need anything or have questions, feel free to ask. There's a folder on the shared drive that has all the information from prior years. It's never a bad idea to familiarize yourself with those. But I know Mr. Ballentine would like this year to be different."

I nodded.

Jackson left my office.

I sagged back into my chair. I had absolutely zero interest in planning and running a Christmas fundraiser, but the woman who'd served as our event coordinator for longer than I'd been working at Ballentine had been diagnosed with stage three breast cancer. Obviously, she needed to take time off and focus on treatment. I didn't disagree with that at all.

But why me?

Noah appeared in my doorway. "Hey. What was that about?"

I gestured for him to come in. "Close the door."

"Ooh." Noah waggled his eyebrows as he did, then he plopped into the chair Jackson had just vacated. "Spill."

"I'm in charge of the Christmas fundraiser."

"Oof. I don't know if that's a compliment or punishment."

I chuckled. Leave it to Noah to sum it up. "Exactly. And with basically three months to get it organized, I'm leaning a little toward the latter. Even though I have no idea what I might have done to warrant it."

Noah shook his head. "Nah, man. Everyone knows you're on track for the next promotion. This is probably the final test—making sure you can handle the glad-handing portion of the job."

I frowned. I wasn't sure who "everyone" was, but I wasn't going to ask Noah. I disagreed though. "I don't think there are any foregone conclusions here."

"Pfft. Please. The rest of us are good employees, it's true, but you've got the knack. And the heart. You really love what you do."

"You don't?"

I had a hard time believing that. Noah was good at his job. Better, in many ways, than me. He actually enjoyed taking potential donors out to lunch and explaining the various things we did here at Ballentine. What Mr. Ballentine had started as a lobbying organization had morphed over the years into a multifaceted Christian nonprofit organization. Yes, we still had lobbying at our core—but we also provided aid and disaster relief internationally either as part of Ballentine or in collaboration with other Christian organizations.

"I do. Just I'm also able to leave it at the door, you know? As much as I enjoy the fact that I have something to do for forty hours a week, it wouldn't be the end of the world if that changed."

I nodded slowly. I sort of understood that. In a roundabout way, I agreed. But only because of my billionaire status, thanks to a friend group that roped me into a stock market scheme a little over a year ago. Having money in the bank—and in the market—was a cushion that I didn't take for granted. I didn't *have* to work. Noah ought to understand, since it was the same for him.

"You're not quitting and going out on your own, are you?"

"No way." Noah gave his head an emphatic shake. "I can't even decide where to move. What on earth would I do if I decided to start my own business?"

Noah's political science degree had a limited number of useful applications in the real world. A lobbying organization was definitely one of the better options. "You could go to law school."

"Ugh. No. I'll leave the lawyering to Tristan, thank you very much. I like it here. I like the level I'm at here. I believe in what

I'm doing and I have time for myself. It's basically ideal. But you, my friend, are definitely on track to be second in command to Jackson when he takes over for Mr. Ballentine. Provided you don't screw up. So, if you need help with this fundraiser, hit me up. I'll do what I can." Noah grinned as he stood.

"You might regret those words." I could pretty much guarantee I'd be taking him up on the offer. Maybe between the two of us we'd be able to do the company proud. "You really aren't finding a place to buy?"

Noah shrugged. "So far the leasing office doesn't mind me being month-to-month. I guess I can step up the search if it looks like that's going to change. Tristan keeps saying one of the condos in his building is supposed to come free, but so far it hasn't happened. And at this point? Since I don't know exactly what I want anyway? I'm content to wait and see."

Noah had always been pretty laid back. It had made him a great roommate when we lived together. It probably made him a great employee, too. "All right. If you're happy, I'm happy. You know I have extra bedrooms in my townhouse."

"I do. But I kind of like having my own space."

I nodded. I did, too. Even as great a roommate as Noah had been, there was something pleasant about rattling around after work, knowing I wasn't accidentally going to annoy someone if I decided to put music on. "Fair enough. December fifteenth. Mark your calendar."

"Already done. You should probably send out save-the-dates soon though, man. December fills up."

My jaw dropped at Noah's parting shot. Save-the-dates? Hadn't those gone out already? The actual invites needed to be in the mail by...I paused and opened up a calendar on my computer monitor so I could count backward. The end of October? I felt like somewhere in all the information Jackson had spouted when he'd brought me the assignment, he'd mentioned eight weeks out for the invites.

I opened a new tab on my browser and searched "when should I send save-the-dates?" The results made me close my eyes and count to ten. Four to six months before? So, basically, last month or, even better, June.

Well, that ship sailed. Probably.

I moved to the shared drive and found the folder for the fundraisers. I blew out a breath. At least there was a folder for this year already. Maybe some work had been done before the whole cancer thing, and I wasn't starting from scratch?

I clicked to open the folder and stared at the single document labeled "Timeline." Well, let's see what the expert recommended. I opened the document, read the first line, and started to laugh. If there was a hysterical edge to it, it couldn't be helped. The timeline was from last year.

It was okay. It was all right. I could adjust it to this year. Of course, I couldn't help but see all the items labeled for June, July, and August. All of which were far in the rearview mirror. Today was the first day of September.

Which meant I needed to kick it into high gear.

Save-the-dates. Did I need a venue first? I scanned the lists. Yeah, there it was. One of the first things. I closed my eyes and tried to remember all the various places we'd had this fundraiser in the past few years. Mostly hotels in DC. They were the typical, ritzy places to hobnob.

There was something to be said for inside. It was going to be December, after all. The weather around here was unpredictable. Some years, December could be in the fifties; others, freezing or below. And there was no way to know.

The safe choice would be that hotel ballroom. Maybe the St. Regis. Or any of the boutique hotels downtown. I opened a new browser tab and started making calls.

"WHAT ARE YOU DOING HERE?"

I laughed as Megan looked down at her watch then back up at me. "Is that how you greet all your customers?"

Her face blazed red. "Of course not. I'm just not used to seeing you here unless you're with the guys. The guys who are, at this very moment, making their way to poker night."

"At Tristan's. Yeah, I know. I thought I'd dash in and get a book first. If that's okay with you? This is a bookstore. Right?"

Megan's eyebrows lifted. I didn't let myself focus on how pretty she was. That way lay madness. "It is. Well done."

I grinned, ignoring the sarcasm dripping off her words. I wasn't what anyone would call a book aficionado. "Hey. I read."

"Uh-huh. Tell me more." Megan leaned forward. "What was the last book you read?"

I cleared my throat and looked away. There'd been talk of reading a Christian living book and expanding our guy time to include more serious discipleship instead of just fellowship and prayer. But we hadn't actually pulled the trigger on anything officially yet.

"Right. That's what I thought." Megan chuckled. "So. What book do you need?"

"Ugh. Know-it-all isn't the best look for you."

"But I do it so well." She batted her eyelashes.

I actually felt my mouth water. That would just not do. I swallowed. "I need an event planning book."

"Excuse me?"

I pinned her with a glare. "You heard me."

"Sure." She stepped around the counter to stand beside me before gesturing to the left. "Follow me."

"Thanks." I fell into step beside her as we made our way through the bookshelves. The brightly colored, glossy covers of the paperbacks under the various genre headings seemed to mock me. Was it really so bad not to be a reader? It wasn't like I couldn't read. I just preferred to watch actors make the books come alive. Was that so wrong?

"What kind of event are we planning? Wedding?"

"Har. Har. Har." I jabbed my elbow into her side.

"Ow. What? Come on, you have to know I'd wonder. It's not as if you're known for putting on soirees."

"Soirees." I rolled the word around in my mouth. "Definitely planning one of those."

Megan stopped in front of a bookcase on the far side of the store and pointed to the bottom shelf. "It probably is ninety percent wedding planning. So if that's not what you're looking for, I might have to order something for you."

I squatted down and eyed the titles. Nightmare. She wasn't kidding about them being mostly wedding planning books. Bright pink, flower-covered wedding planning books. I couldn't buy one of them, just on principle.

My heart sank.

I pushed myself back up and blew out a breath. "Well. It was worth a shot."

"Sorry. I don't get a lot of people coming in for this kind of thing. But I can order you whatever you need. Did you have a title in mind?"

I shook my head. "I don't even know what I should look for. They dumped the Christmas gala on me."

"So work with whoever's doing this year and have them show you the ropes. Learning on the job's probably the best bet anyway. Right?"

My stomach twisted. "That's a great idea. Other than the part where the one I'm in charge of *is* for this year."

Megan's mouth formed an O.

I caught myself staring, just a little too long, at her perfect, pink lips.

"Well then." She tipped her head to the side. "This sounds like a story I need to hear."

I shrugged. "That's it. Basically. Other than the fact that the woman who usually does our fundraising hadn't done any of the legwork at all. And I spent too much time on the phone with hotels today, only to find out that their ballrooms book up for the Christmas season in March. Or earlier."

Megan reached out and rubbed my arm. I ignored the electricity zipping up to my shoulder from her touch. That wasn't what she was going for. I was one of her many honorary big brothers. Period.

"You want some help?" Megan met my gaze. "I'm not a professional. Not by a long shot. But I know how to search the Internet with the best of them. And I have a lot of free time to do that during the day. I don't even mind making phone calls."

I clung to her words like a lifeline. "Are you serious?"

She shrugged. "Sure. It actually sounds fun."

"All right. Thanks." I blew out a breath. I hadn't gotten a book, but having Megan on board was better. For the gala, at least.

I wasn't sure it was going to be the best thing for my heart.

## 2

## MEGAN

I unlocked the bookstore door, stepped inside, and relocked it behind me before reaching for the lights. Most Saturdays I made it just in time to get set up before opening, but not today. Cody would be here in about fifteen minutes to go over all the details for this fundraising gala. I wasn't convinced we could pull it off with only three months to plan, but I was willing to give it a shot.

Especially if it would help Cody.

I wouldn't say I had a crush on him. He was one of my brother's good friends—basically another older brother when the chips were down—so of course I'd do what I could to help.

I'd do it for any of the guys, if they asked me.

But it didn't hurt that, of the five who weren't actually my brother, Cody was the best looking of the lot. In my mind, at least.

Hey, a girl had to have her dreams.

I hurried through the opening procedures. I wanted to make sure I was ready to go, so if things with Cody went long, I could just unlock the front door and we could keep working. As a rule, Saturday mornings weren't super busy.

There weren't any times I'd say the store *was* super busy.

I pushed the constant worry about profit margins and operating expenses back to the far recesses of my brain. Worrying didn't fix things. *Can any one of you by worrying add a single hour to your life?* If I had to repeat Matthew six verse twenty-seven multiple times a day, then so be it.

But it might not be a bad idea to figure out some strategies to increase revenue. Because the way things were going right now, I wasn't going to be able to justify keeping the lights on into the new year.

And then what?

I could always go back to social work.

My stomach twisted at the thought, and I shoved it away, too.

If nothing else, being an entrepreneur had upped my denial game to new heights.

The knock on the door made me look up from the register. I grinned at Cody and hurried over to unlock the deadbolt and let him in.

"Right on time."

"I do try." He grinned and thrust a to-go cup from the café down the street at me. "You like the vanilla cold brew, right?"

I took the cup. "I do. How'd you know?"

"Austin must've mentioned it." He shrugged and glanced over his shoulder at the door. "Should we lock that?"

"Yeah." I moved around him to do so. "Though I'm not expecting hordes of book marauders anytime in the near future."

He chuckled. "Good thing. I'm not sure how you defeat that kind of enemy."

"Me either." I pointed to the sitting area across the store. "Why don't we sit over there? It's more comfortable."

"All right." Cody sipped from his cup and headed over. He settled on the sofa.

I bit my lip. Would it be weird to sit beside him? I could take one of the arm chairs. But what if we needed to look at something together? Annoyed at myself, I sat beside him. "Give me the scoop. Last night you were pretty light on details."

He sighed and raked a hand through his hair. "I don't have a lot of details. We do two big fundraisers each year. The July Fourth barbecue and the Christmas gala. We used to have someone whose entire job was donor relations and development. These events fell firmly into her purview. But she's gone and from what I can tell, she didn't do anything on the Christmas event at all."

"Okay. Maybe this is a good thing."

"How? Because I've got just over three months to get this planned and I don't really think that's enough. So I'd love to see whatever silver lining you've spotted."

I fought a grin. He sounded so dejected. "You get to make this whatever you want. No restrictions. So this is a chance to think outside the box and make it a memorable event, not just another black-tie dinner and dance."

He rubbed the back of his neck. "What if they expect a black-tie dinner and dance? If I don't give them that, then what? I can't afford to go way outside the box and make it so we can't fund all our programs."

I nodded. "Fair. Still. There's gotta be some middle ground. You called hotels yesterday, right? Did you find a venue?"

Cody shook his head. "Everyone's booked up."

"I have some ideas. I did a little web searching last night."

His eyebrows lifted.

It was all the encouragement I needed. I dragged my phone out of my back pocket and opened my browser. "Okay. So my first thought was the arboretum. They have these amazing columns from the first supreme court building. How cool would it be to set up tables there? Maybe set aside some space on the lawn for dancing?"

Cody took my phone and zoomed the image. He cocked his head to the side as he scrolled the page. "It's all outside?"

I nodded.

He handed the phone back. "In December."

"Yeah. That's a potential issue. We could rent heaters and maybe use a tent for the dancing..." I trailed off as I studied his expression. "Or not. Okay. That's fine. Nothing outside."

"I'm sorry. I think it's great. And maybe it's worth suggesting for the summer event—which I'm seriously hoping I'm not going to be in charge of—but I just can't see risking it for December."

"All right." I closed that tab and moved to the next one. "The Torpedo Factory."

His eyebrows lifted, and he reached for the phone. "Just down by the river here in Old Town?"

I nodded. "That's the one."

"They do events there? It's just artist stuff."

I snickered. Artist stuff was exactly how I imagined Cody would classify the gallery and studio space that took up the historic building. "They do events there, yes. The galleries and studios are closed, but you can still see the window displays. It's a lovely space. I know several high schools use it for prom every year. Pretty sure it holds around three hundred easily."

"Hmm. If the weather was nice, people could go outside and see the river."

I nodded. "And if it's not nice, the venue is large enough for people to be reasonably spread out so they can mix and mingle. Even if they don't want to dance."

"I like it." Cody's forehead scrunched up.

"What?"

"Just trying to think of any negatives."

I sipped my coffee and tried to think. "It's not in DC. Do you think that matters?"

"Nah. We have the summer one all over the place. They did it at Mount Vernon two years ago. As long as we're in the metro area, no one seems to care." Cody shot me a hopeful look. "I don't suppose you know if they're available still?"

"I don't. I didn't want to reach out to anyone before you were sure about it." I held my hand out for my phone. "Let's give them a call. It's Saturday, so we might not get an answer until Monday, but it's worth a try."

"Okay. I can do it. I've got the spiel down after yesterday."

I laughed. "All right. While you do that, I'm going to go grab a notepad."

I set my coffee on the floor by my chair and stood. I watched as Cody navigated to the Torpedo Factory web page, and then, content that he had it under control, made my way back to my office. I'd spent a little time last night writing down ideas for the invites after I got home from the bookstore and the weekly girls' night that took place here on Fridays while the guys played poker.

I put my hands on my hips and frowned at my desk. Where had I put the notebook? With a sigh, I started opening drawers. I'd brought it this morning, hadn't I?

I closed my eyes and visualized myself getting ready. I'd definitely put the notebook in my purse. And when I got here, I'd pulled it out and...oh! I went to the counter up front and looked on the shelf under the register. There it was.

I snagged it and strode back to the seats.

Cody was just putting his phone down.

"Well?"

"Left a message. But her recording said she usually checks in over the weekends, so I gave her the dates and everything. We'll go from there. Hopefully, she can get back to me and I can get on with the save-the-dates and all that."

"Why wait?"

His eyebrows lifted. "I mean, I don't have a venue yet?"

"Sure. But a save-the-date is literally asking someone to put the event on the calendar. We can tell them the date and time and what it is and say something like details and invitation to follow. But you need to get on people's December calendars yesterday."

Cody blew out a breath. "You're right about that. You really think people won't be confused when there's no venue?"

I shook my head. I couldn't promise, obviously, but the last save-the-date I'd gotten was for a wedding and it had just had the date and registry information on it. "Even if they are? I still think it's better to get on their calendars now and fill in the details the third week of October. That'll give them eight weeks to respond, which should be plenty."

"All right." He nodded once. "I'll bow to your superior knowledge."

I laughed. "I don't know about superior knowledge. I just rock a web browser. Speaking of which, you wanna look at custom printing sites now?"

Cody groaned and his head fell back. "I don't. I really, really don't."

"Come on. It'll be fun." I nudged him with my elbow, then promptly reminded myself that he was one of many honorary brothers. He didn't think of me as a woman. And I definitely didn't think of him as a man. "It'll be good practice for when you get married."

"Oh, yes. It's important to practice for that eventuality that may never come. Good thinking." Cody shook his head and pointed at my phone. "Show me what you think is best."

"Well…" I drew out the word. "I have a few favorites. It's true.

But since we're hoping to go with the Torpedo Factory for the venue, I thought this one would go well."

I tapped on my phone a moment as I navigated through the saved links until I landed on the one that I wanted. I handed it to Cody.

"Hmm. It looks shiny."

"And wavy. Like a river, right? And the sort of hints of skyline and stars?" I bit my lip. Maybe it was too much. "Of course, you could go with a more standard, heavyweight cream, maybe with a gold accent. I have a couple of those saved if you think traditional is the way to go."

"No. I like this. It's different. And you're right, it'd go well with the location." He looked up from my phone and grinned at me. "What are the options?"

I took my phone back and went back to the product page. "Okay. I think for the save-the-date, you want this postcard style. You still put it in an envelope, mind you, but it's just a flat card. Then when we get to invites and responses, I like the folded version and separate card with smaller envelope for replies. But you should also make a way for people to respond online."

"Online? When we're sending them a card?"

"Trust me. Some people are going to want to respond that way. And you need to figure out your response deadline when you get your catering figured out. Because they're going to need final numbers before the day of. Probably before the week of."

Cody nodded, but he looked a little like a trapped animal.

"Hey. It's going to be okay. Once you get the big things handled, it's going to be a lot smoother."

"Yeah. I get that. I'm just worried about getting those big things taken care of." He ran a hand through his hair. "So how do we order and what's supposed to go on them?"

"Seriously, Cody?" I crossed my arms. "You're not helpless. You've been attending these things for what, five years?"

"I know that. But you act like I've ever paid attention to the mailers. I work there. I know I have to show, so I put the info on my calendar and call it a day."

Men. Good grief. "I don't suppose you have access to the previous year information? It'd be good to copy their wording somewhat."

Cody shook his head. "If it's there, it's not on the drive they gave me access to."

"All right. That's fine. We'll do another web search." I tapped at my phone and scanned the first couple of links that were returned. "Looks like we basically just say 'Save-the-date for the Ballentine Coalition's annual Christmas gala to be held on December whatever' and then something like 'formal invitation to follow.' Seems easy enough. Should I shoot you the link and the wording?"

"Can we order them now? I'd rather know they were under-way. I do understand that these need to be on their way to donors like two months ago."

"You have your corporate card with you?" Because I was not putting these on my own credit card. That poor thing would probably shriek in agony. I ran my finances close to the bone. And sure, Austin would probably love to give me money—but I didn't want to take advantage of my brother. Even if he was a billionaire.

"Nope. But I can use my own." He shrugged. "I can either file for reimbursement or consider it a donation."

Right. Because Cody was also a billionaire. All the guys were. I tried to keep the jealousy down. And the hurt. I wasn't likely to ever really understand why they hadn't invited me to participate in their big stock market experiment in the first place. Sure, I didn't have quite as much liquid cash as the rest of them, but I would have figured something out. How nice would it be to not have to worry about money from day to day?

Whatever. They hadn't asked and, as a result, I was still working to pay my bills. It was fine. I pushed the thoughts away and tapped in the message for the cards. "Double-check this, will you?"

Cody took my phone and read the screen. "We don't put RSVP info on these, right?"

"The Internet says no." I shrugged. I'd been a little surprised by that as well, but the explanations made sense.

"Then that looks great. We need probably close to a thousand."

"Okay." I took my phone back, added them to the cart, and adjusted the quantity. "Rush shipping?"

"Yeah. Please. Fastest possible."

I considered the options and added on rush printing as well. "Where do you want them shipped?"

"I guess to my house? I can just take them into work with me when they show up and that way if they need to be delivered on a weekend they don't get lost in the building's mailroom."

"Smart." I started to type then paused. "I don't actually know your new address."

"Oh. Yeah. Have you even been by?"

I handed him my phone so he could put the info in, and shook my head. "No. You keep having get-togethers when the store is open. It's okay. This is the peril of retail."

"Sorry." He frowned. "I'll plan something for a Sunday. You busy tomorrow night? The weather's still nice. I could fire up the grill."

Was he inviting me or the whole gang? Probably the group. Had to be. Not that Cody and I couldn't spend time together without everyone else around—this morning was a case in point. But why would we? I could admit I wanted to see his place. I'd walked past several times when I'd gone out in the evening to stretch my legs or just get out of my own townhouse.

It was too quiet, too empty now that Austin and Kayla were married and living in her apartment. "I'm always up for a cookout."

"Great. I'll let the guys know. Think you could whip up that apple cake your grandma used to make?"

I grinned, even as subtle disappointment worked its fingers into my heart. Grandma's apple walnut cake was always a winner. "Sure. I can do that."

He flashed a smile at me before digging his wallet out of his front pocket. My eyes were close to bugging out when I realized the card he withdrew was a black American Express.

"What?"

My face heated. "Nothing. I've just never seen one of those in person before."

"One of...oh. Yeah." He hunched his shoulders. "It's kind of nice not to have to worry about limits."

"Sure." It was banal, but what was a better response?

He finished putting in the card information and hit Submit before handing me back my phone. "Thanks, Megan. I don't think I could have made this much progress without you."

I hadn't really done anything, but I also understood that sometimes it was nice to just have someone to bounce ideas off of. "Sure thing. What's next? Catering?"

"Probably? Although I guess I want to wait and hear back from the Torpedo Factory before I start worrying about that. Some of the hotels I talked to sent over info that included their approved vendors. I don't want to choose a caterer and then end up not being able to actually use them."

"Smart." I reached down for my coffee and took a long drink. I checked the time. Why was it awkward all of the sudden?

"Well." Cody stood. "I think that's probably everything I can do until I get the venue locked."

I nodded and stood. "Okay. If I can help more, let me know. I have a lot of time, like I said."

Cody cocked his head to the side. "Is the bookstore having trouble?"

"What? Oh. No." Not really. Probably. But it was my problem. Not Cody's. Definitely not Austin's. I didn't need a billionaire big brother—or honorary big brother—bailing me out.

"You sure?" His gaze seemed to see into me.

I forced a smile I hoped was bright and breezy. "Of course I am. But I like to help, you know that."

"I do." He searched my face again. "And I appreciate it. I guess I'll let you get on with your Saturday."

"Keep me posted, okay? I've got backups for the venue if the Torpedo Factory doesn't work out."

"Will do." He started toward the front door, then turned. "Grilling tomorrow for dinner, right?"

"Absolutely. I'll bring the apple cake." I watched him flip the deadbolt and head out onto the sidewalk. He walked back toward the river, so I couldn't watch him for long. I sighed. There was still time before I officially opened, but I might as well leave the door unlocked. I could take my spot up by the register and if someone came in early, even better.

The bookstore might not be in trouble yet, but I wasn't going to turn away a sale just because it was earlier than my posted hours.

## 3

## CODY

"About time, man." Noah slapped me on the shoulder as he stepped into my living room. He held out the covered bowl in his hands. "Where should I put this?"

"I guess in the kitchen." I shut the door and started in that direction. "I was thinking we could put a sort of buffet line of the sides on the counter here. People could grab a plate, get sides, then come out on the deck for their meat."

"Works for me." Noah set his bowl down on the counter. "I'll leave the foil on until people get here, I guess. It's just a salad though."

"Should it go in the fridge?" I checked the time. Noah was about an hour early. I headed to the fridge and pulled open the door. There was room. "Put it in. And we can both try to remember it's in there."

Noah laughed. "I'm not taking it home if we forget."

I shook my head. When we'd lived together, Noah was the one who would buy veggies and leave them to die in the drawer. Sometimes I'd try to do something with them, but it wasn't as if I was a super healthy eater. Still, a salad was something I could take to work and enjoy for lunches. So it'd be fine. "All right."

Noah carried the salad to the fridge and then looked around. "I like it. You're going to have to learn to cook better to do this place justice."

"Hey." I scowled at him. "I cook. More than you, at least."

"That's not exactly saying a ton. Do I get the tour?"

"You've been over before." Had I really not given him a tour before? He'd helped carry boxes when I moved.

"Sure. But that was before you were set up." Noah shrugged. "I'm guessing you've bought more furniture by now."

Heat crawled up my neck. "Not so much."

Noah began to laugh.

I looked away. Okay, sure. It was a little funny. But maybe not to the split-a-rib level Noah was at. "I don't see you even owning a house, man. So maybe keep the chortles down a level?"

Noah sucked in a breath and blew it out, clearly fighting the last remnants of humor. "Sorry." He held up a hand and cleared his throat. "Sorry. You're right."

"I did get living room furniture." I went through the kitchen door to the living space and gestured to the leather sectional, coffee table, and area rug.

"Nice. Leather's always a good choice." Noah flopped onto the couch. "Comfy."

"I like it." I took a seat in one of the chairs. They weren't as comfortable as the sofa, but they were still nice.

"Did you see that the Potts-Fitzhugh-Lee house is for sale?"

My eyebrows lifted. "I did not."

"You think it's stupid."

"I didn't say that. I just never figured you for a rehab project. I believe you said, at one point in our tenure as roommates, that you weren't changing lightbulbs because that was the super's job." It had turned out not to be the super's job. I'd tried to tell him that, but Noah had been adamant. Sometimes it worked out better if I let him learn things on his own. Even if it had made the two of us the laughingstock of the floor for a while.

Noah's face blazed red. "How long are you planning to throw that in my face?"

"Hmm. Forever?" I shrugged, grinning. "Come on, you have to admit it's hilarious."

"No. I don't." Noah stuck out his tongue. "If I admit I have a long way to go in the home maintenance department, will you at least acknowledge I've made progress?"

"Sure. I can give you that. But it doesn't put you on the rehab-a-historic-home level." I cocked my head to the side. "You're serious?"

"I don't know. I'm serious about wanting to look at it. Maybe I'll walk through and find out it's too much work. But it's not like I can't afford to hire people."

"No. That's true." I studied my friend. "Let me know when you have an appointment and I'll come along. I wouldn't mind getting a glimpse inside."

"Yeah? Cool. Thanks. If you think it's a terrible idea afterward, I'll listen. I might not take your advice, but I'll listen."

I laughed. With Noah, that was a decent concession. I was saved from answering by the doorbell. I pushed out of the chair and answered it. There was no reason for my heart to speed up like it did when I saw Megan.

"Hey."

"Hey yourself." Megan grinned and pushed a glass baking dish into my hands. "One apple cake, as requested."

I leaned close and breathed in the scent of warm apples. "Do I have to share?"

"Yes. But if you're nice, I'll make you another one later this month." She stepped around me and into the living room. "Hey, Noah."

"Megan! You never get to come to things anymore. It's good to see you." Noah patted the seat next to him on the couch. "Cody says there's no point in a tour because he still hasn't furnished everything."

"Pfft. I'm still going to look later. I don't mind empty spaces." She pointed at me. "You know I did most of the decorating at my place. I can help you if you need it."

"Thanks. I might take you up on that." I carried the cake into the kitchen before I could embarrass myself. Austin had suggested asking Megan to help—and everything in me had wanted to do just that. But I wasn't sure how to go about it without giving away how I felt about her. Maybe that wouldn't be so bad?

Ugh. No. There were too many possible bad outcomes to risk it. She was *Megan*. Not only was she my dream girl, she only saw me as yet another older brother. And while Austin might have implied that I had his blessing, the other guys weren't going to go so easy on me. I didn't have the best relationship history. When I'd bothered trying to date, I'd been a bit of a two-date-and-done kind of guy. Although I still didn't see the problem with ending things when it was obvious there was no future there.

And really that was all Megan's fault.

If she wasn't so perfect, maybe someone else would've had a chance to measure up.

I sighed and set the apple cake down on the counter at the far end.

Now that Megan had offered to help, I could take her up on it and no one would blink. Even better? Noah was a witness to her offer.

I went back out into the living room. "I can give you the tour, if you really want."

Megan popped up from where she'd been sitting on the

couch. "You know I do. I like the living room. You did a nice job in here."

"Should I admit I bought one of the setups they had in the furniture store?" I cringed a little. It sounded dumb now that I'd said it aloud.

"You know what? I think that's smart. They have professional designers set those up, so it's not like they're not hoping you'll do exactly that. You probably made the salesperson's day."

Given how overly friendly the woman in the furniture store had been, I was going to go with that. The idea that she'd been flirting with me—despite the enormous wedding set on her left hand—hadn't sat well. So maybe it was just me misreading enthusiastic appreciation? "Let's start upstairs."

"All right."

I started toward the stairs, then gestured for Megan to go ahead of me. "Go all the way up and we'll work our way back down."

She nodded and began the climb.

I couldn't say I minded walking behind her on the stairs. Although it also bordered on torture. She wasn't mine. She couldn't ever be mine.

At the top level, we stepped into an open space. "This is meant to be like a family lounge kind of area. So the living room on the main floor can be more formal and up here is where everyone hangs out. I'm not sure what to do with it right now, honestly. I don't need another place to crash. Because there's the basement area, too."

Megan walked across to the windows and looked out. "It's a good space though."

"Yeah." I pointed to the doors. "Two more bedrooms up here, a bathroom, and a study. There are some nice built-ins."

Megan peeked in the doorways. "You could at least set these up as guest rooms. Get a bed and a dresser. Maybe a chair—they're good enough size rooms they could handle that."

"If your offer to help really stands, I'll take you up on it. We can go shopping or you can send me links or something?"

"Links?" She shook her head. "Oh, Cody. Tell me you aren't buying furniture online."

"Well. Not yet. But I did some looking. Just to kind of get an idea." I hunched my shoulders. Was it really that bad? How was I supposed to know what I was looking for if I didn't at least poke around online first?

She pointed a finger at me. "No buying. You have to touch it first. Otherwise, how will you know what the fabric feels like? Or how firm it is?"

I opened my mouth but closed it again quickly. It wasn't like I knew better. Although I didn't think online furniture shopping was really that bad. But, well, Megan would know.

"Okay. Ready to see the master?"

Megan's eyebrows lifted. "They're called 'primary' now."

I probably didn't want to know why. I just nodded and gestured to the stairs. "It's the whole level. It's kind of nice. Although it's more space than I had in the apartment with Noah. Probably bigger than the whole apartment Noah and I shared, actually."

She laughed. "Why am I not surprised that you don't know for sure?"

I had no answer to that. I just stood at the bottom of the stairs and put my hands in my pockets. "I used the furniture I already had. If it's tragic, we can upgrade. I'm not attached to any of it. It's not heirloom or anything."

"I can tell." Humor laced her words. Megan shook her head as she walked through the mostly empty sitting room area, past the fireplace in the three-quarter wall that divided the sitting space from the bedroom, and into the bedroom itself. "It's big."

"Yeah." I followed behind her and tried to imagine what she was thinking. "Is it bad? It's bad, isn't it?"

"The space? No. Your decor?" She waggled a hand from side to side. "But I can help with that. You really don't mind?"

I got lost, just for a moment, in her hopeful gaze. I swallowed. "I really don't. But keep in mind I'm not trying to get on any lifestyle TV shows. I want comfortable."

"C'mon, Cody. You know me."

"I do."

"So don't worry." She came to stand beside me and rested her hand on my arm. "Let's go see the basement. And then I want to look at the kitchen again, because that's a masterpiece that doesn't need any help."

I laughed. "Glad I did something right."

"Did you do any of it?"

Busted. I shrugged. "I knew enough to leave it alone. Doesn't that count for anything?"

"I guess." She winked at me and started toward the stairs.

On the main floor, I noticed that Austin and Kayla had arrived and were hanging with Noah on the sectional. "Hey, guys. Just giving Megan the tour."

Kayla popped up. "I missed it. Do you mind if I go poke around?"

"Help yourself."

Kayla grinned and took off up the stairs. I looked at Austin. "Are Wes and Tristan coming?"

"Far as I know. Scott and Whitney aren't going to make it. Beckett's throwing up." Austin frowned. "I hope it's nothing contagious."

No kidding. Beckett had sat with us at lunch after church today. And while a kid might bounce back from the stomach flu fast, I never seemed to. Megan had disappeared to the basement.

I wanted to go after her, but it wasn't like she needed me in order to look around.

The doorbell rang and then the front door opened. "Hey."

"Come on in, Wes. Make yourself at home." I gestured to the living room.

Wes snickered. "Please. Like you don't just walk in to my place."

He had a point. And I didn't really mind. "Have you heard from Tristan?"

"Yeah, he's on the way. He didn't elaborate, so I figure it's something with a client." Wes shrugged. "Where should I put the food?"

I spotted the grocery store bag in his hand. "What'd you get?"

"Just some pasta salad. They make it better than even my mom, so I didn't see the point in slaving away in the kitchen."

"Works for me. Then we know we're going to live through the experience, too. So bonus." I pointed toward the kitchen. "Just set it on the counter. I guess I'll go fire up the grill. We're all here except Tristan, and if it is work, who knows how long it'll take him."

Wes laughed.

I made my way through the kitchen, out onto the deck where my oversized grill took up a lot of the usable space. It was an indulgence, for sure, but I justified it based on the size of my friend group. And it seemed to keep growing. I didn't bother grilling when I was cooking for just me. I had a grill pan that worked fine for that.

"This is nice."

I turned at Megan's words and smiled. "I like it."

"Do you see your neighbors out here much?" She glanced around at the backs of the townhouses. All the decks were on this alleyway for residents to access their garages.

"You'd think, right? But no. Not really. It's the area, probably. You know how it is. No one knows anyone else." I shrugged and lit the grill. I didn't necessarily love that about the area—for all Old Town was like a small town in the shopping and historic areas—the residential parts were still full of people driven by their careers. There wasn't time to sit out on the deck and get to know your neighbors for most people. And I couldn't even exclude myself from that.

"Hear anything from the Torpedo Factory?"

She was standing close and her perfume mixed with the smoke of the grill as it heated and burned off the residue from my last experiment. It shouldn't have worked. But for me it did. I needed to get myself under control. She was one of the gang. An honorary little sister.

Completely off limits.

Her elbow bumped mine. "Where'd you go?"

"Sorry. No. Haven't heard anything. Hopefully tomorrow." I bit my lip and pulled the grill lid down before stepping back. "If I don't hear tomorrow, I guess I need to explore some of your other options."

"Okay. You want to come by the bookstore after work tomorrow?"

"Yeah. I can do that." I cleared my throat. "What did you think of the basement?"

"I think setting it up for poker nights was smart. You could probably get a pool table in there if you wanted. Is it going to be a play room? Is that the plan?"

"Play room? You make it sound like I'm a kid."

"Hey, if the shoe fits." She grinned.

I scoffed. "Yes. I think the plan is that it'll be a game room type space. I was thinking of setting it up for movies, too. But I don't want it to be crowded."

Megan nodded thoughtfully. "That's more you than a pool table."

I was a little surprised that she understood so quickly. But she was right.

"I'll play around with it. I don't suppose you have a floor plan?"

I lifted my eyebrows. "I don't think so. But there might have been one on the listing. You could look it up online and see."

"I'll do that." Megan looked around. "What can I do to help?"

"With dinner?" I lifted a shoulder. "Nothing. It's easy enough to throw meat on the grill once it heats up."

"Okay. Let me know if there's something I can do. I guess I'll go see what the gang's up to."

I nodded. When she'd gone inside, I turned back to the grill and lifted the lid. Most of the stuck-on food had turned white. I unhooked the scraper from where I stored it and attacked the grill racks until they were clean then closed the lid again. I checked the temperature gauge. Almost time.

I went into the kitchen to the fridge and got out the burgers and brats. Happy sounds of conversation and laughter floated in from the living room. I smiled. It was good to have a group of friends.

I needed to remember that and not do something stupid that would mess it up.

Because while Austin might say he was okay with the idea of me pursuing Megan, the rest of the guys would definitely not be. They all considered her their baby sister. Sort of a personal mascot to the group. If things didn't work out between us? It would make things awkward at best, tear things apart at the worst. The group of guys was family. They mattered.

# 4

## MEGAN

I glanced up at the movement near the picture window of the bookstore. Was someone finally going to come in? Mondays had never been our busiest day, but it seemed like they were getting slower with every passing week.

The couple strolling down the sidewalk moved along toward the café. At least they'd thought my display was interesting enough to stop, even if it didn't entice them to come in.

I sighed.

Maybe I should close on Mondays. I wouldn't mind having two days off each week. Then Sunday could go back to being a true day of rest instead of the day I tried to do all the things that I couldn't accomplish in the morning hours before I had to get to the store. It felt like admitting defeat.

Which was dumb.

Bookstores in today's world were tricky. Grandma had known it. She'd told me—warned me, really—when I said I was quitting social work and moving to handle the store myself. I was grateful the building was paid for and I just had to manage utilities and inventory and, oh yes, my salary, out of the profits. I could occasionally even hire a part-time employee to give me an extra afternoon or evening off.

I'd even swung a vacation over spring break since everyone else had been headed to the Caymans. An older brother who was a billionaire had some definite perks. Even if it hadn't occurred to him to include me in the whole business to start out.

I wouldn't mind being a billionaire in my own right. Then I could float the utilities—heck, maybe even an employee salary —if I needed to.

But he hadn't and so I wasn't a billionaire and I needed to get over it and move on. I forgave him. I really did. His rationale was sound—I hadn't had the money to go in with them. As much as I'd like to protest that I could've found a way to make it work, Austin was right that I probably couldn't have.

So. Fine.

If watching my brother and his friends over the last year had shown me anything, it was that money could only fix a small handful of the problems in life. And it created new ones. Like losing Austin and Kayla their jobs in the public school where they'd been teaching. Of course, now they were running a new learning center and it was even more fulfilling—at least if you listened to Austin go on about it. God always seemed to work everything out.

For other people.

I winced. *Sorry, God. I know that's not true. You take care of me. I'm grateful.*

The bell on the door jingled.

I glanced up and my face heated even as I smiled. "Hey, Cody."

"Hey. Great news." He grinned and held his phone out to me.

I took it and looked down at the screen. "What am I looking at?"

"What?" He took the phone and laughed as he unlocked it. "Sorry. Torpedo Factory is a go!"

I looked at the email and skimmed the contents. It all looked pretty standard. There was a small part of me that was surprised they were still available. Glad. But surprised. I handed Cody back his phone. "That's excellent. Congrats."

"It's a relief, let me tell you." He clicked the phone off and stuck it in his pocket. "So. I guess now catering is the next thing? The save-the-date cards shipped today, so they'll be here Wednesday. I already printed labels, so if I hustle on Thursday, I can probably drop them off at the post office after work and get them on their way. Since nearly everyone is local, I would imagine people will get them Friday or Saturday. Monday at the latest."

"Make sure you send yourself one. And maybe Noah, too."

He frowned. "Why would I do that?"

"So you know roughly when locals are getting them?" It had seemed like a straightforward idea to me. Maybe it was weird. Sure, it was going to cost an extra stamp, but wasn't it worth about a buck between the two of them to know what delivery times were?

"Oh. Smart." He grinned at me. "Honestly, I don't know where I'd be without you."

I chuckled. "Probably on a lot of wait lists for hotels downtown and on the way to a peptic ulcer."

Cody bobbed his head from side to side. "Yeah. That sounds about right. That means you'll help with the catering. Right? You wouldn't want me to drop the ball now, would you?"

I shook my head. "I don't think you would, but I'm happy to help. It's fun. Especially since you've got a bigger event budget than I can imagine having. Tell me how that works, again, to spend all this money on fundraising?"

"Ugh. Don't get me started. I don't get it either, but

apparently the big donors like to see and be seen, and it helps pry open their wallets." Cody shrugged. "I don't get it. Honestly, if I didn't work for Ballentine and know how frugal we are in just about every area of our operation? I'm not sure I'd give, based on these big galas. It feels like a waste."

"Have you talked to Mr. Ballentine about it?"

"I have. He gets it. Mostly feels the same way. But he also has comparisons for years when we haven't done the two big events each year for whatever reason, and the level of giving is really a lot lower. And since we have a number of donors who sponsor tables, we make back most of our outlay before the fundraiser even happens." Cody blew out a breath. "I've been digging through the files to try to understand, and it's been eye opening."

"Sounds like it." I glanced around the empty bookstore. "We might as well go sit and be comfortable. I'll get my tablet so we can look at the catering options I bookmarked. Did the venue have a list of preferred vendors? We should look at those first, and save some of the fees associated with using someone who's not on their list."

"I think it was one of the attachments. I'll look." Cody headed toward the comfy chairs, already pulling his phone out of his pocket.

I went back behind the register to get my tablet. I'd been looking at caterers off and on today. It was tricky, because it seemed like everyone and their cousin offered catering now. It would probably boil down to what sort of food they wanted to have. Carrying my tablet, I made my way to where Cody sat, and hesitated.

He patted the seat beside him.

It seemed like an almost absent-minded gesture. Definitely just friendly. Why was I so intent on looking for something more there? He didn't think of me that way. He never had. Never would. I was just Austin's little sister.

I sat next to him. "Did you find the list?"

He tilted his phone toward me then frowned. "Why don't I forward the email to you, then you can open it on that and we can both see it more easily."

"Smarty."

He flashed a grin and my heart sped. Why? Why did I react like that to him? He was my brother's friend. One of a group of them. I was basically their adopted little sister across the board. I shouldn't be wondering what it would be like if he were to turn, take me in his arms, and kiss me.

But I was.

"Megan?"

I blinked. Uh-oh. I missed something. "Sorry. What did you say?"

He nodded toward the tablet. "Wanna see if the email came through?"

Email? Oh. Right. Preferred vendor list from the venue. Geesh. I quickly turned on the tablet and opened a browser so I could log into my email account. "Yep. Right there."

"Great. Let's take a look."

I opened the email and scrolled to the attachments. "I'm guessing it's this one, oh so cleverly labeled 'preferred vendors.'"

"That's the one."

I tapped it and waited for it to load before scrolling down a bit to the actual list. "It's nice that they include links."

"Yeah." Cody scooted closer and our legs touched. The heat from his body seeped into mine.

I swallowed and worked to keep my breathing steady. "Do you want to just start at the top and work our way down?"

"In a minute. Could you scroll to the 'S' section?"

I raised my eyebrows but did as he asked.

He pointed. "Season's Bounty. That's Jackson's wife's restaurant."

"Jackson?"

"Oh. Sorry. Jackson Trent. My boss. Seems like maybe it'd be a good idea to see if they have availability first."

"Would his wife want to cater on a night that she'd otherwise be a guest?"

"Oh." He pursed his lips. "That's a question."

"I could be wrong. Or maybe she has people. You said it's her restaurant, that doesn't mean she would have to do the work."

Cody tapped his fingers on his leg. "Maybe it's worth just asking. I can lay it out for her and say we'd like to support her, but we also don't want to take her away from a fun evening out with her husband. Let her decide?"

That sounded reasonable to me. I nodded.

Cody glanced at his phone. "Why don't I call now and see how she responds. Then we know if we need to start at the top of the list and try to figure something else out."

"Before you do that." I bit my lip as he turned to look at me. "Do you know what kind of food she serves? Is it the sort of thing you want for this party?"

He blew out a breath. "That's a good question. I don't even know what kind of food we're supposed to have. They've always been plated, sit-down dinners at Christmas. But between you and me, it's always been relatively unappetizing chicken. Would it be bad to mix it up?"

"I can't answer these questions. Who's in charge of the gala?"

"Me. I guess. Jackson dumped it on my desk and said 'have at it.'"

Okay. To me, that sounded like it was all his decision. He seemed so unsure about the whole thing, which was not like him. At least not in my mind. "So. What kind of food do you want to have there?"

"Not chicken." He shuddered. "Although maybe we have to go with it because of cost? I'd honestly rather have heavy appetizers than a plated meal. More of a cocktail party feel than banquet. Does that make sense?"

"Sure. Is there a program? Speeches or anything?"

"Yeah. Mr. Ballentine likes to give a speech. It's a mixture of thanking them for being there and being a donor, a kind of end-of-year update of what we've been focused on, and then a pitch for more donations."

"That probably explains the plated dinner then. It's easier to keep a captive audience if they're shoving food in their mouth and sitting still."

Cody snickered, then sighed. "So. Chicken."

"Not necessarily." I shifted slightly, stopping the contact between us. It was just too distracting. "What if the majority was the apps, like you said, and a more casual mixing atmosphere—because honestly, I think that's going to work better at the Torpedo Factory anyway. It's not like there's one big ballroom where everyone can be herded together. You'll be spread out over three floors—you could do some fun things like different types of stations in different locations so people are encouraged to move around and mingle."

He brightened. "I like that idea. But what about the speech and plea?"

"Hang on." I navigated to the venue rental page and checked the layouts they had listed. "How many people come usually?"

"We invite around three hundred and end up in the two-fifty range? Why?" He leaned closer to peek at the tablet.

"Okay. So we have tables set up in the main hall. It says two-twenty seated for that space. So you have a few extra tables on the mezzanine—if I recall right, they'll be able to hear fine as long as Mr. Ballentine is mic'd." I glanced at Cody. "You're getting sound, right?"

"Yeah. Of course."

"So for the bulk of the time, it's appetizer stations in the main hall, mezzanine, and third floor. So people can wander and mingle and fill up on several different kinds of finger foods. Then, when it's time for the speech? Plated dessert."

"Plated...dessert?" Cody blinked. "You're a genius."

I grinned. His words warmed my soul. "So they'll sit down at the tables and be served something magnificent. I'm thinking maybe a trio of delights is better than one big slice of cake."

"Trio of delights. Get you." Cody nudged me with his elbow. "But I like the way you think. I guess I need to be open to a separate dessert caterer. Maybe a bakery is going to be better for that?"

"Hmm." That was a possibility I hadn't stumbled on yet. "Maybe? We need a plan."

Cody snorted.

I accepted it as a sound-based equivalent of "duh" and appreciated his restraint in holding off on the word. I cleared my throat. "As I was saying. A plan. First up, type of appetizers and caterer for those. Then we ask that person if they think they can handle some amazing desserts. If yes, bonus. If not, then we look for a bakery."

After a moment, Cody nodded. "All right. I can go with that. I still think we ought to try and use Season's Bounty if we can. Just seems like a good plan to throw business toward the boss's wife if possible."

"True. Which takes us back to the original question: do you know what type of food she serves?"

He shook his head and looked at his phone again. "I have an idea. But you can say no."

"Why does that fill me with dread?"

Cody held up a hand. "It's not scary. I promise."

"And still, the dread persists."

He looked around the store. "Since you're clearly not over-burdened with customers right now, what if you closed early and you and I went to dinner? At Season's Bounty."

I wanted to leap out of my seat and shout "yes!" At the same time, it didn't seem like the kind of thing a responsible business owner would do.

He must have thought my hesitation meant no. "Or I can go by myself. It's fine."

"No. It's not that. I just..." I looked around the empty store. In my experience, it wasn't going to pick up between now and closing. "You know what? That sounds great. Let me print off a note for the door and get things shut down."

"Sure. Can I help with anything?"

I looked at him and reminded myself, again, of all the reasons I couldn't follow through on my desire to hug him. "Nah. It doesn't take me long, and I have a system."

"All right. I'll wait here."

I picked up my tablet and headed to the register and tried to ignore my awareness of Cody's presence in the store. We were going to dinner. Just the two of us. Even as a squeal built up in my heart, I squashed it. It wasn't a date. It was just me, his honorary little sister, helping him out with this fundraiser.

In fact, I should suggest we ask the rest of the group to come along. More opinions was probably better than just two.

But I didn't want to.

I wanted Cody all to myself. And if I spent a little time pretending that we were an item, I wasn't hurting anyone.

A girl could dream. Right?

# 5

## CODY

I f I never saw another address label and stamp again in my life, it would be too soon. Of course, I was going to have to do this all again in a few weeks with the actual invitations. And those were going to require stuffing, too.

Jackson Trent had stopped by at one point during the day to remind me that I could ask for help. As much as I appreciated that, I also knew everyone else was busy with their own work. And the previous person in charge of this had never needed help.

Of course, it had been her sole job. Or at least the bulk of it.

But still. I could do it. And I was staying on top of the rest of my work—mostly. Regardless, I'd gotten the stuff done and hauled them all out to my car so I could take them to the post office on my way home.

I drove into the lane that would take me by the large collection boxes outside the post office and waited behind a minivan whose driver was having trouble figuring out how to reach the mail slot. She finally inched forward, opened her door, and got out to put the mail in.

I chuckled.

When she drove off, I pulled forward and lowered the window so I could put handful after handful of postcards into the box. I was almost finished when the car behind me started to beep their horn. I gave a cheery wave and continued to drop the cards down the chute. Maybe I'd take the actual invitations inside when the time came. Or I could talk to...someone...about how we mailed out our monthly newsletters. As a nonprofit, there were probably cheaper ways to send bulk mailings. Except with something fancy like this, didn't it look nicer to use a stamp?

I'd ask Jackson what he thought.

Finished, I pulled away from the box and out into the post office parking lot. The driver with the horn sent me a less friendly, single-digit wave that I caught in my rearview mirror. I took a moment to pray for him. How frustrating must his life be to feel the need to be that way over having to wait a moment in a line at the post office?

Turning onto the road that would take me home, I considered the evening ahead. Yesterday morning, I'd heard back from Paige Trent, the chef and owner of Season's Bounty, about catering the event. She'd sent me a proposal and suggested that I come tonight for a tasting of her suggested items. Including the desserts.

Megan and I had both enjoyed the meal on Monday night. I wasn't sure if my enthusiasm was because of the food or the company, but I couldn't very well say anything about that. So I was planning to go solo to the tasting tonight. Just to be sure.

But I had two hours to kill between now and then.

I could go home. But if I did that, I'd get comfortable, and leaving again was going to be hard. I could swing by Tristan's and see if I could get him to spill the beans about what was going on with him. He'd been acting off for a few weeks now—

we'd all noticed it—but he brushed it aside as being case related.

What were we supposed to do when faced with the whole attorney privilege thing?

Before I'd consciously decided on it, I was parallel parking a few stores down from the bookstore. When I'd parked, I sat in the car with the engine off. This was a bad idea. A seriously bad idea.

What excuse was I going to use when Megan asked why I was there? Because she'd totally ask. It wasn't as if I was known for reading. In fact, given the option, I'd watch TV or stare at a blank wall before I'd pick up a book.

Everyone knew it.

I could read. I just didn't love it. It took a lot of effort to translate words on a page into the movie that was supposed to take place in my head when I was reading. At least, that was what everyone always told me was supposed to happen. Usually when I read, it was just words. I understood what they meant. I followed the story. But there were no magical moving pictures in my brain.

Which made TV and movies a lot more interesting. Sue me.

I blew out a breath that ended on a half-chuckle. Here I was, getting defensive about something literally no one in our group ever gave me grief about.

But they would if they found out I was suddenly haunting the bookstore.

A knock on the passenger window had me glancing over. I forced a smile when I saw Scott, Whitney, and Beckett.

"Hey, Cody." Scott shot me a look full of curiosity.

Great. Just fantastic. I checked for traffic before opening my door and getting out. "Hey. You guys out for a family walk?"

"Ice cream!" Beckett bounced up and down while holding Whitney's hand. Then he reached for Scott's hand, too, and picked up his feet. His parents lifted him up and gave him a swing without any appearance of conscious thought.

"Yum. Can I join you?" Ice cream was a better idea than bothering Megan. And it wasn't going to spoil my appetite. I'd been so involved in labels and stamps today that I'd had a snack pack of peanut butter crackers for lunch out of the vending machine in the break room. Satisfying and filling were not the adjectives I'd use for that as a meal.

"Sure. More the merrier." Scott gave me a searching look. "Is that why you were parking here?"

I shook my head.

Whitney smirked at me but didn't say anything.

I ignored it. There was no reason to smirk. I hadn't let on to anyone—other than Austin, one time, in a weak moment—about my feelings for Megan.

"Ice cream!" Beckett's voice had less elation and the beginning of a whine in it.

I laughed. "Someone's ready."

"Beck. We're getting there." But even as he chided, Scott turned toward the ice cream shop and reached for the door.

"So. What brings you all out for ice cream on a Thursday evening?" I waited for Whitney to enter the shop before addressing my question to Scott.

"It's kind of an anniversary." Whitney hoisted Beckett onto her hip and approached the glass-fronted case.

Scott grinned. "One year ago, I picked up Beckett at the airport. And got Whitney as a bonus."

Whitney laughed. "I don't think you considered me a bonus a year ago."

"I don't know. I was getting pretty desperate for childcare. Especially when my last hope called to let me know there were no openings when we were standing there in the parking garage at the airport." Scott tucked his hands in his pockets.

"It worked out." Whitney brushed a kiss on Beckett's forehead and sent Scott a look so full of love, I wondered if I should sneak outside and leave them alone.

"It did." Scott returned the look.

The teenager behind the counter cleared his throat, his face blazing red. "Are you ready to order?"

Whitney consulted with Beckett over their scoop choices.

I scooted closer to Scott. "Sorry, man. I didn't mean to horn in on your celebration."

"Don't be stupid. It's ice cream. And we're happy to include you. Especially since I get the feeling that you were looking for something to do that would keep you from doing something else."

I raised my eyebrows. "I was just parking, man."

"Uh-huh." Scott shook his head and lowered his voice. "You're not as subtle as you think you are."

My neck burned. Hopefully, I wasn't as beet red as the kid behind the ice cream counter.

Scott held up both hands. "You're not going to get any judgment from me. I married the nanny. But I'm going to warn you, if Noah, Wes, and Tristan figure it out before you say something? They're going to be ticked."

"There's nothing going on." That was one hundred percent true. I could stand behind it.

"Yet?"

I shook my head. "She doesn't think of me like that."

"You sure?"

I scowled at Scott. What did he mean was I sure? Of course I was sure. It was incredibly obvious that I was just another of her big brothers.

Before I could retort, Whitney spoke. "You ordering, Scott? Cody?"

"Just think about it." Scott stepped closer to the counter and pointed. "Single scoop of strawberry cheesecake in a waffle cone."

Think about it? It was practically all I could think about. Ever. What I needed to do was stop thinking about it. I stared at the ice cream in the case and considered my options. The strawberry cheesecake actually sounded pretty good. It was one of those flavors that, at least in my mind, trended girly, so I wasn't likely to order it. But if Scott was getting it, he couldn't give me grief for trying it.

I waited until the teen looked my way, then pointed to Scott. "I'll have the same as him."

Whitney and Beckett were already sitting at one of the tiny tables. Beckett had a small bowl of ice cream in front of him.

Scott reached for the waffle cone the teen extended. "Thanks."

"Go sit. I'll get this. Consider it my anniversary present." I reached into my pocket for my wallet.

"You don't have to—"

"I know that. You know that. I'd like to, though, if it's okay?"

Scott grinned. "All right. I'll let you. Thanks. Whit's got a milkshake coming."

"I'll bring it." I reached for my waffle cone and slid down the counter to where the cash register was.

The teen rang up the order slowly.

"Are you still in school?"

Startled, the teen looked up at me before nodding.

"Did you ever have Mr. Campbell for math?"

The boy grinned. "Sure. He was great. I'm bummed he's gone this year. And Miss Jones. She's hot."

I chuckled. "You ever go to the learning center they started across the street?"

He frowned. "Is that where they went? I've seen the signs on the road but figured it was a private school or something."

"Nah. It's there for everyone. You ever have trouble and need help, head over there, okay? Or just swing by and say hi to Mr. Campbell. I bet he'd love to see you."

"Here's your milkshake."

"Thanks." I studied the kid a minute before mentally shrugging. He'd either go or not, but I couldn't do much more than I had.

I headed over to the table and gave Whitney her milkshake before snagging a chair and sitting. I sampled my ice cream and nodded. Yummy. Definitely also girly. But so be it. "Any other plans for tonight?"

Whitney shook her head. "Just the usual. Bath and bedtime. You wanna come over and hang?"

"Thanks. I wasn't looking for an invite. I was just curious." I ate more ice cream.

"You're still welcome." Scott tipped his head to the side. "We could watch a movie or something."

"I'm good. I appreciate it, though."

"So you have plans?" Whitney poked her straw up and down in her milkshake.

"Actually, yeah. I'm heading over to Season's Bounty in Arlington for a menu tasting for the Christmas gala."

"Noah mentioned you got saddled with that." Scott sent me a pitying glance. "I figured you'd weasel out of it."

I shook my head. I hadn't even really considered it. I mean, when an assignment came straight from the second in command, was no even an option? "Megan's been a lot of help. It's not so bad now that I've got the venue reserved. Once catering is nailed down? It'll be a breeze."

Whitney laughed. She looked at me, and her laughter trailed off. "Oh. You're serious?"

"Why wouldn't I be?" I pictured the checklist of tasks that I'd typed up. It really seemed like all that was left was the invitations and then managing the responses as they came in. How hard could that be?

"Just seems like a big event probably requires a lot of babysitting. Maybe I'm wrong." Whitney pulled three napkins out of the dispenser in the middle of the table and started attacking the ring of chocolate around Beckett's mouth.

Shoot. Was I forgetting something obvious? Maybe I'd see if someone at work who knew what they were doing could take a look at my list and tell me what I was missing. Of course, the best person to do that wasn't working at Ballentine anymore, but surely there were others who knew what they were talking about?

Or maybe not. If those people existed, wouldn't Jackson have tasked them with this?

Ugh.

I could send the list to Megan. She'd know, wouldn't she?

I should probably leave her alone. Stop trying to involve her in this whole fiasco. If Scott had already picked up on how I felt about Megan, how long would it be before Noah, Wes, and Tristan figured it out?

Although...none of them had a girlfriend. I was pretty sure, given the looks Whitney and Scott exchanged, that he hadn't come up with his theory on his own.

So maybe I was in the clear.

"I guess we'll see." I sighed and frowned at my ice cream. "I really hope I'm not underestimating. Because some of my regular work is slipping while I get this all spun up, and that can't go on indefinitely."

Scott nodded. "You'll figure it out. I'm confused why they don't hire an event planner, though. They surely have the funds for that."

I shrugged. "I imagine they think having someone internal do it is a better use of the money? I don't know."

"The optics matter with a nonprofit." Whitney scooted her chair back so Beckett could climb into her lap. "Even if the cost is roughly the same between hiring someone and using an internal resource, donors like to see it being handled from inside. Because they don't think that means their donation is being used to drum up other donations."

It made no sense. But it also made perfect sense. People had bizarre ideas about things.

"Well. For this event, they get me. I'm hoping I won't make a mess of it. But I figure if donations are down by a lot because I did something wrong, I can just make up the difference myself."

Scott chuckled. "There you are. Pressure's off."

Not really. I was reasonably sure Mr. Ballentine wouldn't be excited about a flopped fundraiser, regardless of whether or not they still ended up with the same amount of money. But I still forced a smile and dragged a hand across my forehead in an exaggerated motion. "Phew."

Beckett snuggled his head into Whitney's shoulder. She looked over at Scott. "We should get him back home before he crashes too hard."

Scott scooted his chair back and stood. He handed Whitney his half-eaten cone and scooped Beckett into his arms. When the boy was settled, he took back his ice cream. "It was good to see you. Thanks for the ice cream. You'll send us an invite to the gala, right? Sounds like a fun night out."

"Yeah. Of course. And hey, happy anniversary of sorts." I hadn't had any intention of inviting my friends to the gala. Other than Noah, none of them were really big into supporting what they deemed political causes. Ballentine did so much more than lobbying, but I also wasn't going to get into it with them. Everyone needed to find the organizations that they could support and then follow through on giving to them. On the other hand? All of them were very gung-ho about supporting members of our group. So maybe invites weren't such a bad idea.

I watched Scott and his little family exit the shop and sighed. I still had about an hour before I needed to leave for the restaurant.

Although...Season's Bounty was surrounded by shops. Maybe the better idea was for me to head over now and just wander a bit in Arlington.

Because I was fairly certain if I sat here eating ice cream too much longer, I was going to end up swinging by the bookstore.

Right now, that seemed like a bad idea. All around.

I was never going to get over this little thing I had for Megan if I kept seeking her out.

Resolved, I stood, took one more bite of the ice cream before dumping the rest in the trash, tossing a wave toward the teenager behind the case, and heading out to my car.

I'd be smart. And before I knew it? I'd have everything with Megan back where it needed to be. I glanced longingly down toward the bookstore as I unlocked my car.

I shook my head and got in.

I was officially pathetic.

## 6

## MEGAN

"Happy Friday." Jenna let the bookstore door close behind her and looked around. "Am I early?"

"A little, yeah." I grinned and forked up another bite of the salad I'd run over to buy at the café a few doors down. I'd packed a dinner, but couldn't face it. It'd work fine for tomorrow.

"You're still eating. I can come back."

"Don't be silly." I picked up my salad and nodded toward the more comfortable seating as I moved from behind the register. "Let's go sit. It's not like Friday night is a happening time around here. That's why the girls hang out."

Jenna headed over and claimed one of the armchairs. "I appreciate you letting me crash your hangouts."

"Please. You can't get out, now. You're one of us. We're like the Borg." At her blank stare, I sighed internally. Why couldn't I find just one girlfriend who also loved science fiction? "*Star Trek*?"

"Oh. Right. The blonde in the spandex with the thing on her eye." Jenna held her hand in an approximation of Seven of Nine's hardware.

"Yeah, I guess. She's not really representative of the species."

Why would Jenna know her but not the Borg in general? These were mysteries that were probably better left unexplored.

"I dated a guy who was obsessed with her."

"Ah." I guessed we were exploring the mystery after all. Not that it was so mysterious. "Pretty sure the guy-drool factor is why she was added to the series."

"More than likely. He used to go on and on about her. Tried to get me to dress up like her for a Halloween party, but finally being tall worked in my benefit and we couldn't find a spandex suit that didn't look like I was wearing capris."

"That's a mental image." I grinned before scooping another bite of salad. "I'm trying to imagine dating someone who wanted to dress up for Halloween when there weren't kids involved."

Jenna shrugged. "It can be fun. I did Civil War reenactments for a while."

I blinked. That absolutely did not compute. "Why?"

"Like I said, it can be fun. You get to know the group of people you hang with and they become a lot like family. Plus, history is important. It's one of the reasons I came back to this area. There's so many historic buildings around that just need someone to put a little time, love, and cash into them. After Austin's project, I'm almost at the place that I can invest in something and have a restoration project."

"I wouldn't even know where to begin with something like that. I guess you have contacts for all the contractors you'd need, being an architect."

"Sure. Although I don't imagine I'll job out much of the work. I like to get my hands dirty." Jenna shifted in her seat. "I did a lot of construction while I was in school. It's a great way to earn some extra money. Bonus, I understand what goes into making architectural dreams a reality."

"Huh." I looked down at the takeout container and flipped the lid closed. I hadn't finished, but it was close enough. I was full. And maybe later the girls would want to send someone out for ice cream. I'd noticed the shop down the street a bit had their strawberry cheesecake this week. They didn't always, but when they did, I made a point of getting a scoop.

"Not handy?"

"I mean, I can change a lightbulb and the furnace filters."

Jenna laughed.

"I know someone who has a handyman out for those, don't laugh."

"Seriously?"

I nodded.

"Man. What a racket." Jenna shook her head.

"So your restoration project. You have something in mind? Or are you waiting to look until you have the cash?" It was such an utterly foreign idea to me, I was curious. "How does that even work?"

"Which question do you want me to answer first?"

"Dealer's choice." I set my salad on the floor and got more comfortable.

Jenna thought for a moment. "I don't have any place concrete in mind yet. I have a filter saved on several of the real estate apps, and I check every couple of days for new listings. There's a great one here in Old Town, but it's way outside what I can afford."

"Which one?" The townhouse I lived in—that Austin had ended up buying from my grandma—was historic. On a street with other historic townhomes. Not that you had to go far to find something classed historic when you were talking about Old Town. Still, I couldn't quite dredge up any for-sale signs in my memory of walking around the neighborhood lately.

"The Potts-Fitzhugh-Lee House." Jenna grinned. "It's got a name, which I love. It was built in 1795, then somewhere along the line it got split into two residences but now it's back to one.

The pictures online..." She shook her head and sighed. "I'd love to get my hands on it."

"What are they asking?"

"Over five mil. So there's no way. I can probably swing two, but I'd rather keep it lower so I have more to put into the restoration. So I'm looking further out, too. I don't really want to live in the country, but I could handle it while I did a restoration. But then I have to sell and look for something else, and I'd really love my first project to be a home. I'm tired of apartment living."

I nodded. I was definitely blessed not to have to deal with that. I still felt guilty that I was living in the townhouse and Austin and Kayla were in her apartment. They assured me they didn't care—that it kept Kayla from having to break her lease and they were closer to the learning center—but I didn't fully buy it.

"You should come see my place sometime. Well, technically it's Austin's—he owns it—but I'm living there. Grandma bought it then sold it to him. Point being, it's historic. The whole street is, practically. I'll keep an eye out for anything that comes up for sale if you want."

"Sure. Thanks."

Jenna and I both looked over when the bell on the door jingled.

I stood. "Good evening. Can I help you?"

The woman, teenager in tow, brightened at my greeting. She nodded toward the boy sulking at her elbow. "He has to read *The Scarlet Letter* by Monday and failed to mention it when getting it from the library was an option. I'm hoping you might have a copy."

I fought a grin and nodded. "Of course. Right over here."

I led the pair to the right bookshelf and tugged out a copy. I offered it to the mom. "Is there a paper or a project, too? Or you just have to read it?"

The mom looked at her son.

He hunched his shoulders even more and muttered, "I have to write an essay exploring themes."

I looked at the mom. She looked defeated. "Essay's due Monday?"

He nodded once.

"All right. The book is short. I have no doubt that you'll be able to finish it tomorrow if you apply yourself. But maybe it's worth getting the notes and analysis as well to help with the essay. Mom can hold onto it until you're finished reading."

The boy looked at his mom.

She sighed. "That's probably a good idea. It's been a while since I read the thing. And I don't remember loving it. Which is not—" She turned to pin her son with a glare. "—getting you out of reading it."

"Aw, man." The boy's impish grin made me and his mom both smile.

I pulled the commentary version I preferred off a nearby shelf and handed it to the mom. "Can I help you find anything else?"

"No. I think this is it. Thank you. We'll be back to browse sometime when we're not facing a weekend marathon of catching up on summer reading that didn't happen." The mom gave her son a fwap on the arm with the books.

"Sorry." He hunched his shoulders.

"You should be." The mother's grin belied her words.

I rang them up and they started toward the door just as Whitney and Kayla pulled it open. I watched my friends wait for the paying customers to leave and waited for the girls.

"Happy Friday." Kayla was already halfway to the comfy seats.

"Hey, Jenna." Whitney plopped onto the couch beside Kayla. "Are we late?"

"Nah. I was early." Jenna stretched her arms up over her head.

"Who has a fun story from this week? 'Cause I could use something cheerful." Kayla tucked one leg up under her. "I had no idea how badly some of the kids needed help even this early in the school year. It's been nonstop."

"That mom and son who left as you arrived? Summer reading that didn't happen. They're the fourth set this week. Different book this time, but still. Who forgets to do their summer reading?"

Jenna raised her hand.

I laughed. "Seriously?"

"Yeah. I would much rather have been outside doing something than inside reading." Jenna frowned. "That's not entirely untrue still today."

"You know you can read outside, right? There's not a law against that." I shifted in my seat. I didn't understand people who didn't love books. And okay, I got that I was an extreme case seeing as I ran a bookstore, but it wasn't like I hadn't been an avid reader before that.

Whitney chuckled. "I actually do have a rule against that at our house."

"What? Why?" I frowned at Whitney. "Reading outside is perfection. If the weather's good."

"Beckett likes to take the books outside to 'read.'" Whitney made finger quotes around the word. "And then he either drops them off the deck, because the hardbacks make a fun splat when they hit the pavement. Or he forgets when it's time to come inside and they inevitably get rained on. Or doused by the neighbors when they're out spraying their planters."

I winced. "All right. I can concede that maybe outdoor reading should only be undertaken by responsible parties."

Kayla laughed. "I like that you didn't put an age limit on that."

"I don't know if it's a fun story, but I'd sure like to hear about Megan's dinner with Cody." Whitney waggled her eyebrows.

I squirmed. "I'm helping him with the fundraiser he's in charge of for work. He needed to check out a restaurant that caters. That's it."

"Uh-huh." Whitney looked at Kayla. "Are you buying that?"

"I'm afraid I have left my wallet at home and am unable to purchase it. Jenna?" Kayla glanced at Jenna. "What say you?"

Jenna sent me a sympathetic look. "As much as I'd like to let you off the hook, I can't."

My jaw dropped. Jenna didn't even know Cody. It wasn't like she'd been doing any hanging out with the whole group—she wasn't always a guarantee on Friday nights. "Wow. I thought we were friends."

"We are. Which is why you shouldn't be hedging like this. Spill the deets." Whitney leaned forward. "The more you stall, the more I think there are good details to be had."

I groaned. "It was nothing. He got this fundraiser dumped on him and asked for help. I've been doing some web searches for him during the downtime around here. So once he got the venue confirmed, he needed a caterer. His boss's wife has a restaurant, it's on the list of preferred caterers for the Torpedo Factory, so we went to check it out. The food was amazing, so he was going to talk to them about the idea we had for the food. I don't know if he has."

Whitney's eyebrows drew together. "He had a tasting last night. He didn't tell you?"

It was like a heavy weight slammed down on my chest, which was dumb. There was no reason for me to feel as disappointed as I did. I shook my head and tried to keep my expression neutral.

"Like I said, I helped him out, is all. And I guess now he's got it all under control."

It wasn't like I could have closed the store early—again—to help him out last night. But gosh, I would have liked to. And not just because the food at Season's Bounty was delicious. I could admit that to myself. I could probably even admit it to my friends. Except I didn't want them to get any ideas about trying to matchmake. With Kayla and Whitney both married now, they seemed to see romance everywhere.

"Cody and I are just friends. You know all the guys think of me like a little sister." I shrugged. It was fine.

Kayla and Whitney exchanged a knowing look, but at least they kept the rest of their thoughts to themselves.

It was time to change the subject to one where I was not in the spotlight. "Did you know Jenna's looking to buy a historic home and rehab it?"

Kayla's eyebrows lifted. "Really? That sounds fun. I guess it makes sense for an architect to do. I have friends of friends of friends who did that in the Southwest part of the state. She bought this gorgeous Gilded Age mansion and fixed it up. Now it's a wedding venue and event center."

"Peacock Hill?" Jenna leaned forward. "I've been down there a couple of times since I moved out here. It's a really well-done restoration."

"Is that the one you showed me on your phone?" Whitney looked at Kayla. "For the women's retreat at church?"

"Yeah." Kayla nodded. "I hope we can make it work. It'll depend on how many people end up interested. If we can get twenty, the price drops enough that it shouldn't be out of anyone's reach."

"Twenty doesn't sound hard. You've got four here, right?" I glanced at Jenna. "Or maybe three, but you're certainly welcome to join us. I know you don't come to our church. Yet."

Jenna laughed. "Subtle. Noah keeps making that same offer. I like streaming the big church in Loudon from the comfort of my bed. Not tied to a particular schedule."

"Well, the offer stands." I looked at Whitney. "So three here. Just seventeen more."

"You make seventeen sound like such a small number." Whitney smiled at me.

"You should get it in the weekly email. Have you talked to the front office about that?"

The idea of a women's weekend retreat was growing on me fast. Of course, I'd have to find someone to cover the store, but I had a few people on reserve who could probably make it work. It'd just be two days, since I was closed on Sunday anyway.

"I have. I guess I'll ask the pastor about it, though. The secretary keeps giving me the runaround." Kayla's mouth tightened. "She doesn't like me because I didn't end up marrying Luke, and so he left the church, because I got together with Austin."

"What? That's not at all how that went down." Whitney crossed her arms. "Maybe let me talk to her this week."

"Sure. But don't say anything about me or the Luke thing. She's made up her mind. There's no point in arguing with her." Kayla touched Whitney's arm. "I'm serious."

Whitney scowled.

I fought a grin.

"Whitney?" Kayla held Whitney's gaze.

"Fine. I promise I won't say anything to her. Unless she brings it up."

"If that's the best I can get, I'll take it. But it really is fine. It all worked out in the end. In fact, I got an email from Luke the other day. He's doing great. He's found a wonderful church home in Colorado and the new ministry he's helping kick off is almost ready to launch. They've got a lot of financial support behind them, and it sounds like he's happier than ever." Kayla clicked the button on her phone like she was checking the time. "Anyone else feel like dessert?"

I raised my hand. "The ice cream shop has strawberry cheesecake this week."

"They do. Scott had some last night. I managed to snag a little taste. It's amazing."

"I'm in." Jenna shifted and started to stand. "I don't mind going to get it if you all tell me what you want."

"I'll come and help carry." Whitney popped out of her seat. She looked at me. "You want the strawberry cheesecake?"

"I do. In a bowl."

"Kayla?" Whitney looked at her.

"Yeah, sure. That sounds refreshing. I'll do the cake cone though."

I wrinkled my nose. Why anyone would take a cake cone when there were literally any other options was beyond me. "Hang on. Let me go get some money."

"Nah. My treat." Jenna stood. "We can call it a thanks for adding me to your crew gift."

"You don't have to—" I stopped when Jenna glared at me. "Thank you."

Jenna nodded. "Better. You ready, Whitney?"

"Absolutely. Not sure about ice cream two nights running, but I guess I'm going to live on the edge."

Jenna chuckled.

I waited until Whitney and Jenna had left before looking at Kayla. "Are you okay?"

"Yeah. It's just busy and somehow harder than teaching was."

"Do you think it's because you just get the struggling kids?"

I'd wondered about that when my brother first got this idea. He'd always told me the bright kids—the super achievers—

made things more bearable on days when he wasn't sure he was reaching the kids who struggled.

Kayla shook her head. "Actually, no. We've got a couple classes running in the late morning and early afternoon for homeschoolers. They're more like a typical classroom with that mix of students. It's nice to see kids who are excited about learning, too."

"All of them?" I lifted my eyebrows.

Kayla snickered. "Well, no. They're still kids, after all. But it's still been fun to mix things up that way."

I could see that. "Maybe it's just change. You know, now that you're in the middle of it and you have to face the reality that you're not in your classroom like you thought you'd be."

"That could be it." Kayla sighed. "Either way? I'm glad I've got Austin with me. I don't think I would have liked it if I'd stayed at the school and he wasn't there."

Aw. I loved how much Kayla loved my brother. And how much he loved her. They really were perfect for each other.

Maybe someday, God would see fit to bring me someone who would love me the same way.

And if it happened to be Cody? I wasn't going to complain.

# CODY

The church service finally wound to a close, and contemporary Christian music, like the local radio station loved to play, drifted through the speaker. I glanced down the row of my friends until my gaze landed on Megan, and I tried to catch her eye.

"So subtle." Austin's elbow in my ribs accompanied his whisper.

I glared at him. "What? I need to talk to her."

"Uh-huh. So go talk to her." Austin raised his eyebrows. "Will you be joining us for lunch?"

"Don't I always?" I actually looked forward to hitting up the diner after church with the crew. Sometimes the women sat at a different table. Sometimes we pushed tables together for a big, rowdy crowd. Either way was fine. I just liked the fellowship and sense of family that it brought.

"Just thought you might have other plans."

I huffed out a breath. "I want to ask if she'll go try a bakery with me after. For the gala. Is that acceptable? I didn't realize she—or I—needed your permission."

Austin chuckled. "Touchy, touchy. You know, I like bakeries.

You could invite me. Pretty sure Noah and Wes also are fans of baked goods. Tristan—well, he's on a health kick, so maybe not—but you get my point."

I did get his point. In fact, I'd spent most of last night tossing and turning and reminding myself of that same point. Not that it had done any good. I wanted Megan to come.

Just Megan.

"Yeah. I'll keep that in mind."

Austin snickered and clapped my shoulder. At least he didn't say anything else.

I hurried to catch up with Megan as she and a tall—wow, that woman was tall—lady made their way toward the foyer.

"Meg. Wait up." I jogged the last few steps after she stopped.

"What's wrong?" Concern clouded Megan's face.

My face heated. Of course she was worried something had happened. This was unlike me. Completely out of character.

I cleared my throat. "I was wondering what you were up to after lunch. You're coming to lunch, right?"

"Oh. Well." Megan glanced at the woman then back at me. "Have you met Jenna? She knows Noah. And she did the learning center design for Austin."

Jenna smiled and stuck out her hand.

I took it. "Nice to meet you. Maybe again?"

Jenna chuckled. "I think again. You look familiar. But it might be because Noah has talked about you."

My eyebrows lifted. Was Noah spending time with a woman? I'd have to give him a hard time about that. "You're joining us for lunch, right?"

"I hadn't planned to." Jenna glanced over her shoulder at the exit. "I really hadn't intended to crash the service. I told the girls on Friday that I preferred streaming, but they can be persuasive."

"Were we wrong?" Megan crossed her arms.

"No. You weren't wrong. It *is* better in person." Jenna's lips turned down at the corners. "Just not as cozy."

"Yeah well, you can't have everything. Come to lunch. I know the diner's better than any sandwich you could drum up out of your fridge." Megan glanced over at me, and I read a silent plea for backup in her expression.

"She's right. The food's good. Affordable. Filling. And you can't beat the company." I gestured toward the rest of the crew, who were finally making their way toward us.

"If you're sure I'm not intruding." Jenna bit her lower lip.

"Jenna! You're coming to lunch, right?" Noah joined our loose circle and shot her a welcoming smile. "And you'll come back next week? Be part of the gang?"

I studied Noah a moment before turning my attention to Jenna. She was probably three inches taller than him, but he didn't seem to care. Was there something going on there? I didn't often miss having a roommate, even though Noah had been the best roomie ever, but for a few seconds I got a little pang in my chest.

Jenna groaned a little. "How about I agree to lunch as a place to start?"

"All right. If it's the best we can get." Noah bumped his shoulder into her arm. "You want to follow me? Or did you catch a ride?"

"No. I have my truck." Jenna shrugged. "I can follow you, I guess?"

Megan made a shooing motion. "That's fine. We're all headed the same place. I'll see you in a bit."

The group began moving off.

"Hmm." I wasn't aware I'd made the noise aloud until Megan frowned at me. I held up my hands. "Just thinking. You have any scoop about there having been something between her and Noah in the past?"

"Jenna?" Megan shook her head. "She's never said anything other than that they've been friends forever, even though they lost touch for a while."

"Okay." I was going to let it go. There was no need to see unrequited love everywhere I turned simply because I was struggling with it myself. Well, not love. Unrequited...interest. Yeah, that was a more accurate word. I fell into step beside Megan as she headed out to the parking lot. "Hey. You up for trying desserts at a bakery this afternoon?"

"I might be. You sure you wouldn't rather go alone?"

I winced. That was a definite jab. I didn't have to guess who'd spilled the beans. I shot a glare over my shoulder at Whitney. Although it was probably Scott's fault, since I figured he'd told his wife, who'd then passed along the info. All because I was weak when it came to ice cream. "Should I apologize? I didn't think you could close early two nights in the same week."

Megan stopped and heaved a sigh. "No. You're right. I couldn't have gone. But I would have wanted to."

"I'm really sorry. I thought I was making it easier by not tempting you." Awesome. Way to completely mess that one up. Was I second-guessing and making all the wrong moves because I was trying so hard not to let on how much I enjoyed spending time with her? Which was, of course, making things weird between us.

"I'm a grown woman, Cody. I can make decisions for myself. At least I can when I'm given the opportunity." Her eyebrows lifted so high they practically disappeared into her hairline.

I hunched my shoulders. "I'm sorry. Again. I really would love for you to come to the bakery with me."

She frowned at me for several seconds before nodding. "You'll have to tell me about the Season's Bounty choices and why their desserts didn't work. Which bakery?"

"There's apparently a Swiss bakery near Shirlington. Paige

recommended them when I wasn't excited about her dessert options."

"What were..." Megan held up a hand as she stopped talking. "Hold that thought. Let's head to the diner, and you can fill me in there. We don't need to keep everyone waiting."

"Sure. See you there." I gave her a slight smile before I headed to my car.

In a perfect world, the group of us would be better able to figure out rides to church so we weren't all coming separately. At least with Scott and Whitney and now Austin and Kayla married we'd cut down some. But I always looked around the smallish parking lot and grimaced when I realized just how much of the space we took up.

My route to church took me right past Megan's townhouse. Maybe I should offer to pick her up. If I explained, she probably wouldn't think anything of it, would she? More to the point, would any of the guys?

My stomach knotted as I unlocked my car and climbed in. Scott and Austin both seemed to suspect—well, *know*. I'd all but confirmed it to them. How long, really, was it going to be before Tristan, Wes, and Noah figured it out?

I was going to have to say something to them, wasn't I?

No.

I started the engine.

No. I didn't need to talk to the guys because there was nothing going on. Megan and I were friends. It was all we could be. She didn't want anything more from me, and I was a fool to even consider that it could be any other way.

So. No need to talk to the guys. No need to do anything that I hadn't already been doing. Just keep on keeping on.

Megan would help me with the desserts today, and then I wouldn't need her to help me with anything extra and everything would go back to normal.

I switched lanes so I was behind Megan as she drove to the diner. Everyone else was already here and hanging out by the entrance. The diner got busy enough after church that they didn't seat until the whole party was there.

A little tendril of guilt and embarrassment wrapped itself around my throat. Good thing Megan had been thinking.

"Finally. I was beginning to think you two weren't going to join us after all." Whitney sent Megan a pointed look as we approached the group.

"Sorry. We got caught up."

I sent Megan a grateful glance. "It was my fault. I can go in and let them know we're here."

"No. I'll do it." Whitney, with Beckett hoisted on her hip, headed inside.

"Nice going, bro. Make the hormonal one's hangry even worse." Scott shook his head. "You're lucky she found crackers in her purse."

"I'm pretty sure she'd beat you up for calling her hormonal. I'm guessing that, for one, it's never actually appropriate to call a woman that and, two? It's not information that, even if true, a woman wants her husband sharing with her friends." I shook my head and sent Scott a pitying look. "You better hope she doesn't find out."

"Who shouldn't find out what?" Kayla leaned closer, grinning.

"Nope." I mimed drawing a zipper across my lips. "Look, Whitney's back."

"Come on, guys. Our table is ready." Whitney had poked her head out the door just enough to speak. Then she disappeared back inside.

The group filed through the doors and toward the large table the waitstaff had set up for us on the far side of the room. I wormed through until I snagged a chair to Megan's right. Jenna was on her left. Then on the other side of Jenna was Noah. Austin plopped down beside me and nudged me with his elbow.

I glanced over and had to fight not to roll my eyes as he sat there wiggling his eyebrows at me. He was such a pain. Beside him, Kayla hit him on the arm and hissed for him to stop.

Great. So four people knew. And if two of them were women, was there any chance at all that Megan didn't already know? I wasn't completely sure what the woman code was on stuff like that, but even guys would be rushing to spill details if they hadn't been sworn to secrecy.

Sometimes even if they had.

Megan touched my arm to get my attention. "Okay. Tell me about Season's Bounty and why their desserts won't work."

I ignored the warmth from her fingers and tried to organize my thoughts. "The hot food is all perfect. There were these chicken lettuce wraps that I honestly could have just eaten for days. Three kinds of bruschetta. Stuffed mushrooms. Some kind of skewer that had vaguely Greek seasoning to it and a dipping sauce that was a lot like what you get with a gyro."

"Yum." Megan held up a finger as the waitress approached our table.

I waited while we all ordered, got our menus collected, and conversation resumed around the table.

"Okay. Keep going." Megan clasped her hands together on the table. "It sounds fabulous."

"It was. I was disappointed that crabcakes weren't an option, but Paige explained that she only uses local, in-season ingredients and crab season ends before the gala."

Megan frowned. "Bummer. The crabcake I had when we went on Monday was divine."

"It was."

Megan had let me have a bite since we'd been there to check out the restaurant. In fact, we'd spent the entire meal sharing bits of each thing so we got to taste more than just what we ordered.

I cleared my throat and forced my mind away from the casual intimacy of that meal and back to the present. "Let's see. She did this thing she called a bacon puff—basically thick bacon in flaky pastry. Deviled eggs."

Megan snickered. "No way."

"They were good. And they were classier than your grand-mother's deviled egg." Of course, now I was worried. "Should I cancel those?"

She shrugged. "If you think they're fine, they're probably fine."

Except I could hear the derision in her tone. Shoot. I should have taken her with me. I could always call and set up a second —no. I'd given Paige the go-ahead. The food was good. And the layout ideas that she'd had when I explained the venue had seemed logical. Fun, even.

I took a breath. "Okay. The desserts were mostly fruit. And I mean fruit is good, but to have fruit in December, she was explaining, it was all basically canned."

Megan wrinkled her nose. "Gross."

"Not like store canned. Like granny canned. But yeah." I didn't completely get the fascination with only using local, in-season food, but it was the thing at Season's Bounty so it wasn't as if I was going to change that. Nor did I want to. People could do what they wanted with their businesses.

"Anyway, she suggested this bakery and a couple of other restaurants that have, in her words, phenomenal desserts. I thought the bakery was probably the best first choice. Thus my excursion this afternoon. You game?"

"Sure. I like dessert. We should see if anyone else wants to tag along."

I winced.

"What?"

"What what?" I wasn't sure I could pull off playing dumb, but I hadn't meant to react visibly.

She cocked her head to the side. "You winced. You don't want to invite the gang?"

"I don't want a committee." That sounded harsh. I blew out a breath. "Just...so many opinions is going to make it take longer."

"But you'll get a whole bunch of opinions and then you'll be confident that what you land on is the right mix. What if you and I like the bakery options, but the restaurants would have been even better? You're going to try them all before you decide, right?"

I shook my head as my stomach sank. "No?"

"Is that a statement or a question?"

I glared at her. "Statement. I already chose Season's Bounty for the food. I didn't try anything else. I liked what she presented and went with it. Maybe there's something better out there, sure, but where does it end? There's always the possibility of something out there being better, but at some point, you have to choose."

Megan's eyebrows lifted. "So you think the two of us, who like a lot of the same things, are going to be able to make a decision that'll appeal to everyone at the gala?"

"I think we'll be able to make a decision that everyone at the gala will agree was reasonable." It was a bit of a hedge, but how unlikely was it that we were going to be able to come up with something to appeal to everyone? I didn't think we'd get there even if we visited every restaurant in the area with a group of fifty. "People have different tastes. Different dietary needs. At some point, we have to decide the majority will be happy and run with it."

After a moment, Megan gave a slow nod. "All right. That's reasonable. I still think inviting everyone along would be fun."

I wanted to sigh. At the same time, I couldn't explain why I wanted to spend time alone with her. For all that I didn't believe the cat would stay in the bag forever with two couples in the know about my feelings, I didn't need to be the one spilling the beans. With any luck, when someone did tell her? Megan would laugh it off as ridiculous.

"I guess if they don't have plans, they're welcome to come."

Megan brightened and clapped her hands. "Yay! This is going to be great."

"Yeah." I hoped my smile was brighter than it felt. It wasn't going to be great. It was already an epic fail, as far as I was concerned.

# 8

## MEGAN

I was puttering through the bookshelves, dusting and straightening the books, when the bell over the door jingled. I looked over and grinned when I saw Whitney. "Hey, you. What brings you out on a Monday afternoon?"

"I needed out of the house." Whitney made her way over to where I was working and leaned against a shelf. "Beckett had a rough morning. He's down for his nap now and Scott basically kicked me out."

I frowned. "That seems extreme. Maybe you need a nap, too?"

Whitney shook her head. "No. The fresh air was better. And the walk."

I watched as Whitney's eyes filled and reached for her hand. "What's going on?"

"I miscarried again this morning."

"Oh, Whitney." I pulled her into a hug and squeezed. I couldn't imagine what that would be like, but I knew it wasn't happy. "You hadn't said anything."

"No. We were going to wait until twelve weeks. I was seven." Whitney swallowed and looked away. "I went to the doctor on

Friday to get checked. She warned me that my HCG numbers weren't what she'd prefer. But I really thought this time..."

I waited to see if she'd say more. She didn't. What was I supposed to say? What could I say? I didn't know how any of this felt. "I'm so sorry."

"Thanks." She gave me a tight smile that belied her shiny eyes.

"What if you held down the fort and I ran down to get us ice cream? Or coffee. I can go either way." I'd had half of my peanut butter and jelly around lunchtime. I still wasn't super hungry, but food was always comforting, wasn't it?

"Maybe an iced coffee? It's warming back up out there. Scott thinks our slightly cooler temperatures were a fluke and we're heading back to summer temps for a bit."

"We probably are. Seems like we do this every year. Early September brings a little relief and then, *wham!* We're back to the swelter until mid-October." I studied Whitney. She was pale and drawn. Somehow, she seemed fragile, which was definitely not a word I tended to think of when it came to my friend.

"What if you, Scott, and Beckett went home for a bit?"

She glanced at me, puzzled. "We are home."

I shook my head. "To your parents. Or to his. Or hey, why not spend a week or two with both? Get away and regroup with people who love you?"

Whitney blinked rapidly, clearly battling tears.

"Think on it. I'll be back in a jiff." I darted into the office to grab my wallet and keys. When I came out into the main bookstore, Whitney had curled into a corner of the couch. I snagged my cell phone from the register area on my way out, pausing to lock the door behind me. For all that she was willing, Whitney was in no shape to man the bookstore. It wasn't as if I tended to get a bunch—well, any—of customers on Mondays. But I didn't want to risk it.

As I strode toward the café, I called Scott.

"Hey. Did Whit come to the bookstore?" Worry frayed the edges of his words.

"Yeah. She's curled up on the couch. I'm running down for some coffee. I might go ahead and close and just hang out until she's done."

"You're the best, Megan. Thanks."

My heart broke for Scott. He sounded so unsure. And sad.

"You know I love both of you. All three, actually. Is Beckett still napping?"

His chuckle was strained. "Yeah. Hopefully, he'll wake up in a better mood than when he went down."

"He probably senses the tension and hurt."

"You think? We've been so careful not to let him hear us talking about it."

I tugged open the café door. "Kids are smart. They pick up on more than we realize. Hang on a sec."

I put my phone down by my side and approached the counter to order. Whitney's suggestion of iced worked for me—especially after that short walk through heat and humidity that belonged in July, not September. I paid and returned to the call as I slid down to the order pickup area.

"Sorry about that."

"It's fine. I appreciate you letting her crash at the store. This spring, it wasn't as hard. This time..."

I cleared my throat. "What if you went away for a bit, the three of you?"

"Hmm."

At least he hadn't jumped straight to a no. "I know you've got consulting and stuff, but can you do it anywhere? I feel like Whit might enjoy seeing her folks. And yours. And it'd be extra help with Beckett while she recovers."

"That's...not a bad idea. I'll reach out and see if they're up for it. And if not, maybe we'll just go to the beach ourselves. I've been looking at vacation properties in the Caymans. We could go down and see them in person. Maybe even stay in them."

The barista called my name and waved as he put the coffees on the pickup counter. I slid my phone away from my mouth so I could say thanks as I picked them up, then headed toward the door.

"You could always see if the grandparents wanted to come along—make it the best of all worlds."

Scott's laugh was brighter than he'd been the whole call. "I'll see what they think. Thanks, Megan."

"Don't make firm plans until you talk to Whitney though, okay?" I chewed my lower lip as I walked back to the bookstore. The last thing I wanted to do was railroad her into a trip she didn't actually want.

"No. Of course not. I do know a tiny bit about being in a relationship."

I snickered. "Just double-checking. I'm gonna go. I'm letting Whit stay as long as she wants."

"Appreciate it. We're fine here. If she asks, remind her of that, okay?"

The concern in his voice made me smile. Scott was a good guy. Of all my brother's friends, he was the one I would've chosen to be an insta-dad. He was pretty good at rolling with the punches.

"Will do. Later."

I ended the call and put my phone in my pocket so I could unlock the bookstore door. I was grateful the café had put the coffees in a drink carrier so I could hold them with one hand. I guess being rude and continuing a phone call while I was in there had paid off. Since I didn't make a habit of it, I didn't figure they'd hold it against me.

When I was inside, I headed to the sitting area. I opened my mouth to speak and then realized she was asleep. I set the coffees on the floor and went through the store to the back room. I kept a lap blanket at my desk for the days when the AC got overzealous while I was doing paperwork. I grabbed it and took it back to where Whitney was curled up. As carefully as I could, I draped it over her, then I bent down to wiggle my coffee out of the tray, and headed back to the register.

I was caught up on my paperwork. This morning, I'd even managed to get a little ahead on the ordering that I needed to do —thus why I had been dusting the bookshelves when Whitney came by. I hadn't finished that task yet, but it could wait until I drank my coffee. Or longer.

Of all the things I did at the store, dusting was my least favorite. It had to be done. I got that. But there was nothing saying it all had to happen on the same day, right?

I slipped the paperback I was reading out from under the counter and opened it at my bookmark. It was a good story. Not one of my usual genres, but I was trying to broaden my scope there. A bookseller needed to be able to recommend titles across the board. And I had a vague notion of doing a blind date with a book kind of thing in October except theming it more like a costume party slash masquerade for books. I hadn't completely fleshed out the idea, but if I did it, I'd need good recommendations beyond my perennial favorites.

Maybe I'd ask for the gang to make suggestions as well. I could also put out a call in the bookstore's e-newsletter.

I scribbled a reminder on the notepad I kept nearby for this exact purpose and returned to the book.

I got lost in the story, only surfacing when a sleepy-looking Whitney shuffled up to the counter, the blanket draped over one arm, coffee in hand.

"I guess I was tired." She sipped the coffee, frowned at it, then did a sort of spinning and shaking motion to try and mix it.

"Maybe I should have stuck that in the fridge so less ice melted. Sorry." I scrutinized her. "You look a little better."

"Gee, thanks."

I grinned. "That was a compliment."

She chuckled. "I'll take it as such. But since I know what I look like when I wake up from a nap, I'm now marginally terrified about what I looked like before."

"Pale, tired, and sad."

Whitney sighed and leaned against the counter. "I guess I can't complain, since that sums up how I feel pretty well."

"So." I stuck my bookmark between the pages and set the paperback aside. "I should probably mention that I suggested a trip to Scott, too."

"He called? How long was I asleep?" Whitney fumbled at her pocket before pulling out her phone. "Oh, wow. It's been almost two hours."

"You were tired. But also no. I called him when I went to get the coffee."

She seemed to think this over for a moment before nodding. "All right. I think I probably would have done the same, if the situation was reversed."

I exhaled. Phew. I wasn't trying to make her mad, but also? She needed time to process. And heal. And Whitney was a family gal, hands down, which meant seeing her folks and Scott's folks was the perfect cure.

"I don't like feeling this way."

"What way is that?" I cringed inside. Talk about awkward. Except I really didn't know. I'd never been pregnant. I'd never miscarried. The one time I'd been worried I was pregnant was something I pushed far, far away into the back recesses of my mind, because God promised that He kept the memory of our sin as far as the east was from the west. And if He didn't remember it? I shouldn't keep dredging it up, either.

Whitney was quiet for so long I wasn't convinced she was going to answer. Then she said, "Broken."

"Oh, Whitney." I reached out and rested my hand on the one she'd placed on the counter.

She shrugged, but I could tell it cost her. She wasn't nearly as nonchalant as she was trying to be. "Statistics say one in five detected first pregnancies end in miscarriage. One in three is more likely if you take undetected pregnancies into consideration. So I could sort of roll with the one in the spring, you know? I mean, it hurt. Even though we weren't trying, I would have been okay with it. But this one?"

I nodded, a lump in my throat keeping me from offering words that would inevitably have been dumb or unsuitable.

"I'm scared. What if it keeps happening? What if I can't ever get pregnant and stay that way? What if—"

I held up a hand and arched an eyebrow. "What if monkeys land on the moon?"

Whitney blinked.

"Grandma always used to ask me that when I'd start down that road. Then she'd start singing *His Eye Is on the Sparrow*, which I will not do, as one, I don't really remember the words and two, you've heard me sing."

Whitney snorted half of a laugh. "Your voice is fine."

"Exactly." I pointed at her. "It's fine. That old hymn requires more than fine to do it justice. Did people just sing better in the early 1900s?"

"I think people were more used to singing. And maybe everyone was a little less critical about it, too." Whitney shrugged. "But I wasn't there, so maybe not. You shouldn't be self-conscious about your voice, though. It's strong and on key, which is more than many can say, and even if it wasn't, we're told to make a joyful noise. It doesn't say make a professional quality song."

I tipped my head to the side. "I hit a nerve."

"A little." Whitney held up her fingers a tiny bit apart. "Scott barely sings at church. Same reasons as you—he says he can't carry a tune in a bucket. But he's wrong, just like you, and I want Beckett to grow up and keep belting out the words like he does now. Even when he doesn't always know the words, he sings out, loud and proud, because it's coming straight from his heart."

I smiled. I'd heard Beckett sing—anymore, he was liable to sing instead of talk—and Whitney was right. He did belt it out unapologetically. He still struggled occasionally to find the words he wanted if he was on the spot, but he was doing so much better than he was a year ago when he and Whitney had showed up on Scott's doorstep.

Whitney took a long drink of her coffee, then set it down. "You don't think I'd be running away?"

It took me a moment to figure out that she'd returned to the idea of vacation. "I don't. You're regrouping. Recuperating. And Scott mentioned the idea of combining the trip with looking at vacation homes, so you could even call it reconnoitering, if you wanted to keep with the 'r' theme."

Her smile actually reached her eyes this time. "I like those three Rs better than the usual ones."

"Don't get me started on 'rithmetic." I shook my head. "We have a hard enough time teaching people to spell. Do we really need to get cutesy with the foundations of schooling?"

"Sounds like you're getting yourself started."

"Sorry. I'll stop. I'm just saying." I took a breath and let it go. "My original point was that you shouldn't feel guilty about needing time to recover and rest—more 'r' words for you—and Scott is happy to take you wherever you might be able to do that better. And Beckett has two sets of grandparents who are more than happy to help while you do."

"You're right. Maybe we can all go to the island and look at the properties together. My folks could use a break. My sister's at a point now where I think they'd be willing to leave her and not worry." Whitney bit her lip. "I guess I'll head home and talk to Scott. Thanks, Megan."

"You know I love you, right?" I stepped around the counter and held open my arms.

Whitney rolled her eyes, but she let me hug her. "Back atcha."

"You're such a guy."

Whitney laughed as she stepped back. "I love you, too. Better?"

"Much. Give Beckett a smooch from me."

Whitney studied me. "I hope I didn't scare off your customers sleeping on the couch like that."

"No one even looked like they were going to stop in." I shrugged. "I'm thinking of closing Mondays anyway."

"You should. You deserve a two-day weekend like everyone else." Whitney opened the door but stopped and sent me a smile. "Thanks. Really."

"I want to say 'anytime.' But also? Not for this reason if we can help it."

"Amen." Whitney waved and stepped out onto the sidewalk.

I watched her until she disappeared from sight then blew out a breath and looked around the store. I should finish dusting and straightening the shelves. And then? I was going to go ahead and update the website with new hours. Closing on Monday wasn't going to hurt the bottom line. With savings on the utilities, it might just improve it.

# 9

# CODY

"Chocolate or strawberry?" I put the two samples of mousse down on the counter by the register and dug the two individually wrapped spoons I'd brought along out of my laptop bag.

Megan's eyebrows disappeared under her bangs. "Hi. Nice to see you, too."

I grinned. "Sorry. Hi. How are you?"

"Good. It's been slow today. I officially decided to close Mondays as well as Sunday, and now I'm wondering if I just need to close all together."

She looked so despondent I wanted to gather her into my arms and just hold her for the rest of the day. But that would only bring a whole host of questions I wasn't willing to answer. Even in my own mind. I settled for resting my hand on her arm. "I'm sorry."

Megan shrugged one shoulder. "I know it's how things go. Every day can't be Christmas. At the same time? I wish it could. Maybe I need to have a sale."

"That might get people in the door. Flip side, of course, being that then they won't come back until your next sale and then you have people who only buy things when they're discounted and maybe that's just as bad as having a smaller number of full-price customers?" I didn't know for sure that was how retail worked, but it seemed likely.

"Eh. Sort of. Sometimes the discount buyers turn into regular buyers when they realize I have the same prices as the big online store who shall not be named. Of course, I don't drop it on their doorstep within twenty-four hours. They have to drag themselves out of the house and come to me." She gave her head a firm shake and looked down at the desserts I'd brought. "Tell me why I'm eating this?"

"Because the bakery called and they can't do the custard on that big of a scale after all. I guess they talked to their chef and he was adamant that it only worked in small batches so it was too much work for the price we already contracted." I hadn't really bought that explanation, but what was I going to do? It wasn't like I could prove any of it. And I really wanted to stay with this vendor, if only because the idea of finding something else made me want to hop on the plane I shared with the guys and see what living in Bora Bora was really like. "This is their suggestion as an alternate."

"Did you try them?"

I nodded.

"And?"

I gestured to the samples in front of her. "And I need you to tell me which one."

Megan scowled at me, but she peeled the lids off both containers and took one of the spoons. After wrestling with the wrapper for a moment, she finally got it free and dipped into the chocolate mousse.

I could see she was taking her job seriously. She pondered, then took another little bite of chocolate before nodding and repeating the procedure with a new spoon and the strawberry mousse.

"Well?" It was good the guys didn't invite the women to play on poker nights. Megan would clean us all out. Either that or she genuinely didn't have a strong opinion either way.

"Strawberry."

"Really?" One corner of my mouth poked up. "That was the one I liked better, too, but I thought maybe I was being dumb. It feels like chocolate should be a no-brainer. But..." I didn't know how to finish the sentence. There was nothing *wrong* with the chocolate mousse. It just wasn't as good as the strawberry.

Megan held her hand up for a high five. I slapped it.

She picked up the strawberry and scooped another bite. A much bigger one this time. "I liked the chocolate. I'd eat it if it were all there was and I wanted something. But the strawberry? I feel compelled to finish it, and I know I'm going to want more when it's gone."

I chuckled. "That's a pretty good summary. All right. I'll let them know. Thanks."

"That's it?"

I nodded. "Yeah? Unless...never mind."

"Gah. Don't do that. Unless what?" Megan set down the container and crossed her arms.

Me and my big, dumb mouth. "I know you can't leave, but what if I brought you dinner? We could eat and hang out a little."

It was like Megan's gaze was boring into my soul. "You don't like living alone."

"Yes, I do." Sort of. Some of the time. I shrugged. "It's an adjustment."

She started to laugh and had to sit down on the stool behind the counter because she didn't seem able to stop.

"Glad I could provide some entertainment." I frowned. "I guess I'll see you later."

"Wait." Megan held up a hand and took a deep breath. Then another. "I'm sorry. I just know exactly how you feel. I thought it was going to be so great not having Austin around all the time. I mean there were days when I just wanted to go home and have some peace while I watched TV, but there was Austin asking about my day and all that. I miss it now, though. I get home and the house practically echoes."

"Yes."

I came back to the counter. Megan was batting a thousand today with her ability to put my thoughts into words. Not that it was all that unusual. It was one of the reasons I'd noticed her in the first place. After the initial, "wow, she's cute" reaction that I figured any guy would have when they looked at her. Then, as I got to know her—because she and Austin were peas in a pod and you couldn't know one without the other—well, I'd just say she'd carved out a part of my heart and claimed absolute owner-ship of it.

"I thought about getting a dog, but it doesn't seem fair when I'm gone all day. I don't think Mr. Ballentine would be on board with me bringing an animal into the office."

"Aw." Megan looked around. "You could get a cat instead. I could get a cat for the shop."

I wrinkled my nose. "That doesn't seem like a way to attract patrons. Allergies are a thing."

"Yeah, I guess. There are all these books about funky book-stores that have shop cats named Lizzie and Darcy or Jane and Rochester." She shrugged. "It's adorable."

"Sure. In a book. Do you want to go buy books covered in cat fur?"

Megan chuckled. "Probably not. All right. No shop cat. I don't even like cats all that much. I'd rather have a dog, myself."

I made a big checkmark on a list I hadn't realized I was keeping of all the ways Megan was perfect for me. "Small, medium, or large?"

"Are we talking dinner or dogs?"

"Dogs. But we'll circle back to the food in a sec."

"You're going to make fun, but I love Yorkies. Maybe a schnauzer."

I grinned. "So, a purse dog."

"Schnauzers don't fit in purses." She squirmed a little. "Okay, maybe they could go in a big shoulder bag. You probably want a big, goofy thing like a lab or a boxer, right?"

I shuddered. "Nope. I am not a fan of large dogs. I'm probably more team schnauzer than Yorkie, but I could be persuaded to go that route."

Her jaw dropped. "No way."

"Way." I didn't need to explain the whole big-dog-jumped-on-me-and-scarred-me-forever story, did I? It wasn't the manliest story in my arsenal and I'd rather not get into it if I didn't have to. I cleared my throat. "So. Dinner?"

"Yeah, okay. But not from the café. I go there entirely too often and I'm kind of over it. I feel bad saying that, but it's true."

"That's fair. I'm in the mood for Italian, anyway. What if I got takeout from Mia's?"

"I'm so in." Megan grabbed her phone and opened a browser. "Hang on and I'll tell you what I want. I can give you some money."

"Please." I waved that off. "One of us happens to have no issue on that front."

She visibly bristled. "I don't have money issues."

"No offense intended. I know you're a strong, competent, capable woman."

Megan squinted at me and I got the impression she was trying to decide if I was teasing her. I wasn't. Or not much. Just a tiny bit. The fact was, she was all of those things. And I loved her for it.

Wait, what?

Not loved. Liked. Appreciated, actually, would be an even better word.

Admired? Sure. That worked, too.

She turned her attention back to her phone, and I slowly let out a breath. I wasn't positive she still didn't plan to toss money at me, but seriously, what was the point of being a billionaire if I couldn't pick up the tab for dinner when it was my idea in the first place?

Megan set her phone down. "Chicken parm, a house salad, and if they can do that strawberry lemonade they do as a take-away? I'd love that."

"Garlic bread?"

The look she gave me practically shouted, "Duh!"

I chuckled. "Just checking. All right. I'll be back...well, I'd say in a minute, but it'll probably end up being closer to an hour by the time I get there, order, they make it, and I get back."

"That's okay. I'm not in a rush. You're sure you don't want me to—" She broke off when I shot her a look. "Sorry. Thank you."

I nodded once and headed for the door. I debated the merits of driving over. It might make bringing the food back simpler. At the same time? I had a good spot on the street and those were hard to come by. Megan said she wasn't in a rush, so I'd just walk. It was a nice evening for it.

I liked the small-town feel of Old Town. The cobblestone streets were charming, if a bit of a pain for walking. Trees lined the street and added interest to the brick buildings that made up the bulk of the shopping area. If I concentrated just a little, I could forget I was just a hop, skip, and jump from DC, and that outside the borders of Old Town was a bustling metropolitan area, complete with ridiculous amounts of traffic.

Mia's patio seating was bustling. If Megan didn't have the bookstore evening hours, I'd definitely want to spend an evening out there with her, enjoying a meal and watching the people walk by.

Gosh, I had it bad.

I needed to get over it, though. She was my friend's little sister. All the guys in the group considered her an honorary sister. And beyond that, we were friends. Sure, watching Kayla and Austin stop dancing around one another and admit they were in love had been great. They were living, breathing proof that friends could turn to more without ruining things.

But how likely was it, really?

"Hey, man."

I spun. "Wes? Hey. What are you doing here?"

Wes pointed to the restaurant. "Probably the same as you? Getting dinner. I was going to get takeout, but if you're here, I could eat with you. The patio's hopping."

Uh-oh. "I'm actually getting takeout. I told Megan I'd bring her dinner at the bookstore."

"Yeah? That's nice of you. Are you going to eat there?" Wes had his hands in his pockets.

"That's the plan."

"Cool. Okay if I join y'all?"

I wanted to growl. Or shout, "No!" Instead, I heard myself saying, "Yeah. Of course. More the merrier, right?"

Wes grinned and offered me a fist bump.

I popped my fist against his and pulled back while making the sound of an explosion. I reached for the door and tugged it open, gesturing for Wes to go in ahead of me.

We ordered at the bar. I went ahead and picked up the tab for all three of us. Not that Wes didn't have the same billions I did, but if I was going to fight with him about something, it wasn't going to be a twenty-five-dollar entrée.

"How's the dive shop coming?"

Wes perked up. "Good. I should be able to open in January. At least that's the plan."

"So you have your space?"

He nodded. "Yeah. I opted for the bigger one that's technically outside of Old Town, but still in Alexandria. It's got the space for me to get an indoor pool in the back."

"A pool? In a retail space?" How did that even work? I couldn't quite wrap my head around the idea. Maybe Wes had been spending too much time diving and was suffering from some kind of weird delusions.

Everything about Wes seemed to lift and brighten. "Yeah. It's going to be so cool. No having to rent time at the community center pool or anything like that for classes. It's pretty easy to do —even with a retrofit like this. There's a company who works with a ton of the swim lesson franchises, and now they have the whole thing down."

"Won't the whole place smell like chlorine?" I still had less than amazing memories of the indoor pool at the Y where I'd learned to swim when I was little. I shuddered. "And the humidity?"

"Nah, man. That's old school, but it's not like that anymore." Wes shook his head to underscore his words. "No smell and the pool is in a separate temperature zone, so while it's a little more humid in the pool area, that won't permeate the rest of the shop."

"I'll take your word for it." I couldn't picture it, but I guessed I didn't have to.

"You'll see. I need to get info on Noah's architect. I'd like her to help with the design, if she will. I think I can have a classroom, the main retail space, and the pool."

"The space is that big?"

He nodded. "I think it'll work."

"Cool."

A server came by with a giant paper bag. She set it on the bar. "Gentlemen, here's your food. Enjoy your evening."

"Thanks." I reached for the bag. "Oh. Strawberry lemonade? Can I get that to go? I was supposed to ask."

"Sure. I'll be right back." The server hurried off.

"Sorry."

Wes shook his head. "Don't be. It's good stuff. Megan wanted it?"

"Yeah."

"She's always had that sweet tooth."

Had she? I rolled the idea around in my head and tried to make it stick. It wouldn't settle. Sure, she liked an occasional sweet, the same as most people, but that was it. Thankfully, I didn't have to comment because the server came back with a large to-go cup.

"Here you go."

I took the cup and reached for my wallet. "How much?"

"Don't worry about it. Your tip more than covers it." The server smiled and wandered off.

"What did you tip her?" Wes jabbed me in the side. "That your new way to get girls to look in your direction? It's a good angle."

"No." I glanced in the direction the server had headed. Had she thought I was hitting on her? "I was just being nice."

"Uh-huh." Wes shot me a knowing grin. "Come on. Let's get this food back to the bookstore before Megan begins to wonder if you were just joking with her about buying her dinner."

I didn't bother to sigh. As we crossed the bar to the door, I thrust the bag of food at Wes. "Since you're crashing this party, you can at least make yourself useful."

He took the bag. "Where'd you park?"

"I walked from the bookstore." I wasn't going to explain any further than that unless he asked. Even then, I was sure exactly how to phrase things. Megan had been helping me with the fundraiser. Had I technically needed her input? No. But it would still pass as an excuse.

Probably.

"You want a ride?" Wes pointed to where his car sat.

"How'd you swing that spot?"

"Clean living?" He grinned at me and started toward his ride.

I fell into step beside him. "Clean living, huh?"

"Sure. You should try it." Wes's words were full of laughter. "Or maybe I happened to be driving by just as someone else was leaving and took it as a sign to eat here."

"Aha."

That was much more likely. Not that Wes was a bad guy. He loved Jesus the same as the rest of us in the group. But he'd also been the most enthusiastic about embracing his new life as a billionaire. The Tesla model S I climbed into was one of many cases in point.

"This is new."

"Yeah. It just came. I like it. The acceleration is amazing." After he checked the traffic, he proved his point by tearing away from the curb.

"You're going to get so many tickets."

"Nah." Wes shook his head. "Anyway, I like it for driving around town. It holds a decent amount in the trunk, too."

"Your other cars don't get lonely?"

He sent me a bland stare. "You could always get another car yourself, instead of being jealous of mine. There's no law that says you can't spend the money. You know that, right?"

"Hey. I bought a house."

"True." Wes pulled into a spot near the bookstore. How he had such great parking luck was a mystery. "Isn't that nicer than walking?"

"Faster, at least." I grinned and pushed open the car door then grabbed Megan's drink from one of the cup holders. "You got the food?"

"Yeah, yeah." Wes opened his door and got out. He reached into the back seat for the bag holding our meals.

I closed his door and waited for him to make his way to the curb, then walked beside him to the bookstore.

"That was fast." Megan looked over as we stepped inside. "Hey, Wes."

"Hey. I ran into this clown buying dinner and figured I'd save you from being alone with him." Wes gave a mock shudder, as if hanging out with me was the worst fate anyone could imagine.

Megan's smile looked forced, but she batted her eyes. "Gosh. Thanks."

"Any time. Seriously. If he's lurking around and you're getting bored, never hesitate to call. You know I live close."

"Hey." I punched Wes in the shoulder with a little more force than I might normally use. Sure, joking around was par for the course, but I definitely didn't need him trying to convince Megan that I was some kind of creeper. It was bad enough that the group kept horning in on things that I set up as a way to spend time with her.

"Ow. Watch it, man." He looked irritated.

Good. At least he was feeling the same thing I was. Massive irritation. "Should we set up over on the comfy chairs?"

Wes had already started in that direction. "Where else would we sit?"

"In the back?" Megan nodded toward her office area. "But this makes it easier for me to help if someone comes in."

I studied her as we walked over to join Wes. Something in the way she'd said that was off. "Business bad?"

Megan shrugged. "It's fine. It's Wednesday night. Not exactly prime bookstore hours, you know?"

When were prime bookstore hours? She frequently mentioned when they weren't. But did she ever get a crowd?

"You should have an event and get some people in. Remind everyone that you're here." Wes looked up from digging in the bag of food. "When I get the dive shop's retail space set up? I'm having a massive grand opening to make sure people know I'm there."

Megan's smile looked tight. "How nice for you."

"What?" Wes frowned. "I'm not saying you should do that. But you could do something, right? What makes you a better bookstore than the big chain at the strip mall?"

Wes needed to shut it. Immediately. Couldn't he see that everything he said was making it worse? Not that I disagreed with his point, necessarily, but there had to be a better way to go about it. And Wes—Mr. Bull-in-a-China-Shop when it came to expressing his opinions—was not the one to help.

But I could.

For now, I'd change the subject. "Is there plasticware in there?"

"Yeah. Here." Wes tossed me a set, then lobbed another at Megan. "You two really got the same thing?"

"Apparently." I reached for a takeout container and handed it to Megan before collecting my own. "Is that a problem?"

"Nah." He peeked in the bag. "Ooh, garlic bread. Did we order that, or did the waitress with the hots for you throw it in as a bonus?"

My face was on fire. I was *not* going to look at Megan though. I clenched my jaw and spoke through gritted teeth. "I ordered it. You were right there. And she was being nice."

Megan snickered. "Maybe you were being clueless."

I groaned. With Wes horning in, this whole evening was devolving rapidly. Maybe I ought to grab my food and head home. That was probably an overreaction. But gosh, it was what I wanted to do.

Wes was already stuffing food in his face.

I looked at him and lifted my brows. "Not going to wait to pray?"

Color blazed across his cheeks and he swallowed hastily. "Sorry. You're right. I get distracted."

"I'll do it." Megan closed her eyes and folded her hands over the container in her lap. "Jesus, thank You for food and friends. Keep us focused on You and in Your will. Amen."

I mumbled a quiet, "Amen" and flipped open the lid on my food. The rich scent of tomato and cheese filled the air. It was almost enough to distract me from obsessing about Megan's choice of words. Friends.

Not that she was wrong. We were friends. All of us.

But man, I wanted to be more than that to her.

# 10

# MEGAN

"Thank so much. Have a great night." I smiled at the customer as she hoisted a bag bulging with books off the counter.

"Oh, I will. The problem is going to be deciding what to read first." The woman grinned. "I'll be back, I promise!"

"I'll look forward to it." I watched her leave and blew out a breath when the door closed behind her with a cheery jingle. I could use two or three sales like that every day, but I sure wasn't going to complain.

Wes's words from Wednesday had been haunting me all week. What *did* make my bookstore better than the big chain at the strip mall?

For Old Town residents, I was right here. But I wasn't even really competing with the chain store. The online giant was the real competition. I couldn't beat overnight delivery to someone's doorstep. Or e-books.

And the thing was? I loved e-books, too. So I got it. I did. They were convenient and didn't take up space in the house. Sure, there were downsides. There was something relaxing about the weight of a physical book in my hands and the smell of the ink. The quiet whisper of a page turning.

I sighed.

I loved books in all their forms. It made running a bookstore the perfect career. Unless, of course, I couldn't figure out how to get the bottom line up to a level that removed the challenges of keeping the lights on every day.

"Happy Friday!" Jenna called out as she pulled open the door.

"You're cheerful."

Jenna grinned. "It's Friday and I've got a line on a renovation project. I'm going to see it tomorrow and, if it's as perfect as it looks like it's going to be, maybe I can get the purchasing ball rolling."

"Congrats. Where is it?"

Her smile dimmed. "That's the only slight issue. It's in Georgetown."

I winced.

"Yeah, I know. I never thought about moving into DC proper. But if I hate it, I can always look for something else and sell it." Jenna shrugged. "Maybe I'll get out there tomorrow and it won't be what I'm looking for after all."

I forced myself to be cheerful. "It could be perfect. And it's not so far on the Metro. Or in a car, although that probably takes longer."

"There you go." Jenna nodded. "So I'll see what happens. Either way, it's nice to find something I'm actually interested in seeing in person. What about you? How's your Friday been?"

"Good." Ish. Apart from the one big sale, I'd had a few browsers walk in and leave with a book or a pack of gum. Everything counted, as far I was concerned. "Let me ask you something."

"All right."

"What makes my bookstore better than ordering online or heading to the mall?"

Jenna's eyebrows winged up. "What brought this on?"

"Wes said something." I waved it off. "It got me thinking. I need to do something to bring in business. And that means I need a hook, right? Something that makes me a destination more appealing than the convenience of never having to leave the house."

"I guess I can see that." Jenna turned to look out over the store. "You could expand your local interest section."

I'd thought about that. "Those books only sell to tourists who happen by."

"That's surprising." Jenna moved closer to the books featuring, primarily, the history of colonial America.

I shrugged. "Most of the titles there are also carried at Mount Vernon. Or any of the other historic sites that have a gift shop. Usually when I sell one, the conversation is along the lines of how they looked at it when they were visiting such and such a place, but now seeing it again they had to have it. Sometimes, I'm tempted to get rid of it all together. But they do sell in small quantities."

"You carry independently published books, right?" Jenna turned back to face me.

"Some, yeah. I've been thinking I could expand that, somehow. The question is how." I sighed and leaned my elbows on the counter beside the register. "I've had a few authors stop by and ask about selling on consignment. I don't really want to do it that way."

"Why not?"

I frowned and struggled to organize my thoughts. "I guess because it somehow makes the books feel less to me. Does that make sense?"

Jenna wiggled a hand from side to side.

"You think I should do that? It's less risk for me. I can give the books back if they don't sell. But then, I feel like I'd have to keep them on a separate shelf, not mix them in with their genres on the regular shelves, and then the only people who are going to find them are the ones who are already interested in an indie title. Which means fewer people will discover the amazing stories that are getting published outside of the traditional publishers these days."

"Unless they're looking for local authors."

I pursed my lips and considered Jenna's statement. On the one hand, the people stopping by to suggest selling on consignment had to be local. On the other? If I was going to buff up my support of indie authors, there was no reason I couldn't put that on the website and make it possible for any independent author to send their books. "I guess I could limit it to local authors. Or, what if I agreed to buy say ten copies at an agreed-on wholesale amount? Then they'd be my books to do what I wanted with and if they sold, I could get more. If they didn't, I wouldn't. But ten is a nice number for an author to sell, and it cuts down on reorder frequency. Maybe."

Jenna laughed. "Sounds like you already know what you want to do."

"I guess it does." I couldn't explain why I was still so unsure. So tentative. The bookstore was mine to run as I wanted, but it had belonged to Grandma for so long before that, I was used to having someone else give the final say. "Is it unique enough?"

"I think you should try it and see." Jenna pushed off the bookshelf she'd been leaning against. "I'm going to go sit in the comfy seats. Am I chronically early or is everyone else late all the time?"

I snagged my phone from under the counter and followed her. "It's more that the Friday thing is a loose, unstructured meet-up. Everyone shows up when they can. If they can."

"Ah." Jenna settled into a chair.

I waited for her to elaborate, but she didn't. Sometimes, Jenna was hard to read.

"Are you working on any fun projects for your firm right now?"

Jenna launched into a discussion of the remodel of a 1980-era ranch in Falls Church she was designing. I tried to follow along, but it didn't seem like she actually cared. She was just happy to talk about load-bearing walls and beams and combining rooms to make them larger and more functional.

She was in the middle of describing how she was going to re-do the bedroom layout to make space for the primary bedroom to have an *ensuite* when the bell over the door jingled and Kayla and Whitney arrived. Together.

"Hey, guys. Sorry to be late. Beckett." Whitney rolled her eyes. "I really thought the phrase was terrible twos, not fearsome fours."

I laughed. I couldn't help it.

"Gee. Thanks." Whitney scrunched her face at me. "So much sympathy."

I held up a hand and tried to get my chuckles under control. "I'm sorry. Sorry. My mom says it never gets better. It just gets different."

"Yeah. That sounds about like what my mom keeps telling me." Whitney blew out a breath. "I'm looking forward to seeing her. And heading to the beach."

"When do you leave?" I was glad Scott had taken my advice and arranged the trip. Some time away would be good for all of them. Maybe even Beckett.

"Tomorrow afternoon. My folks couldn't get away until then and I thought it'd be more fun—plus a little more efficient with the plane—to all go together." Whitney sagged onto the couch.

"Maybe it's all the packing and rushing that set Beckett off. He's excited. I know he is. I just wish…"

Kayla rubbed Whitney's arm before turning to look at me. "How are Cody's event plans going?"

"Good, I think. He ended up back here on Wednesday with another dessert choice."

"Seriously? After we all helped at the bakery?" Kayla frowned. "What did he get rid of?"

"The custard."

I closed my eyes and tried to drag up the explanation Cody had given. Sometimes when he talked, I missed the actual words because I was focused on his mouth. Which was stupid for a thousand reasons. He didn't think of me that way. And I wasn't going to ruin my relationship with him—the only one of my brother's friends who didn't treat me like I was an annoying little sister—because of my misguided crush.

"I think he said the chef wouldn't do a big enough batch. Something about it not working like that."

"I can see that." Jenna leaned forward and propped her elbows on her knees. "My *abuela* makes flan. It's delicate. Custard is similar."

I studied Jenna. "I like flan. Any chance you have her recipe?"

Jenna snorted. "You do *not* want me trying to bake. I don't starve, but flan? Nah. It's way outside my wheelhouse."

"Your grandmother didn't teach you?" Dang it, I really wanted flan now, and finding a restaurant that did a good, not rubbery, job was next to impossible.

"She tried. I'm hopeless. Gingerbread houses? Those I can do." Jenna grinned. "Architecture for the win."

Kayla chuckled. "If we do a competition this year, you're on my team. Mine always breaks apart."

"That's because you try to make a skyscraper." I shook my head. "You're never satisfied with a house."

"Guilty." Kayla shrugged. "Maybe this year I'll make a model of the learning center instead."

"Are you going to let Austin help you?" I smirked. Austin always lost the gingerbread competitions. He was hopeless.

Kayla sucked a breath through her teeth. "Do I have to?"

"He is your husband." Whitney jabbed her elbow into Kayla's arm. "Winning isn't everything."

"Says you. You haven't even seen how heated these competitions get." Kayla frowned. "I guess I have to. If we're doing this? I need to know now."

"Why? Are you going to practice or something?" I laughed, trailing off as I watched Kayla's expression. "Oh. Wow."

"Talk to the group. If we're doing this, we should get it on the calendar. Would we do it in the Caymans?" Kayla reached to the bag at her feet and dragged out a thick planner. She flipped it open and started turning pages. "Austin and I have been talking about closing the center for the month of December so we could spend longer in the islands. He's starting to get serious about finding a place to buy down there."

"I thought he wanted to go different places?" I bit my lip. I really thought I remembered Kayla mentioning that at one of our girls' nights in the winter. She'd been on a crusade to get everyone to commit to a mission trip to Mexico during spring break, and Austin had balked.

"He does." Kayla leaned back, her fingers tapping the page in her planner. "I do, too. Kind of. I also like the familiar and low-key hang-out-and-do-nothing vibe we have at the beach."

Whitney nodded. "I like that, too. Thankfully, Scott and I are on the same page. We're looking at places to buy when we're down there. I'll keep you posted on what looks good, if you want."

"I want. But I guess I should double-check with Austin and make sure he's not just doing it because I pushed him. It's not like I'd mind seeing Germany or whatever, but in winter? It's cold there at Christmas."

I thought it sounded magical. Snow on the Alps? Yes, please. "Don't you like to ski?"

"There's that." Kayla blew out a breath. "Would everyone want to do a ski vacation instead? I mean, it's not like we have to spend all of our Christmas breaks together. But I like the idea of spending time with our group for some of it. We're family."

I grinned. "We are. And we'll definitely spend time together. But I imagine Scott and Whitney wouldn't mind time with their folks and Beckett without the rest of us hanging around. Same for the rest of the guys. You're stuck with me, though, since you had the bad taste to marry my brother. Although not at Christmas, sadly, because retail."

Jenna snickered. "I feel like you were on board with that whole thing. Granted, I'm new here, but really."

"Okay, fine. I'm thrilled. Truly. But also, he's my brother. So ew."

Kayla wiggled her eyebrows suggestively.

I pretended to retch.

"Children, please." Whitney's voice was full of laughter. "I think, at the end of the day, we're not ready to write in your calendar, Kayla. So you probably need to tuck that back away. But if we're all doing different things for Christmas, maybe we could do a gingerbread competition at Thanksgiving. Most of the guys don't bother to head back to see their parents for that, so it might be an easier sell."

"Genius." Kayla shot Whitney a grin and flipped back a page of her calendar. "I'm writing that in. Who's hosting this year?"

"I think it's Cody's turn." They all turned to look at me, and I worried my face resembled a tomato. I tried for a nonchalant shrug. "He said something about it when we all visited his new place."

"And you just happened to remember it?" Kayla's gaze was penetrating.

I looked away. I remembered a lot of what Cody said, but I didn't need everyone knowing that. Especially not my sister-in-law. Whatever Kayla knew, Austin was bound to find out sooner or later.

For what seemed like forever, Austin had had ideas about me dating. Or even being interested in guys. He was a big part of why I hadn't had a serious boyfriend in...too long to remember. Unless you counted Reuben, which I totally did not.

I glanced over to the door as the bell jingled above it and my stomach sank. It was as if I'd conjured him with my thoughts.

Whitney's eyebrows lifted.

I shrugged. He hadn't been in to the store for a while. Maybe he just needed a book. I stood and headed toward the register. "Hi, Reuben. Can I help you?"

"Nah. Just came to look around and see what's new." His gaze cut over to where the girls were sitting. "I see it's time for your Friday night gossip fest."

I bristled. "We're not gossiping. We're friends hanging out."

"Uh-huh. And talking about what's going on in everyone's life. Kind of the definition of gossip, don't you think?"

I clenched my teeth together and tried to stay polite. "Not when we're all talking about our own lives. There are some new books in two of the fantasy series you like. And I saw that the final book in the long-running series has a release date now. I can place a pre-order for you so it's here as soon as it's available."

"Oh, I ordered that online." He waved away my words as if they were no big deal. "They have that pre-order price guarantee, and I'm pretty sure I got a discount. But thanks."

"Sure."

He looked at me and seemed confused. "Did I say something wrong?"

"No. No, of course not. It's always great to hear about customers enjoying the perks of my competitors." I couldn't stop the words. I should have. It was unprofessional. And my tone had definitely crossed the line into snotty.

Reuben shook his head and gave me a look that would've been more appropriate if I was a small, misbehaving child. "Oh, Megan. Competition is how businesses thrive. If you can't handle that, maybe you're in the wrong career. It didn't even occur to you to offer me a bigger discount to pre-order with you? I can cancel the online one, you know."

I wasn't going down this rabbit hole. I'd tried it once or twice in the past. The fact that he kept coming around was probably because of that. Well, that and I'd actually gone to coffee with him a couple of times in the spring. What had I been thinking? Mostly that I wanted him to keep buying books from me and not completely tick him off. I'd held out the ridiculous hope that he'd decide we weren't a good match on his own and leave me be.

I didn't know how to respond, so just offered a tight smile.

"Well?" He crossed his arms.

"Let me know if I can help you find anything." I moved around the counter to stand by the register. I wanted to head back to the girls and reclaim my seat. They looked like they were having a good conversation that I was missing. But I also didn't completely trust Reuben at this point and the best vantage for the store was by the register where I could physically see people *and* I had access to the monitor displaying cameras for the hidden areas.

Reuben frowned. "You're not even going to try?"

"I'm not, no. It's not my policy to offer individual discounts that aren't part of a store-wide sale or publisher promotion." At least I'd managed to keep my voice steady. I really wanted him to leave.

"But I bought you coffee."

I studied his incredulous look a moment before responding. "I'd be happy to pay you back."

"No." He scowled at me. "But good luck staying in business. I know people who read, and I'm going to fill them in on how hostile you are."

"Okay." My stomach clenched into a tight knot. The store wasn't going to survive a big campaign against it. I wasn't sure Reuben actually had the kind of clout to do anything more than tell the basement dwellers he played D and D with every Saturday, but I also really didn't want to find out.

He stabbed his finger in my face. "You'll see."

He jerked the door open and stormed out. I waited until he'd marched down the sidewalk as far as I could see before letting my shoulders sag.

The girls hurried over.

Kayla grabbed my hand. "Are you okay? We were debating calling the police."

"I'm fine. I'm glad you didn't." I mustered a small smile. "I think I just lost a customer, though."

"Ugh. Good riddance." Whitney wrinkled her nose. "I still can't believe you went out with him."

I closed my eyes on Jenna's shocked expression. "Can we not get into that? Please?"

"Fine. Sorry. Still." Whitney patted my arm. "Come sit down. Did I really hear him threaten to start a smear campaign?"

"Basically, yeah." I bit my lip as I followed the group back to the sitting area. "I'm not sure he can do much damage. But just in case, I need to figure out how to make my bookstore stand out."

"We're going to help." Jenna gave a decisive nod.

Whitney and Kayla murmured agreements.

With a tight smile, I made my way back over to the sitting area with them. My thoughts were muddled and swirling around. But the one that popped to the forefront more than any of the others?

I wished Cody were here.

# 11

---

## CODY

I stood outside the expansive front of the red brick townhouse at the address Noah had texted me. It was big. Bigger than anything I—or any of the other guys—had. Which wasn't a big deal. It wasn't like we were in some house size competition. But what was he going to do with that much space? I was rattling around in my place and it wasn't even half this size.

I glanced down the street and caught a glimpse of Noah jogging my way.

"Sorry!" He called out as he checked both ways before darting across the quiet road. He came to a stop near me and raised his arms up over his head, linking his fingers. "Sorry. I couldn't decide if I should drive or walk. Nothing in Old Town is far, you know? But then when I started walking, I realized the apartment was actually a bit of a stretch from here."

I laughed. "All good. You made it. The real estate guy?"

"He's on his way. He called a minute ago and said he was running late. But he also said it was okay if we wanted to walk around back and look at the gardens. It's got almost half of an acre." Noah took a deep breath and let it out slowly. When he spoke again, all evidence of his jogging was gone. He pointed to the right side of the building. "Let's go that way."

"What are you going to do with that much land?" I couldn't quite picture Noah spending his free time mowing grass or digging in garden beds.

He shrugged.

I understood the desire to have a place of his own. I'd bought something in the spring. He was the only holdout still in a rental. But for all of that, none of us had gone this crazy. "I guess you could put up a swing set so Beckett could come over and play."

Noah chuckled. "I'd be okay with that. Although they enjoy the park near their place from what I gather."

He pulled open the gate in the low, wrought-iron fence that surrounded the property and gestured for me to go through.

I stepped onto the brick walkway and looked around. "It's pretty. You're going to need a gardener. And someone to fix up the paths."

Noah looked where I'd pointed to the three bricks that had been tossed to the side of the path, nearly under the bushes that lined it. He squatted, grabbed one, and fitted it into the pattern. "That's not too hard. But a landscaping company isn't a bad idea. I might like pushing a mower now and then, though."

I snorted. "Sure. In the middle of July, when it's ninety-five degrees and ninety-eight percent humidity, that's going to be super fun."

"You don't do it in the heat of the day. You get up early. Or wait until after dinner."

"Right. Got it. Then it's cooled down to ninety. That makes sense."

Noah laughed and punched my arm. "Maybe I like the heat and humidity."

"Uh-huh." I shook my head and we walked along the path to

where it opened on a large patch of grass. "Are those crepe myrtles?"

"They're trees."

"Do you know anything about plants?" I looked at the row of trees—I was almost positive they were crepe myrtles—that lined the edge of the brick path along the back of the house.

"I can learn, same as you. There's the Internet now, had you heard?" Noah squinted at the trees. "Maybe Megan has a book about this place in her local Virginia history section."

I doubted it. This wasn't a tourist attraction. Didn't look like it ever had been. I'd read the historic marker out front while I was waiting and, since it was going on about some famous poet and playwright living here in the middle of the twentieth century, it just didn't seem like the kind of place people had been flocking to visit. Plus it was a private home now for sale so it could continue being just that. "You can ask her."

"But you think not." Noah shook his head. "You're so easy to read."

"Then why do I beat you at poker practically every week?"

Noah just scowled at me instead of answering.

I grinned back. "When is the agent getting here? This is a nice lawn and stuff, but you're not going to live out here."

"I might. For the seventeen days a year when the weather is nice enough to do so." Noah pulled his phone out of his pocket. "Looks like he's here. We can head to the front door and he'll meet us there."

"Sounds like a plan." I tucked my hands in my pockets and continued to eye the green space as we worked our way back around. It was really nice. Was I being negative because I was jealous? I had plenty of space in my townhouse—but absolutely zero ground that could be called mine. The little patch of lawn out front was community space. On the positive side, that meant the association did all the mowing and weeding and whatever-elseing needed to be done. On the other hand? It wasn't mine.

"Noah. Great to see you." The man I assumed was the real estate agent extended his hand as we approached the steps to the front door. "Hi. You must be Cody. I'm Steven. Glad you could come along."

"Happy to do it." I shook Steven's hand.

"Let's go on inside. I won't bore you with the historical details—I'm sure you read the listing, right, Noah?"

"I did. I'm not sure I could pass a test, if it came to that, but I have the basics. Seventeen ninety-five, right? And Robert E. Lee grew up here."

Steven glanced up from his phone with a grin. "That's right."

After the agent fiddled with his phone for a moment, the lockbox on the door clicked. Steven reached for it and removed a key before unlocking the door and pushing it open. "After you."

Noah stepped through first. I followed. I barely registered Steven coming in behind and pulling the door shut.

"As you can see, the entry is stunning. The previous owners had started on a renovation-slash-restoration project, but ran out of funds. But they did a wonderful job on this space."

I glanced at Steven then turned back to the foyer. They had, indeed, done a fantastic job here. Gleaming wood doors stood to either side of the street entrance. More wood lined the bottom quarter of the walls, making them seem even taller than they were. "This is fancy."

"Yeah." Noah blew out a breath. "And I realize 'historic' means people go for restoring instead of changing. I'm for that. Mostly. But the colors…"

"They're not bad. The wallpaper is what, cream? That's what I'd call it, anyway. And the carpet matches. It looks like any federal historic home I've ever toured." I shrugged.

If Noah was going to finish the renovation, it wasn't like he had to keep what the people before him had done. But he probably needed to try and stay somewhat within the realm of historic accuracy.

"Are there rules that go into what he can do since it's a registered home?"

Steven wiggled a hand from side to side. "There's leeway. The damask wallpaper might not be your style, but it's a good choice from a historic standpoint. Let's go left, into the living room. It's the other room that's been finished. For all the other spaces, I have drawings and plans I can share of what they'd worked out with their architects and designers. You don't have to use them, but they are included in the purchase price."

We wandered into the living room and I winced. It was done in a sort of apple green. Sure, very seventeen hundreds if everything I could drag out of my memory of entirely too many trips to Colonial Williamsburg was to be believed. But also not a color I could see living with.

"Where does the flat screen go?"

Noah laughed and looked my way. "Right? I'm trying to picture comfortable furniture in here and failing."

Steven looked pained. "Why don't we move on across the hall?"

I trailed behind Noah and Steven as they went through the dining room, family room, breakfast area, and kitchen. The designs for the family space and kitchen were modern enough while maintaining some of the historic feel, but I still couldn't picture Noah living here.

The stairwell in the foyer was open all the way up. I stood at the bottom just gazing at the twists of stairs. How did you get furniture up there? Maybe some kind of hoist system, since it was open?

It took another hour to make our way through the rest of the property and look at the various plans for renovation and restoration. Thankfully, once we moved out of the formal rooms on the main floor, the space became a lot more livable.

But it was still so much space.

"How many square feet is it?" I looked at Steven as I stepped back down off the bottom step into the foyer.

"Just over eight thousand."

I looked at Noah and fought a laugh. "I rattle around in my place, man, and it's just two."

Noah raked a hand through his hair. "I know. I get it. But I just..."

Steven cleared his throat. "Why don't you think about it and get in touch? We can come back and walk through again any time. Obviously, properties like this don't tend to fly off the market, so there's no reason not to take your time."

"Yeah. Okay. Thanks, Steven. I appreciate it." Noah shook Steven's hand.

I nodded at the guy and followed Noah out onto the street. We stood by the historic marker sign, hands in our pockets, as Steven locked up. He sent Noah a cheerful smile as he walked past us and down the street to a silver sedan parked near the end of the block.

"Dude."

"I *know*." Noah blew out a breath. "Is it weird that I kind of love it, though?"

"Yes. It's weird. Possibly delusional. It's *eight thousand square feet*. What are you going to do with that? You have a family of twelve stashed somewhere I don't know about?"

Noah chuckled. "No. Flip side, there's a lot of work that would still need to be done. So it's not all ready to live in anyway. Maybe by the time it's done I'll know more what I'm doing."

"And what? You sell it and move into a condo?" I honestly

couldn't see where he was going with this. "Since when do you want to live in a reno anyway?"

Noah shrugged.

I narrowed my gaze. "Wait. Does this have anything to do with Jenna?"

"No. Why would you say that?" Noah shook his head and crossed his arms.

"Defensive much?" I let out a short laugh. "I don't know why I didn't see it."

"There's nothing to see. Jenna and I are old friends." Noah turned to look at the front of the building. "But you have to admit, renovating a place like this would be right up her alley."

"You should come back with her and get her take." I wasn't sure why I didn't drop it. I was the last person to start pushing about someone else's relationships. I sure didn't want anyone doing that to me when it came to Megan. At the same time, there was that whole saying about too much protesting, and it fit Noah to a T.

"Maybe. She'd have ideas. She could even tell me if the plans the sellers are leaving are the right way to go. Some of the ideas seem dumb—did you catch that dressing room?" Noah laughed. "Why would anyone in their right mind need a space that big to get dressed in?"

"It's also the walk-in closet for the master." But yes, he had a point. It was a big room that could easily be another bedroom. Not that the house needed to have seven bedrooms instead of six.

"Maybe I will talk to Jenna about it." Noah faced me. "I still appreciate you coming along."

"Still happy to do it. Especially since you're going to help me stuff invitations for the gala in exchange."

"What? No." Noah held up his hands and backed away two steps. "Not happening. I don't want to have anything to do with that. I don't want Mr. Ballentine or Jackson getting the idea that I'm their next sucker. Event planning is not, nor will it ever be, my forte."

"Like it's mine?"

"You seem to be making it work, so yeah." Noah shrugged. "Those save-the-date cards were top notch. All the women have been chattering about how excited they are to have it at the Torpedo Factory. So you sure picked a unique venue. Maybe you ought to volunteer to do the summer fundraiser, too."

"No. I didn't come up with any of this on my own. It was all Megan. If there are props to give, they go to her." I hoped my voice was neutral, but given how Noah was looking at me, I might have let too much warmth seep in.

"Megan, huh." Noah eyed me. "Been spending a lot of time with her, I guess?"

My shoulders wanted to hunch. "Maybe a little more than usual. But she's been a big help. Like I said, anything I've managed to make happen has been her. Well, and I guess the rest of you when you helped choose desserts last week."

"That was fun. If you need more help like that, be sure to let me know." Noah grinned. "What are you doing with the rest of your Sunday afternoon?"

"Not sure. Go home and hang out, probably. See what's on TV. You?"

"My folks are in town. They're staying at the Marriott downtown. I'll head that way and hang out with them. Maybe we'll hit the pool or go walk around the Smithsonian Mall. Whatever they want to do." Noah checked the time. "I guess I should get going. I told them I'd be there, for sure, by three."

I glanced at my phone and laughed. "Yeah. You've got an hour. Why did you schedule this walk-through today with your folks in town?"

"You think I knew they were coming?" Noah snorted. "You've forgotten how they are. They just call and expect me to be free."

I guess I did vaguely remember that. "Drive safe."

"Thanks. See you in the office tomorrow." Noah lifted a hand before he turned and broke into a light jog. Maybe I should have offered him a ride?

I went to my car and climbed in behind the wheel. Then I just sat there. I didn't want to go home. I hadn't been kidding about the fact that I rattled around in the place. Sometimes, having my own space with no roommate or anyone else around was great. But most of the time? I had the TV on just to keep it from feeling ridiculously empty.

Lonely.

I turned on the car and checked for traffic before pulling out of the parking spot. I should go home. Maybe I could find a series to stream from the very beginning. That would give me something to look forward to every evening.

And yet, instead of turning where it would take me to my place, I found myself on Megan's street. There was a spot right in front of her door. I took it as a sign and made quick work of parallel parking.

I shut off the engine, unbuckled, and pushed open my door.

Maybe she was out. She could be busy doing paperwork at the bookstore or hanging out with the girls—although Whitney and Scott had taken off yesterday for an extended vacation, so it would just be Kayla. And maybe Jenna.

I doubted Kayla was spending her Sunday afternoon away from Austin. Did newlyweds do that?

Better not to think about it too hard.

Nerves jumped in my belly as I approached her front door, which was dumb. We were friends. I was just a friend stopping by to say hi. That wasn't weird at all.

Right?

# 12

## MEGAN

I almost ignored the doorbell again when it rang the second time. It was Sunday afternoon and I just wasn't in the mood to buy wrapping paper or candy or popcorn or whatever the little kid who was out there not taking the hint was selling.

I groaned.

I wasn't old enough to be this obnoxious. Next thing I knew, I'd be yelling, "Get off my lawn!" and shaking my fist at the children skateboarding or riding their bikes on the sidewalk in front of the townhouses. Of course, it'd be nice if their parents paid attention every now and then, because some of them...

I stopped that train of thought and forced myself up off the couch. This was ridiculous. I was going to answer the door, smile, and buy at least two things to prove—to myself if no one else—that I wasn't some crazy old lady.

With a glance in the mirror of the hall stand that was beside the door, I fixed on my brightest grin, winced a little, toned it down so it didn't look borderline insane, and opened the door.

I blinked at the back of the man walking away from my door. "Cody?"

He turned and cocked his head to the side. "Hey. You are home."

"Yeah. Sorry. I was…" How was I supposed to explain that bit of temporary madness? I wasn't. So yeah, leave that alone and move on. "Did you want to come in?"

"Not if you're busy. I was, ha ha, in the neighborhood."

I snorted. My hand flew up to cover my face as it burned. I could only imagine the fire-engine red pulsating through my pores now.

"Nice." He chuckled.

"Yeah, well. You're always in the neighborhood. You basically live in the same neighborhood. We all do. You've never stopped by before." Oh, man. I shouldn't have said that. The slight undercurrent of accusation was uncalled for. Because why would he have stopped by? Maybe to see Austin. But Austin was always busy, so the guys made plans to get together. They weren't a group of random, spontaneous hanger-outers.

Hanger-outers? Ugh. What was wrong with me? I needed help.

Obviously.

I cleared my throat. "You can come in. I'm not busy."

"You're sure?" He took a hesitant step toward the door while watching me like I was a skittery cat.

Great. I stepped back to make room and made an elaborate flourish with my hand, beckoning him in.

He flashed one of those knee-weakening grins and slipped past me so close I could feel the warmth of his body.

Which I should absolutely not be focusing on. He was a mammal. As was I. Mammals were warm blooded. So of course there was warmth when he passed me, if there wasn't, then he could be sick. Or have a thyroid condition or something and oh my word, I was babbling in my brain and it needed to stop.

I shut the door and turned the top bolt.

He looked at me, one eyebrow lifted.

"Habit. Sorry. I'm not locking you in or anything. You can leave whenever you want. Promise." I closed my eyes. Could I be any more of an idiot? "Like now, because I'm being weird, and I wouldn't blame you for a minute."

"You are being a little weird. I'll give you that. Are you okay?"

I peeled open one eye and looked at him. He was watching me, but not in a "What's wrong with the crazy lady" way. I'd take it. "Yeah."

He waited. To be fair, he was probably expecting—and probably deserved—more of an explanation. But what was I supposed to say? I was sitting in the living room flipping channels and letting my mind concoct romantic fantasies about you before you showed up?

No. Way.

Ever.

"Um. Would you like something to drink? Or a snack or something?" I headed into the kitchen without checking to see if he'd follow. I wasn't the best hostess in the world, but I had some manners.

What I didn't have was a lot of drink options.

"What do you have?" Cody pulled out a chair at the kitchen table and settled in it, looking completely at ease. Completely at home.

What would it be like to have him there? My mind took off—those fantasies came easier and more frequently these days than ever before—and there he was in pajama bottoms and a snug white tee, hair tousled, and sleep still clinging to his features.

I turned away so fast I hit my face with the fridge door.

Ouch.

"Are you okay?"

I couldn't look at him. The laugh that came out of my mouth bordered on hysteria. "Fine. I'm good. Just a klutz. I have water."

I stared at the contents of the fridge and reached in to shift a few of the condiments. "Oh hey. I have fancy sparkling water from something. You want?"

"Sure. That beats tap water." Humor laced his words, but also concern.

I grabbed the two cans of La Croix that had been lingering in there for who knew how long and shut the fridge. "I really am okay."

"Uh-huh." He took the can from me and his fingers brushed mine and my whole system went on alert. He popped the top and took a drink, then wrinkled his nose. "Why do people like this?"

I moved to sit across the table from him—no way was I sitting on the same side—and opened my can. I took a drink and shrugged. "It's bubbly like soda, but without all the sugar and calories?"

"But it's not sweet. It's honestly almost bitter. And this is supposed to be lemon lime?" He shook his head. "I don't see it."

I took another sip. Maybe he had a point. It wasn't the strongest flavor out there. But then again, it was water, not soda. "I like it. I can get you some tap water after all, if you'd rather."

Cody shuddered. "No, I'm good. I don't get how you drink the tap water here without some kind of filter first."

"I guess it's what you're used to." The tap water had never bothered me. Was it as good as out of a bottle or this fancy sparkling water? No. But it didn't taste bad or leave a weird after-taste or anything, so why not drink it?

I set my can down on the table. "So what really brings you over? Something up with the Christmas event?"

"No." Cody's shoulders hunched slightly. "I really was just in the neighborhood. Noah and I went to look at that historic home that's for sale a few streets over."

"Seriously? Jenna was talking about that on Friday. She's

drooling over it, but can't swing the nearly six mil they're asking. I guess that's not a big deal for Noah."

What would that be like? None of the guys—well, maybe except Wes—threw their money around or made a big deal out of the fact that they could drop six million on a house without blinking. But it was a fact that was never super far from my mind. It would be so easy—so nice—to just ask Austin for a cash infusion for the bookstore. But then where would it stop? I was already pretty sure he'd bought the building from Grandma. Neither had said anything, but Grandma was a lot less interested in how things were going these days and I couldn't chalk it all up to me taking over the whole thing instead of having employees.

Cody's cheeks were pink. "There's that."

"Is he going to buy it?"

"Not sure. He likes the lot. And okay, I can give him that the backyard is pretty impressive, especially for a place in Old Town. But I don't know what he'd do with eight thousand square feet of house and a half acre of yard. It'd be great for a family of twelve or something, you know?" Cody spun his seltzer can on the table. "I rattle around in my place, and it's what? A quarter of that? Maybe a little more. No yard."

I nodded. "I get that. Since Austin and Kayla got married, I've been wondering if I should have agreed to let them live here and taken over her apartment. I don't need this whole place to myself."

"Did they want to do that? Swap places?"

"I'm not sure what their preference would have been. They gave me a list of options they were okay with and let me choose." And I'd chosen to stay here. Why?

Cody frowned. "Why'd you pick to stay?"

I chuckled. "Mind reader. I was just asking myself that. I guess because change is hard and moving is a drag."

"Fair." He grinned. "You know, you can probably tell them you've changed your mind, and they'd be willing to trade."

Would they? They were closer to the learning center in the apartment. On the other hand, it was a one-bedroom apartment for the two of them and Kayla's two cats. Not that cats took up a lot of space or anything, but they were still creatures sharing the place.

I blew out a breath. "I like walking to work. Not having to deal with parking, all that. But yeah, I'll think about it a little more. It's probably the right thing to do."

"Driving and parking—any other cons? It would cut down on the rattling around."

I bit my lower lip. "I've never actually lived in an apartment. So there's the whole going into the unknown thing. What's it like to have people on the other side of basically all your walls?"

"It's not so bad. Most places are pretty well soundproofed." He frowned. "Although Kayla's in an older building, so don't quote me on that."

I laughed. "If it was bad, we'd be hearing about it from Austin. Improving the barriers between our shared walls was the first thing he did when we took over this place from Grandma. He doesn't like neighbor noise."

Cody grinned, and I thought my heart was going to stop.

I looked away. "So do you regret buying your house?"

"Nah. I love it. I love being able to see the water and watch TV whenever I want at whatever volume I want—being mindful of the neighbors, of course." He winked.

My face heated again and I quickly took another drink to ease my suddenly dry throat. I needed to get over this...whatever it was. Crush? Infatuation? I tried to keep my voice natural when I spoke.

"Of course. I'd expect nothing less."

Silence settled between us. But it wasn't strained or weird—at least not to me—it was comfortable. Pleasant, even.

I got another little mental flash of him as I imagined he looked when he woke up in the morning, and with it a subtle yearning from somewhere in the vicinity of my heart.

"Can I ask you a question?"

I pulled my thoughts back from flights of fancy and focused on Cody. He was leaning forward, arms on the table. He looked serious. My heart sank a little. He'd noticed and was going to let me down easy. Because of course he was. What else would he do?

"Sure. Always."

He licked his lips and his gaze darted around before returning to settle on me. Was he nervous? Cody made a quiet sort of throat-clearing sound. "How would you define our relationship?"

"Our relationship? You and me?" I gestured to the two of us, like a moron. I was buying time, because I wasn't sure what the right answer was. "I don't understand."

"Are we friends? Acquaintances? Just people who end up in the same place because we have mutual friends?" Cody spread his hands apart. "Something entirely different?"

I swallowed. "Maybe a combination of things? We started out as people who ended up in the same place all the time because of Austin. I'd like to say we've gotten past that and are friends in our own right, though. Why?"

"So just friends?"

I studied Cody's face. Was he asking what I thought—hoped—he was asking? But what if he wasn't? What if he was completely good with being friends and I opened my mouth to tell him I thought more than that and he was like, eww, no?

"How would *you* define us?"

It was a cop-out answer. The kind of answer parents gave

when they were too busy or distracted or annoyed to just answer. And for the first time in my life, I understood a tiny bit why they did it.

"Definitely we're friends. I just wonder, sometimes, if that's all we are?" Cody's eyebrows lifted and he leaned forward a smidge. "If it's all we can be, or if there's a chance for more."

A thousand different answers flickered through my brain in the space of two heartbeats. I wanted to take the time to think through the repercussions of each and then choose the very best one. The one that posed the least risk to either of us. But that wasn't what my heart wanted. My heart saw its chance and circumvented my brain, and I had one of those strange out-of-body moments when you see and hear yourself doing something that isn't well thought out.

"I'd really like there to be."

## 13

---

## CODY

My heart stuttered. Had she really said what I thought I'd just heard? I couldn't have stopped the grin that spread across my face if I'd wanted to. And I definitely didn't want to.

"For real?"

Megan wouldn't meet my eyes, but she nodded.

It was all the encouragement I needed. I reached across the table and took her hands in mine. There was no way to describe how long I'd wanted to hold her hands like this—and more, but there'd be time for that. I wasn't going to rush her. Or me. It wasn't like we could announce to the world that we were dating. It wouldn't go over well in the group at large.

Austin might have said he was okay with it when it was all some nebulous, up in the air idea. I didn't know how he'd respond to it becoming reality.

So we could wait on that some.

"How do we do this?" Now she looked up and met my gaze.

I laughed and squeezed her hands. "Now who's the mind reader?"

She smiled. "It's complicated, right? It was complicated in

my head when I thought there was no way on earth that you'd ever be interested in me like that."

"I've always been interested in you like that." I gave a small shrug. "Just to be clear."

Her brow furrowed. "What do you mean?"

"I mean pretty much from the moment I met you, when you were way too young for me to be thinking about you as anything more than an annoying little girl, I was doing it anyway." I winced. That came out creepier than it had sounded in my head.

"Yeah? Well, same goes." She chuckled, head shaking. "Why do we make things harder than they need to be and miss out on so much?"

"Do you want to go sit in the living room?" I really wanted to be closer to her. At least on the couch, she could be next to me. I could put an arm around her. Maybe she'd rest her head on my shoulder. All the things I'd imagined—well, okay, not all of them—for so long.

Megan's answer was to stand and come around the table. She'd kept hold of one of my hands the whole time. Maybe she *had* been hoping for this as long as me.

We moved to the living room and settled on the couch. Megan tucked herself up beside me, head on my shoulder. I wrapped my arm around her, and laid my cheek on the top of her head.

"This is perfect."

She chuckled. "I think that's my line."

"We can share."

Megan sighed. "That doesn't explain what we do from here though. Austin..."

"Of all the guys, he's not one I'm worried about. Mostly. I sort of have his permission."

She twisted her head so she could meet my gaze. "What do you mean?"

"This spring, when I was looking at my house before I bought it, I kind of let it slip that I had a crush on you. He seemed cool with it."

"And you didn't make a move?"

It seemed stupid, now. "I should have. Definitely."

"But you didn't because?"

Her direct, steady gaze made me want to shrink into myself. "It boils down to being nervous. Maybe Austin was okay with the idea. But what's he going to think about the reality? What about the rest of the guys? I can guarantee Wes and Noah are going to have problems with it. Tristan might not care either way. Scott—well, he seems on board."

"You've talked about this with Scott?"

"Not on purpose." I didn't like the censure in her tone and scrambled to explain. "I was debating asking you to join me for the tasting at Season's Bounty. Actually, I was sitting in my car at the curb talking myself out of asking you to come along. Scott, Whitney, and Beckett showed up to get ice cream. I joined them. Scott, it turns out, sees more than you think he does."

Megan grunted. "Whitney, too. Well. That explains a few things she said the other day."

"Do I need to apologize?"

"No. I get it. It's not like I haven't been trying to act like there's no interest on my end, too." She sighed. "Why do we have to have a group of friends who are all so...invested in everyone else's life?"

I laughed. Invested was the perfect word. "In the long run, it's probably a good thing."

"Yeah, probably. But if we're going to hide our relationship from them, it's going to make things a lot trickier than it would be otherwise."

I wanted to tell her we didn't have to hide it. I certainly didn't *want* to sneak around like we were doing something bad. Maybe

—just maybe—there was a tiny thrill at the idea of keeping it to ourselves, but mostly it was a big complication. "What if we told everyone?"

"Ugh. Drama." Megan shook her head. "You said Wes and Noah would have an issue. I can see where you're coming from. Wes, especially, acts more like a big brother than my actual big brother ever has. I think he likes the idea of getting to beat someone up if they're mean to me."

"That sounds like Wes. Can I just say I was so mad when he horned in on our dinner from Mia's the other day? I spent the whole walk over there thinking about how great it was going to be to have you all to myself. How maybe I could see if you felt anywhere close to the way I did. And then, *wham!* Enter Wes. Ruiner of all things."

Megan patted my leg. "Aww. He doesn't ruin *everything*. Just most things."

I laughed, but it ended on a sigh. "He's not going to take it well."

She blew out a breath. "I don't know if the girls will care. On the flip side, they're probably going to tease me mercilessly. I've kind of protested about not liking you. A lot."

I clutched a hand over my heart dramatically. "Ouch. I'm wounded." I grinned and kissed the top of her head. "I'm sorry. Is this a situation where we need to rip off the bandage and deal with the fallout?"

"No. I'm not ready for that. Can we keep it to ourselves? Enjoy being together without it being this big thing? For a little while at least?" Megan tipped her head back to meet my gaze. She was biting her lip.

I nodded slowly. It was what I wanted, deep down. Not only did I want to savor having something with just the two of us for a while, but there was an element of excitement that came from it only being between us. And there was the whole thing about not being sure how the guys would take it. Maybe they'd be cool, but...

"I don't want us to lie. If someone asks, outright, we come clean."

"Okay. I'm not good at lying, anyway." She managed a small smile. "It makes it hard to sell someone a book I hated if they ask what I thought. Usually, I can come up with another recommendation, though, so it works out."

I laughed. "At least you have alternatives. I bet you also can find things that did work about the book."

"Most of the time. There are a couple though—" She wrinkled her nose. "—with no redeeming qualities. But other people love them, so I can just say something about them being super popular."

"See? Not a lie. Just not a ringing endorsement." There was a small part of me that wanted to ask Megan when we would be able to be out in the open. I understood—even embraced—the idea of keeping things quiet for a while. But not forever.

When would we know the time was right?

Because when I looked at Megan, I saw the woman I wanted to spend forever with. And sure, it was way too early to say something like that out loud if I didn't want her running away as fast as her legs could carry her. But it also meant clandestine love affair was not the long-term solution.

Megan shifted, her chin tipping up just a bit more.

My gaze darted to her lips.

Was it too soon? We'd been friends forever. I'd been crushing on her in secret for forever.

I swallowed and looked away.

"Cody?"

I looked back.

"Is there a reason you won't kiss me?"

I shook my head. The few flimsy reasons I'd thought I had

evaporated like mist in the sunlight of her words. I lowered my mouth to hers and the time for worrying was over.

I COULDN'T STOP my grin as I pulled into a parking spot a few shops down from Megan's bookstore. Everything between us had changed on Sunday. For the better. Yesterday, I'd joined her for dinner at her place and she'd told me all about her day off. We didn't have official plans to see each other today, but I hadn't wanted to go home without at least saying hello.

"Hey, Cody." Jenna stepped through the door of the ice cream shop with an enormous scoop of something chocolate in a waffle cone. "What brings you out on a Tuesday night?"

Dang it. Already my brain was scrambling to come up with a lie. And that was something we weren't going to do. "Thought I'd swing by the bookstore on my way home."

Jenna nodded. "That was my plan. Then I saw they have double chocolate chunk as their flavor of the week and I had to stop in. I really wish Megan's store wasn't so close to this one. Their ice cream is the best."

"It is." I walked beside Jenna. "Did you need a book?"

"Nah. Just figured I'd say hi to Megan. Maybe spend an hour or so. I don't like the idea of her being here at night on her own after seeing this dude Reuben harassing her on Friday."

My eyebrows shot up and all my muscles tensed. "Someone's harassing her?"

"Maybe that word is too strong, but he definitely couldn't take a hint." Jenna licked her ice cream. "And since she doesn't mind if I eat in the store, I can have dinner and some company."

I chuckled, but couldn't say if it sounded normal. Inside, I was seething. Why hadn't Megan mentioned she had someone making life difficult? Now that I was her boyfriend, that was something I needed to know.

I pulled open the bookstore door and let Jenna go in ahead of me.

Megan was helping an older woman, but she glanced over and her eyes lit up when they landed on me. She held up a single finger before returning her attention to the customer.

Her response eased some of my tension. But not all of it. Even before we were dating, if someone was hassling her, she should have said something to me. Or one of the guys. We would have...I paused that train of thought. Huh. Maybe that was why she didn't say anything. Because we absolutely would have handled it.

And Megan was capable of handling herself. It was one of the things I loved about her.

I sat in one of the comfy chairs across from Jenna. "Megan mentioned you were looking at the Lee-Fitzhugh house."

"Only in my dreams." Jenna dug a napkin out of her pocket and wiped her lips. "I ran the numbers again this weekend and there's no way to make it a profitable flip. And I just don't need a place that big for myself. It's too bad, though. It's a great house. Great lot. Even better? The landscaping in the back is fine. I wouldn't have to do much—if anything—there."

"Have you talked to Noah?"

Jenna looked at me, confused. "About the house? No. Why would I?"

"I actually toured it with him on Sunday afternoon. He's thinking about it."

"Seriously?" Jenna's eyes lit up and it was a startling transformation. Then she frowned. "What would he do with a house that big? Is he dating someone I don't know about?"

"No. Or, I guess if he is, no one knows about it." I don't know why I added that bit. Probably a guilty conscience because I'd started to realize just how easy it was to end up in a secret relationship. Especially if you started with a secret crush. I cleared my throat. "So probably no. Noah's not exactly someone who keeps secrets well."

"True. Although he did date the prom queen for about two weeks in high school with no one the wiser."

"Noah? The prom queen?"

How had I never heard this story? I glanced quickly over my shoulder, looking for Megan. She was still with the customer. I should be glad—books needed to be sold so she could keep the store going. But I'd rather she had time to hang out with us. Or, well, me. I returned my attention to Jenna.

"I need to know this story."

Jenna shook her head. "I shouldn't have said anything."

"No way. You have to spill the tea. Come on."

She rolled her eyes. "Fine. It's not that great of a story. She asked him out—I think she'd just broken up with the football player she was dating."

"Of course she was dating a football player. Was she a cheerleader?"

Jenna chuckled. "You'd think, but no. She played lacrosse. You didn't want to mess with her. Anyway, she asked him out, he said yes—I think maybe because he was scared to say no, honestly. They went out two or three times over the course of like two weeks, then she dumped him and got back together with the football player."

"Ouch." I'd been hoping for a story I could tease Noah with, but that one was maybe a little too harsh. Oh, who was I kidding? I'd be looking for a way to mention it. But I'd stop if he asked me to. Probably.

"He didn't seem too broken up about it when it all came out. I guess she'd told him he couldn't say anything to anyone, but she told a few key people so it got back to her ex. Really, she was using him to make a point." Jenna shrugged. "Noah never dated well in high school."

"I'm a little surprised he dated at all. He never talks about it."

"Not surprising. He was awkward." Jenna shoved the last bit of cone and ice cream into her mouth. It was a big bite, so she held up a finger while she chewed, covering her mouth with her other hand. Finally, she swallowed. "Don't tell him I said that."

I mimed zipping my lips. I wasn't going to tease Noah about being awkward in high school. We'd all been awkward at some point. But the prom queen thing? That was going to have to be mentioned.

"Hey. Sorry." Megan flopped onto the sofa beside Jenna. "I love customers, but that woman needed more help than seems reasonable when she was just trying to pick up a copy of her book club's latest selection. It wasn't as if there was a choice involved. What brings you two out tonight?"

"Oh. No. It's not like that." Jenna held up a hand and shook her head vigorously.

"Wow. Thanks." I chuckled as I clasped a hand over my heart.

Jenna's face blazed red. "Sorry. I didn't—I just—you know what? I should go."

"Don't be silly." Megan grabbed Jenna's arm and tugged her back down. "I didn't mean it like that, either. Either way, it's nice to have company."

"That's why I came." Jenna lifted a shoulder. "I'm still a little worried about that Reuben guy."

Megan's gaze darted over to me.

I lifted my eyebrows.

Her lips thinned. "I'm fine. He's not a threat. But I appreciate your concern."

"I got ice cream out of it, so I'm not complaining. And now that your customer is gone, I might pick your brain for another good steampunk series. Your last recommendation was fantastic, but I finished them. Why do some authors stop at three?" Jenna drummed fingers on her knee. "Don't they know readers want more?"

"Some do." Megan looked out over the bookshelves. "I have an idea, but I'll have to order them. You trust me?"

"Yeah. Absolutely." Jenna started to reach into her pocket.

"Stop. You can pay when they come. Give me a week, okay?"

"Okay. Thanks."

Megan grinned. "Not only is it my job, but I enjoy it. So you were out for ice cream and worrying unnecessarily. What about you, Cody?"

Really? She was doing that? I gave her a long look. "Just thought I'd stop by on my way home."

"I could recommend a book or two for you, if you wanted." Megan's eyes danced with humor.

She was really putting me on the spot. I didn't love to read. Everyone knew this about me. And even dating a bookseller wasn't likely to change it. But two could play. "You know what? Sure. Hit me."

Megan blinked. "Oh. Okay. Hmm."

I watched as she furrowed her brow. After a moment, she popped out of her seat. "I'll be right back."

I felt Jenna's gaze on me and turned casually. "What?"

"Not a reader?"

I shook my head. "Everyone knows it. Everyone makes jokes."

"Well, good for you for giving it a shot." Jenna blew out a breath. "Noah's really considering that house?"

"Yeah. Or at least he was on Sunday."

"I'm gonna go call him. He shouldn't buy a reno like that without talking to someone who knows what she's doing. Tell

Megan I'll catch her Friday, okay?" Jenna stood and strode from the store, her long legs carrying her quickly from view.

I couldn't help but think Noah was in for it.

I also couldn't help being glad that Megan and I were finally alone.

It took a couple of minutes, but Megan returned with two books. "Where's Jenna?"

"She ran out to call Noah. I mentioned he was looking at that house." I reached for Megan's hand, took it, and tugged.

Megan tumbled into my lap with a laugh.

"That's better." I cupped her cheek and drew her close for a quick kiss. "Hi."

"Hi back." She leaned away, but stayed on my lap. "I think you'd like both of these. They're thrillers. One is about a police officer. The other is military. Both are fast paced, edge-of-your-seat stories."

"Am I going to have nightmares?"

Megan laughed. "No. But if you do, call me."

"You better believe it." I took the books and set them on the floor beside my chair, then twined my arms around her waist, locking her in place. "Tell me about this Reuben guy."

"He's not a threat. I promise. I can handle it."

"I never said you couldn't." I held her gaze. I believed she could handle it. I did. "I just want you to tell me about him. Okay?"

Megan sighed. "Fine."

I leaned forward to kiss her. I meant for it to be brief. But, well, it was a little while before she got around to giving me those details about the weirdo.

# 14

## MEGAN

Nerves danced in my belly as I walked through the bookstore making sure everything was ready. I'd gotten here three hours early, but it had seemed like the better idea at the time. The other alternative had been continuing to lie in my bed, staring at the ceiling, praying that this wasn't going to be a colossal flop.

After some long conversations with Cody—and the girls, but those conversations weren't as delicious to remember, so of course I focused on the ones with Cody—I'd taken the plunge. Grandma had always been happy to carry an independently published title, but she hadn't gone looking for them.

I did.

And oh boy was the response incredible.

Apparently, indie authors were super excited to have the opportunity to put their books on the shelves of a store. It made sense. Browsing online was a completely different thing than browsing in a store. And there were still those holdouts who wouldn't buy a book if the publisher name on the spine wasn't one they recognized.

Sad.

Anyway. I'd ultimately gone with the plan of purchasing the books outright so I could shelve them by genre with all the other titles. No one was going to be able to tell at a glance which ones were from the big publishers, so why not give the stories inside a fighting chance?

I'd also mentioned that I was open to book signings for anyone local—or willing to travel—and wow had I underestimated the desire for that kind of thing. I'd started with offering two Saturdays a month, and I was booked solid through March.

Today was the first one.

The author was local. She actually lived in Alexandria, just not Old Town, and her focus was on what she championed as noble bright fantasy. Basically, fantasy that was full of good conquering evil with a lot less focus on the darkness and more emphasis on the light.

I was a fan.

I'd read several of her books that featured the Fae and couldn't get the next one fast enough.

I had a pretty good audience for fantasy at the store, so it made sense to start with an author who could feed those voracious readers. Now I just had to pray they'd actually show up. I'd only been advertising C. J.'s appearance for a week and a half.

Maybe I should have waited to start at the end of October so I had more time to try to build buzz? But I worried that the more I delayed, the easier it would be for me to talk myself out of doing any of them at all.

I might have been secretly hoping no one would sign up for the first spot, but she had. So.

I took a deep breath and slowly let it out.

It was going to be okay. Good, even. Maybe even great.

Okay, I couldn't quite get myself to great. Positive thinking when it came to the bookstore was still a bit of a work in progress.

I'd shifted the comfortable seating out of the way to make a signing area. It didn't look too awkward having the couch and stuffed chairs moved over against the wall. I'd set up a four-foot-long rectangular table and covered it with a black cloth that reached to the floor in the front and on the sides. I'd stashed boxes of C. J.'s books underneath. It was probably better to just set out a few of each title and restock them as they sold rather than making huge piles, right?

I'd ask her when she came. She did a lot of craft fairs, apparently, so she probably knew more about this than I did.

Everything was ready. I checked the time and groaned. I still had too much time before C. J. was going to show up. And she was supposed to arrive at nine, about an hour before we opened for the day.

I went to the back room and dug my wallet out of my purse. I'd go down to the café and get coffee. Maybe a treat of some sort. That would kill a little time. And then? Well, maybe I'd be able to focus enough to do some of the paperwork that was waiting for me at my desk.

I locked the front door and enjoyed the quiet of a Saturday morning as I made my way down the brick sidewalks to the café. There was some traffic—foot and cars both—but that wasn't unusual. In the DC area, and Old Town was no exception, there was always traffic of some sort. Even at three in the morning.

The café was bustling. The clientele was different than a weekday, though. Saturdays brought out the families with kids dressed in sports uniforms and parents sharing amused glances as the children babbled.

I got into line and checked my phone. I itched to text Cody and see what he was planning to do today. This was the major downside of retail work. I hadn't really had a serious relationship...well, *ever*. So it hadn't been a problem that my Saturdays were long and consumed by my job.

It wasn't as if Cody could just take off on Mondays so we could spend a day together, either. Which left Sundays.

And Sundays were hard because we had a group of friends who expected us to be at church and go to lunch with the group. All the while, we were pretending that nothing in our relationship had changed.

It was hard.

And kind of fun.

But mostly just hard.

"Heya, sis."

I turned as Austin poked me in the ribs. "Hey. When are you going to outgrow that?"

"How about never?" Austin grinned.

I shook my head and scooted forward as the line moved. "What brings you out to get fancy coffee on your day of rest?"

"I don't know if you heard, but my sister's bookstore is having its first ever author event. My wife and I are excited and wanted to come to support her."

"Aw." I fluttered my eyelashes at him. "Where's Kayla, then?"

"She's parking. We didn't want to take a spot near the store—better to leave those for the paying customers—so she dropped me off to get eats and went down to the garage."

I reached the front of the line before I could respond. So I placed my order, then stepped out of the way and gestured for Austin. "My treat."

"No way. That's not how us supporting you works out." Austin reached into his pocket and pulled out his wallet. "But I'll get yours."

"I can—"

I broke off as Austin told the cashier his order and handed her his credit card at the same time.

"Thanks."

"My pleasure."

I waited while he finished the transaction then slid out of the way and down closer to the pickup area.

"I'm proud of you. I think this is going to be great for the store."

Everything in me warmed. I didn't *need* my brother's approval, but I certainly craved it. "I hope so. The authors seem excited about it. All the spots I made available are taken."

"Nice." Austin nudged me with his elbow. "I knew you'd figure out what you needed to do."

"Let's not be hasty. I don't know if this is going to be everything I need." In fact, I worried that it was going to end up being just another expense. I'd bought the books outright—again, because it seemed like my job to handle and because I could put anything that didn't sell into inventory. So there really was no cost to the authors unless they decided to bring some kind of swag with them to give away. Maybe that was why the authors were excited to sign up? It basically guaranteed them quite a few paperback sales right out of the gate.

"Well, I'm praying it's the start of something amazing." Austin cocked his head to the side. "Are things worse than you're letting on? You've seemed preoccupied lately. I chalked it up to this new venture—change, that kind of thing. Is there more?"

I swallowed. It was good I had these changes to blame, because I was fairly certain any preoccupation was coming from my new, secret relationship with Cody. Honestly, most days I was like a giddy teenager—completely incapable of focusing on anything without extreme effort. I figured that would settle down in time. It had to, didn't it?

"Hey. You in there?" Austin waved his hand in front of my eyes.

"Gah. Are you six?" I smacked his hand. "You're right about it being change. I'm fine. Good, even."

"All right. You know I'm here for you if things are bad, right?"

"You always have been."

"That's never changing."

I met his gaze and smiled. I believed he meant it. But I also knew, deep down, that his primary focus was Kayla and the life the two of them were building together. Which was absolutely as it should be. I was capable of taking care of myself and my business. And I really was happy that my brother and his best friend had figured things out.

And now with Cody...was I finally getting closer to finding that for myself?

It was too early to make that kind of leap. It was also incredibly difficult to avoid.

"Order for Austin!"

"That's us." Austin started toward the pickup window.

I hurried to catch up—he'd always had long strides—and grabbed the paper bag of pastries and my drink. "Thanks."

"Happy to do it. I guess Kayla's waiting at the store. Or we'll see her on our walk back."

I nodded and started toward the door.

It wasn't a long walk back. The air was already warming as the sun cleared the tops of the buildings. Kayla was, in fact, leaning against the wall beside the bookstore door.

"Took you guys long enough." Kayla reached out, and Austin put one of the to-go coffees into her hand. She sipped and let out a satisfied, "Ahh."

I chuckled and held out my coffee. "Can you hold this while I unlock the door?"

"Of course." Kayla took my drink. "Are you excited? This is going to be so great. I downloaded one of her books last week when you said she was going to be your first author, and I've already recommended the series to a couple of my students at the learning center."

I glanced over my shoulder before pulling the key out of the lock. "Yeah? Which one?"

"*The King's Sword*? It's the first in a trilogy, I think. I really liked it. I'm planning on buying it and the rest of the series in paperback today. You have them, right?"

I grinned at Kayla and her bubbling enthusiasm. That was definitely her defining characteristic, and I loved it about her. I also didn't mind that she could tone it down when it got to be too much. "Pretty sure, yes. I ordered some of everything she had. We worked out a deal where she gave me her author price plus a little, but if I charge a little less than you can get them online, I still make a decent profit. Everyone wins."

"I have a pretty smart sister. I've always said it." Austin reached for the door. "Why don't we go inside and continue the conversation."

"Sounds good to me. Did you get the turnovers?" Kayla handed me my coffee before she stepped into the bookstore and headed toward the seating area. She stopped when she saw the new setup. "This is different."

"Good or bad?" I looked over the area and tried to decide. I didn't know where else I could set up for an author signing, but if we were going to try something else, we needed to do it now.

"Just different." Kayla went to the couch and sat. "I'm not sure where else you'd set up."

I laughed. "That was my exact thought. It's not like I'm keeping it this way. It was easy enough to push things around."

Austin frowned as he sat beside Kayla. "Next time, ask for help. You shouldn't have to do this on your own."

I nodded and tried to keep my voice casual. "Cody happened by while I was working. He did a lot of the heavy stuff."

"Good. That's good then." Austin opened the bag of pastries and took out one of the turnovers. He handed it to Kayla then reached in the bag again. "I'm glad you've been able to help him with the Christmas gala. He was upset when he got that dumped on him. It's going okay?"

I took the bag from Austin when he held it out and looked inside. My chocolate-filled croissant didn't look nearly as amazing as their turnovers. But it was what I'd wanted, so I'd deal. "Seems to be."

Kayla's eyebrows were almost all the way to her hairline as she looked at me. I sent her a questioning look. Her gaze darted to Austin, and she gave a tiny shake of her head.

Shoot.

The only thing that could mean is that she had questions she didn't want to ask in front of Austin, but that I wasn't going to get out of answering.

I bit into my croissant. I wouldn't lie. Cody and I had agreed on that. But man, it was going to be tempting.

The three of us chatted about nothing important while we finished our pastries and coffee. Then I dragged out the vacuum to get rid of the flaky crumbs that Austin—well, all of us, but mostly Austin—had managed to get on everything. I was coming back from putting it away when the bell over the door jingled.

I hurried to the front. "Good morning. We're not quite open yet."

"I know. I'm sorry. I'm early—well, I was supposed to be early, but I'm earlier than that. I'm C. J. Brightley." The tiny woman held out her hand.

I shook it and smiled. "Of course, you are. If I'd taken even two seconds, I would have realized it. Thanks for doing this. And for, apparently, being excited."

C. J. laughed. "I haven't been in here before. This is a great space."

"Thank you. I've got you set up over here." I gestured to my right. "We can change or tweak whatever you think we need to. I haven't done this before and I'm really hoping it'll be good. For all of us."

C. J. wandered to the signing area I'd created and looked everything over. She peeked under the table and grinned. "I think it's going to be great. I have a pop-up banner in my trunk. Do you mind if I set that up on one side?"

"Not at all."

"I can get it for you, if you want." Austin stood, brushed off his hand on his jeans, then held it out. "I'm Austin Campbell, Megan's brother."

"Nice to meet you." C. J. took his hand. "I'd love some help. Thanks."

Kayla leaned forward on her seat. As soon as the door closed behind Austin and C. J., she pounced. "Cody just happened to be by? What's going on?"

I hunched my shoulders. "He came by. I needed help. He helped."

She squinted at me. "You're hiding something."

My eyes darted over to the door.

"I knew it!" Kayla jumped out of her seat. "You and Cody are a thing."

"Shh." I squeezed my eyes shut then opened them. "You can't say anything. We're not telling anyone."

"But...why not? This is great." Kayla frowned. "You know Austin won't mind, right?"

I shook my head. I couldn't launch into the explanation I wanted to, because C. J. opened the door, setting off the bell, and Austin came in, lugging a box.

"Please?"

Kayla huffed out a breath. "Fine. But I'm not happy about it."

Austin brought the box over and set it on the table. "There's no way you were going to carry that."

C. J. flexed a bicep. "I'm small, but mighty. Also I have a dolly."

I chuckled. "Smart woman. Can I do anything to help you get set up?"

"I think I've got it. But I really do appreciate this." C. J. reached into the box and started extracting metal poles.

"Here's hoping it's a success. For both of us." I stepped away from the table and jerked my head toward the cash register. "Let's get out of her way. Holler if you need anything, okay?"

"You got it." C. J. grinned and started screwing poles together.

"I've got a good feeling." Austin leaned against the checkout counter. "She's great."

Five minutes before our official opening time, I double-checked that C. J. was ready. I took some quick pictures for the bookstore's social media and newsletter, promised to send them to her as well, and shooed Kayla over to the table. "Go buy your books and we'll get this officially underway."

# 15

## CODY

I paced by the front door. Megan should be here any minute, and I couldn't wait. Sundays were hard.

It was hard to resist reaching for her hand during church. Or slipping my arm around her shoulder as we listened to the sermon. I didn't like eating lunch in the diner with the girls in a booth across the restaurant, and the guys at a table too far away for me to make eye contact.

I'd thought—hoped—that with Scott and Whitney enjoying their month or so in the islands that we'd be able to do more combined eating. But today, there hadn't been room to put enough tables together, so we'd had to deal.

No one but me had minded.

Of course, I hadn't let on that I cared, because that was opening a huge can of worms that didn't need opening. But man. We were only two weeks in with this secret relationship, and it was already harder than keeping my crush quiet had ever been.

Finally, the doorbell rang. I rushed to open it and grinned when I saw her standing on my porch, looking over her shoulder.

"Hey. Come in." I reached for her hand.

Megan looked at me with a worried smile. "I thought I saw Tristan walking by the water with someone. I don't know if he saw me."

"Don't worry about it." It wasn't completely unrealistic for Tristan to be wandering by the water near my townhouse. *With someone* was a twist, but he took client meetings in unexpected places sometimes. And he'd been talking about hiring security. So maybe he'd followed through on that.

After the press that had cost Austin and Kayla their jobs in the spring, all of us had struggled a little with the idea that we might need to hire personal security. I really didn't want to go that route. I wasn't sure what Mr. Ballentine would think of it, to start off, and beyond that? I was just a guy who happened to have some money now.

But the money was the thing.

I pushed those thoughts aside and shut the door behind Megan.

"What if he saw me?" Megan toed off her shoes and stepped into my arms. "I'm already dodging Kayla."

"Kayla?" I eased back so I could see her face. "Why?"

Megan sighed. "I mentioned that you'd help set up for the author signing, and I guess since it was after the girls had left on Friday, she made a giant mental leap that meant the two of us were together, and we aren't lying so...I hedged, but I think she knows."

I pulled Megan close and rested my cheek on the top of her head. It wasn't the end of the world. Of course, I'd rather just about anyone other than Kayla know, since she was married to Megan's brother, but... "It's going to have to come out eventually."

"I know. But I'd rather it was because you and I decided it was time." Megan blew out a breath. "Why is this complicated?"

Maybe we were the ones making it that way? "I don't know."

I waited, holding her, to see if she was going to say more. When she didn't, I stepped back and linked my hand with hers. "Tell me about the author signing."

Everything in Megan brightened. "It went so well. C. J. was the perfect person to go first. She does all kinds of other in-person events, so she knew what to tweak and the best way to arrange traffic flow. And she was so personable and easy going."

I grinned and squeezed her hand before tugging her over to the sofa so we could sit. "That's fantastic. How were sales?"

"I over-ordered, but only by a little. I have two copies each of three different series. But I'm pretty sure I'll be able to sell them without a problem. She signed them and she's going to mention in her newsletter that there are signed copies available at the store for her local readers. Since a lot of the in-person events have tapered off for a bit—until the Christmas craft fairs start up —it's a great chance for people to get them." Megan snuggled up next to me. "I'm optimistic."

"That's good. I'm sorry I didn't come. I wasn't sure what to do —I figured a lot of the gang would be coming in and out, and I wasn't sure if there would be questions."

Megan snickered. "There were still questions. 'Did Cody come yet?' 'Isn't he going to come?' I finally told Wes he should call and ask you himself, because I wasn't your keeper."

I laughed. "Oh man. Wes did call. I didn't answer—I ended up riding the trail down to Mount Vernon and then back up all the way to Gravelly Point. I watched the planes take off and land for a while before riding back home."

"Fun. I might like to join you if you do that again." Megan bit her lip. "But you'll probably have to look over my bike first. I haven't ridden in a while, and I have no idea what kind of shape it's in."

"I can do that. It'd be nice for you to have the option to ride to the store, too. You could park in your back room without any trouble. And it's faster on days when it's super cold."

"On super cold days, I'll probably drive, but I get what you mean." Megan tipped her head back and met my gaze.

I brushed a quick kiss across her lips. "What would you like to do with our afternoon?"

"I guess snuggling on the couch isn't a very good plan."

It sounded pretty perfect to me, honestly. But it was still a bad idea. There was entirely too much temptation for things to get heated and lines to be crossed. Both of us enjoyed kissing too much for that to be the only thing on the agenda.

I sighed. "Probably not. We could watch a movie?"

"That's not really any different, is it?" Megan shook her head. "I'm still curled up with you with your lips right there."

"Hmm." I leaned close and kissed her.

I always lost track of time when I kissed Megan. There was no room in my head for anything other than her.

Megan put her hand on my chest and pushed as she eased back. She took a deep breath before scooting to create a little more physical distance between us. "We definitely need to figure out what we're going to do."

I nodded. "We should go somewhere. I'd say we could take a walk by the water, but if we're going to try to keep this for us just a little longer, maybe we should head into DC?"

"Okay. Let's do that. The museums are open until five. Pick one."

I stood and offered her my hand. She took it and I tugged her to her feet.

"I need to run upstairs and get shoes. I don't really have a preference, though, so you choose. Please?"

Megan wrinkled her nose.

I took it as agreement and darted up the stairs for my sneakers. Downtown was a good idea. We were unlikely to run into anyone there—if one of the gang was headed to a museum, or even the National Mall, we would have heard about it at lunch. I didn't get downtown to play tourist as often as I ought to. Why was it that living near these amazing museums and monuments meant I didn't take the time to see them?

I guessed because life was busy, no matter where you lived, so things like that got pushed aside.

I hurried back down, shoes on my feet, and tucked my hands in my pockets. "Well?"

"Let's go to the National Gallery."

I chuckled. "You're hoping that'll make me regret letting you choose, aren't you?"

Megan shrugged, but she had an impish gleam in her eye that told me I was right.

"Too bad for you, I like art." I gestured for her to go down ahead of me. "And I happen to know where good parking is near there. Double win."

"Triple win, then, since I'm actually pretty excited about going. I haven't been in...forever. We live right here. You'd think we'd be there constantly."

"I had that same thought when I was getting my shoes. Do you think people who live in New York City go to the Statue of Liberty?"

Megan frowned and pulled open the door that led out to the garage. "Good question. I have no idea. Probably not. Life, right?"

Megan had already gone around to the passenger side and gotten in. So much for a chance to be chivalrous. On the other hand, it was maybe a little silly when we were in the garage? She didn't seem to care either way, so I wasn't going to overthink it.

I'd wasted too much time overthinking things when it came to Megan.

I got in, punched the garage door opener, and then reached

for my seat belt. I glanced over at her and the jolt of emotion that surged through me made me freeze for just a moment. Was it too soon to tell her I loved her?

More than likely.

She lifted an eyebrow. "You okay?"

"Yeah. Of course. Ready?"

"Let's do it." She grinned.

It wasn't long before we were on the GW Parkway, driving along the Potomac on our way into the city. It was a sunny and clear fall afternoon, and I got to spend it with Megan.

If life could get better, I wasn't sure how.

I'D RIDDEN along on the high from my Sunday afternoon with Megan all week. Nothing at work had been able to get to me—even though there had been some hiccups that would probably have frustrated me in the past. I'd gotten them smoothed over. Everything was on track with the gala. The invitations were in house from the printer and looked great. Even Mr. Ballentine had remarked that they looked good.

I should probably bring them home so I could stuff, label, and stamp them while I watched TV in the evening. There were a couple of weeks yet before they needed to get in the mail, but given how everything else with my regular job duties was going, I wasn't going to be able to devote a day—or two—to doing it like I had with the save-the-date cards.

Bleh.

Maybe I could talk the guys into trading out a poker night to help.

I laughed. Given Noah's response when I'd half-joked that he was going to have to help me, I didn't see that going over super well.

So. Lugging them home and doing it during TV time it was. Would Megan want to help? I'd ask.

I'd been spending more time at the bookstore in the evenings than in front of the TV lately anyway. So far, no one had dropped by and noticed, but I didn't think we could keep that going too much longer.

The question, of course, was when and how we broke the news.

I sighed and looked around the basement room in my townhouse. I'd set it up for poker nights and left it. Scott and Whitney were still out of town, so I was doing a lot of the hosting. I didn't mind. I actually kind of enjoyed it. I had more space than Tristan. Wes's place was always a wreck. The guy was a slob. Noah hadn't settled on something yet. And Austin and Kayla were in a one-bedroom apartment.

So yeah. I was the default winner for hosting.

The doorbell rang. I was halfway up the stairs when I heard the front door open.

"Cody? It's Noah and Wes."

I jogged up the rest of the way. "Come on in. We're set up downstairs still."

"Nice. Can I grab a soda?" Noah pointed toward the kitchen.

"Yeah, of course. I got snacks, too. You can help bring them down." I glanced at Wes. "You need a drink?"

"Sure. I can carry stuff, too. Is everyone coming tonight?" Wes trailed after Noah as we made our way to the kitchen.

"Tristan texted the group saying he'd be here. I'm not sure about Austin."

I grabbed one of the bags of chips and waited while the guys dug through the fridge for the sodas they wanted. When they'd also snagged snacks off the island, we headed down to the basement game room.

"Just put the snacks over here."

I opened the chips and set them on the smaller table that was pressed against the wall. I thought it was supposed to be used as an end table. Or one of those things that sat behind a sofa. But it worked for this, too.

Musing about it reminded me that Megan had offered to help me decorate. I needed to see where she was with that. If nothing else, it would give us an excuse to hang out together.

"You really need to figure out what this room is going to be." Noah pulled out one of the folding chairs and took his spot at the table. "I bet it's depressing when you're not set up for poker."

Wes shrugged. "I still don't have all of my rooms figured out. It's not a big deal. Just get some stuff, throw it in. If, down the road, you decide you don't like it, toss it and try again."

I winced. I might be a billionaire, but I wasn't going to waste money just because I had it. "I'd rather take my time and get it right."

"Your choice." Wes popped the tab on his drink. "I'm doing that with the dive shop. So I get it. But it's a lot easier to redecorate than to decide you didn't dig the pool deep enough at the start."

"You're really doing that? Putting a pool inside your shop?" Noah shook his head. "I don't see how that works."

"It's going great. You should swing by someday. Let me know when and I'll clear it with the crew. I'm on target to open in January." Wes took several swallows of soda. "I was hoping for sooner, but we ran into some shipping delays for various materials."

"Sorry. That's no fun." I was curious what, exactly, Wes was doing with his days. But I also didn't want to ask. He'd get annoyed and offended, I guessed because he thought I was judging him, and that would ruin the night before it started.

"Eh. It's fine. I'm finishing up the business classes I think I'll need this semester. I'd like to squeeze in a few more dive certifications before we open, but I don't think that's going to happen. I should have pushed harder over the summer, but I needed to be here to get the building taken care of and the remodel started. I can always get the certs once we're open. It just means hiring instructors in the interim." Wes reached for the deck of cards in the middle of the table and started to shuffle.

"Let me text Tristan and Austin and see where they are." I slipped my phone out of my pocket and started up the stairs. Maybe they were close—or even waiting at the door. Although I should have heard the bell if they rang it. I hadn't missed it yet.

Tristan texted back almost immediately. He was parking and would be right here. Austin finally replied that he wasn't going to make it after all.

I frowned. Hopefully, everything was okay.

I watched out the front window for Tristan and finally spotted him as he walked around the corner from the street side of the townhouse row and started up the steps to the front door. I pulled it open as he was reaching for the doorbell.

"Hey, man. Glad you could make it." I gripped Tristan's hand and pulled him close for a back-slapping hug. "Feels like you're always busy."

"Tell me about it." Tristan shook his head. He kicked off his shoes inside the door and then shrugged out of his suit jacket. "I didn't even make it home yet. I'm grateful I still have so many clients. It's good to be busy. But I wouldn't mind if they didn't all end up in crisis at the same time."

I chuckled. "That would be good. You need more than chips and cookies? I can throw a sandwich together or pop a burrito in the microwave."

"I'd kill for a sandwich. I never got around to eating lunch— too busy. Anything you've got. I'm not picky." Tristan shot me a grateful smile. "You want me to hang here while you make it?"

"Nah. Head down to the guys. Wes is already shuffling. You

can tell him to go ahead and deal. I'll just be a minute." I hustled into the kitchen where I made quick work of a ham, turkey, and provolone sandwich. I even had lettuce and sliced tomatoes in the fridge, thanks to a recent grocery order and the fact that you could buy it all in ready-to-use packaging. After a moment's thought, I tossed a dill spear on the plate beside the sandwich. I always appreciated a pickle. Maybe Tristan was the same.

I snagged one of the soda boxes out of the fridge and carried it and the plate down with me. I set the sandwich in front of Tristan, then put the sodas over by the chips.

"You didn't offer us a sandwich. I see how it is." Noah grinned and reached toward Tristan's plate.

Tristan smacked Noah's hand. "Try and die."

Wes snickered. "That looks better than what I had. When did you become the sandwich king?"

"This guy?" Noah pointed at me. "He's always had that crown. When we roomed together, he basically lived on them."

"Still do. Mostly." I shrugged. "They're quick, easy, and have endless variety. It's impossible to get tired of sandwiches."

"I'm not sure I agree with all of that." Noah sneered. "I got pretty sick of them."

"You were always more than welcome to make something else if you didn't like what I fixed on my night. Those were the rules." I shook my head. Ungrateful. That was what Noah was. "And now that we're not roomies, what are you fixing yourself for dinner most nights?"

Laughing, Noah held up his hands. "Fine. You win. Sandwiches. But I buy Swiss cheese and roast beef. I might never eat ham again."

Wes barked out a laugh. "That's going to be an issue at Thanksgiving, Christmas, and Easter."

"Just Easter, but yeah." Noah picked up the cards Wes dealt. "I'm hoping to be over it before then."

Tristan lifted half the sandwich and took a big bite. He chewed a minute then asked, "Has anyone heard how Megan's author signing went? I meant to get over there but didn't manage it."

I froze. It felt like everyone's eyes were on me. My neck burned. So did my cheeks.

"I dropped by for a bit. Looked like she had a pretty steady crowd coming in and buying." Wes burned a card and flipped the next into the middle of the table. "I was surprised I didn't see anyone else there."

This time, I wasn't imagining the pointed look. "Yeah. I didn't make it. Sorry. It slipped my mind and I took my bike out on the trail. By the time I was back, I was exhausted and stinky."

"Nice. Way to support a friend, man." Noah tossed chips into the pile. "I was there for about an hour. She said I just missed Wes. The author was nice. Easy to talk to, super personable. I ended up buying a four-book urban fantasy series from her and I don't even really know what urban fantasy is."

Tristan laughed. "I like it. Text me the titles and I'll grab the e-books."

"Or, you could swing by and see if Megan still has some copies. Support your local bookseller, and so forth." I shot Tristan a pointed look.

"Right. I'll do that. Do you think she's going to have extras?"

I nodded. "Yeah. She mentioned she did."

"You still picking her brain for the Christmas gala? I would have thought that was basically done at this point." Noah shook his head. "If I didn't know better, I'd say you were looking for excuses to spend time with her."

Tristan shot me a considering glance.

Wes scoffed. "Nah. You know Cody."

I wasn't sure what that meant. I also wasn't going to ask, because I was ready for the conversation to shift away from

Megan. They were too close to saying something that would open up the bag of cats. "Are we playing poker here, or what?"

"Yeah, yeah." Tristan tossed chips into the center of the table.

Wes burned another card and flipped over the next.

I let out a breath and, for just a moment, wondered if Megan was having as tricky a time at her girls' night as I was here.

We needed to figure out what our end game was.

Soon.

# 16

## MEGAN

Whoever was ringing my doorbell needed to get a life.

Okay, sure, it was a Monday morning and just after nine, so it wasn't unreasonable for people to be out and about. But it was my only real day off and I'd given myself permission to sleep until ten. Or later.

I'd tried ignoring them, but they weren't taking a hint. So fine.

I threw my legs over the side of the bed and glanced down. My pajamas were as modest—maybe more—as what a lot of women called workout gear. Bonus, the pants were loose and roomy instead of tight like leggings.

And sure, I wore leggings—were there people who didn't? But I didn't kid myself that they were in the running to win any "put together and professional" awards.

"Yeah, yeah, yeah." I hurried down the stairs, turned the deadbolt, and pulled open the door. "What?"

Cody laughed and held out a coffee cup. "Not a morning person. Check."

"I can be a morning person. Just not on my day off." I took

the coffee, sipped, then scowled at him. "Shouldn't you be at work?"

"It's a holiday. What we grew up calling Columbus Day, but I'm pretty sure it's been renamed. Or they've added something to it." Cody shrugged. "I just know I get the day off and I couldn't think of anything I wanted to do more than spend it with you."

My heart melted. I stepped back. "Sweet talker. You'd better come inside."

He grinned and shook the white bakery bag in his other hand. "I also have bear claws."

My mouth watered. "Dibs on the toes."

Cody shot me a quizzical look as he passed me and headed into the kitchen.

I closed the door and followed, sipping the coffee as I did so.

Cody had already gotten plates out of the cabinet and was putting them on the table. I reached for the bakery bag, opened it, and breathed in the tantalizing smell of sugar and yeast.

"These are huge." I reached in and put one on each plate. "They're not from the café. Where'd you get them?"

"Nuh-uh." He grinned. "That's my secret. I don't need everyone flocking over there and buying all the goods."

I sat and peeled one of the bear claw "toes" off and popped it in my mouth. It was the perfect combination of crispy outside and chewy inside. I eyed the rest of it. It didn't look like there were going to be too many pieces with the wrong bread-to-crust ratio. "But if enough people don't go, they won't stay in business, and then none of us will get these amazing treats."

"Hmm." Cody picked up his pastry and bit in.

I winced.

"What?"

"You don't—that's not how you eat these. Ever."

Cody snorted. "It's how I eat them."

"But...but...you just..."

Cody started to laugh. He set his pastry on his plate and clutched his stomach as he cracked up.

"So glad I could amuse you." I shook my head and pulled off another perfect bite. "You realize this could be a deal breaker, right? But I guess you're not worried."

He worked—hard—to rein in his mirth. After several deep breaths, he was down to sparkling eyes. "You'd really dump me because of how I eat a bear claw?"

Would I? I drummed my fingers on the table. "Probably not *just* that. But it's a definite mark in the negative column, so you'd better watch out, buster."

He grinned and leaned forward, invading my space. "Tell me more about these columns. What else am I working against? Or, you know, you can fill me in on all the things you do like about me."

I laughed and waved him back. "Goofball. I'm not feeding your ego."

"But I brought you a pastry. I feel like that at least earns me a peek at one item on the 'Why I love Cody' list."

"No one said anything about love." I batted my eyelashes at him and tried to will my racing heart to slow. He was just teasing. Because the big L hadn't been anything we'd discussed yet. We'd barely started dating. And sure, we'd been friends for what felt like forever. And he—and I—had had feelings and interest for about that long. But that didn't mean we jumped straight into love.

There were steps. And we needed to take them.

Or we at least needed to be open with our friend group about where things stood between us first. Right?

Cody clutched his chest dramatically and slid to the floor. He let out a gasping, strangled moan.

I scooted back and looked under the table at him. "You okay down there?"

"Just dying from the heart shot. Don't worry about a thing." He folded his hands neatly on his chest.

If I squinted an eye and tried hard, I could picture him holding a single, white lily. "You'd make a beautiful corpse."

"Beautiful?" He shook his head. "The hits just keep on coming."

"Oh. Sorry. Manly. Very manly and macho. For a corpse."

"Better." He gave a single nod before closing his eyes. "Your floor is hard—did you know that?"

"Well, it is a floor. You could get up. Or are you a fairy and you need me to applaud?"

"Wow. I'm a beautiful fairy." Cody pushed himself to a sitting position, narrowly avoiding cracking his head on the bottom of the table. "An unlovable, beautiful fairy apparently."

"I never said you were unlovable." I crossed my arms. "I said no one had said anything about love."

"Fair enough." Cody got to his feet, brushed off the back of his jeans, and came around to the side of the table where I was sitting. "What if someone did?"

I bit my lip. "Is it fast? It feels like it might be fast."

He sighed quietly before leaning in to brush his lips over mine. "Then we'll wait. Even though I don't want to."

I closed my eyes. I didn't either. Not really. "Don't you think our friends deserve to know before we go there?"

"I don't know why. This isn't about them. It's about us." He waited until I met his gaze. "I love you, Megan. There's no question in my mind that you're the woman I want to spend my life with. But I've been waiting for you this long, I can wait some more."

"I love you, too." My words came out as a whisper, practically unbidden.

His grin flashed again before his mouth covered mine.

The kiss wasn't nearly long enough. Before I was ready, Cody had eased back and moved to the other side of the kitchen table. With a cheeky wink, he picked up his bear claw and bit into again.

I just shook my head and broke off another perfect bite for myself. "Maybe, since you're such a beautiful fairy prince and everything, I will excuse the barbaric way you eat pastry."

Cody rolled his eyes.

I reached for my coffee. "Other than eating amazing food from a location you're going to share with me, what did you want to do today?"

He pointed at me. "Not telling you. Maybe it'll be my wedding gift to you. We'll have to see."

I was glad I hadn't taken a drink yet, because I surely would have choked when he so nonchalantly threw out the words "wedding gift." I wasn't sure what part of taking things slow and waiting that fell under, but I was guessing it didn't. It was, in fact, the opposite.

It didn't seem like Cody had noticed my stillness, because he'd continued talking. "I was thinking maybe a movie marathon while we stuffed invitations for the gala?"

"Ah, romance." My hand flew up to cover my mouth.

His shoulders fell.

"Sorry. I'm sorry. It's actually not a bad idea and I don't mind helping you at all."

"It's fine. I can do it at night. That was my plan. And actually, that's why they're in my car. But then I realized I was off today and thought it would be something we could do together. But you're right. It's lame. We could go downtown again."

I shook my head and reached across the table to grab his hand. "I do not want to go downtown on a federal holiday. Neither do you. Talk about crowded. The invitations are fine. And it's a good plan to get them done well in advance of them needing to be in the mail. But I get veto power on the movies."

"Bzzzt." He flipped his hand over so he could lace his fingers through mine. "We will find a movie that is mutually acceptable. No one gets veto power. I'm not worried though. I think the two of us like enough of the same things that we'll be fine."

He was probably right. I squeezed his hand. "We can order something in for lunch. I was planning on hitting up the grocery store today, so I don't have much on hand."

"Sure. Then maybe go grab Thai together for dinner? If anyone sees us and asks, we can tell them the truth."

I cocked my head to the side. "The truth...as in we spent the day stuffing gala invites together?"

He nodded. "And the rest. If you want."

My mouth went dry. It was all well and good to say I thought we needed to tell people. But faced with a timeline for doing it? Now I wasn't so sure. "Let's play it by ear."

I OPENED the bookstore on Tuesday still giddy from my day with Cody. Choosing a movie franchise had turned out to be simple. He'd suggested *The Lord of the Rings*. I accepted. Easy peasy. Maybe things would have been different if he'd tried for *The Hobbit*. I'd watched those—you couldn't love fantasy and books and not at least try—but I was pretty sure I'd never willingly experience them again. Not even the voice of Benedict Cumberbatch could tempt me, and I'd previously said I'd be willing to listen to him read the phone book.

Of course, now he was doing movies and using an American accent and really, there was just no reason for it. It was ridiculous.

Whatever.

I pushed thoughts of Benedict and movies from my mind and booted up the store computer. We were getting a steady stream of online orders for C. J. Brightley's books since her appearance. I'd need to get in touch with her and arrange for another box or two. She didn't mind signing them, and I liked being able to offer that as a special thing. Everybody won.

Our next author event was this Saturday and I was feeling much more confident about it, having seen how well the first one went. This was a Christian romance author, so maybe the audience would be smaller, but I liked the idea of showcasing the genre so people understood that romance didn't always equate to super descriptive sex on the page.

I already carried a few of Heather Gray's books—Grandma had made it a point to have a larger-than-usual Christian fiction section—so I'd taken them home to read last week. They were really quite good. And not over-the-top preachy, which is how I thought most people viewed Christian fiction.

I'd made a point of mentioning that in the store newsletter when I made the announcement that she'd be here.

Her books should be arriving today if the email with tracking was to be believed. So that would be something I could do during the inevitable long stretches between customers.

The bell above the door jingled. I locked the computer and made sure to pull the door to the back room closed behind me as I hurried to the front.

"Good morn..." I would have liked to stop and just ask him to go, but I forced myself to finish the greeting, albeit with less cheer. "...ing, Reuben. How can I help you?"

He looked around, a smirk on his lips. "Seems pretty dead in here today. Feeling the pinch yet?"

"This is pretty typical for a Tuesday right after we open. Were you looking for something particular or did you want to browse?" I had to force my hands to remain relaxed. I didn't want him to see how nervous he made me. I mostly thought he was harmless. But recent interactions with him were changing that opinion somewhat.

Reuben leaned against the counter holding the register. "I got a great book online the other day. E-books. I don't know how I lived before I discovered them. I can get them instantly, even the middle of the night, and I'm not ever going to run out of storage again. Too bad for you, of course."

I was gritting my teeth so hard my smile hurt my cheeks. "E-books are a wonderful invention. I'm glad they work for you, though of course I'll be sad to lose your business."

"Oh, well now, we could still work something out. You could close for lunch and meet me at the café. I could probably bring myself to come back after and pick something up. As a thank you of sorts."

"I'm afraid that doesn't work with my schedule. And if you're not going to browse or buy, I'm going to have to ask you to leave." This was the problem with running a business that was open to the public. There really was very little I could do about it if he decided he wanted to hang out in here. That was what bookstores were for to some degree.

And he knew it. He shot me a look of disbelief before shaking his head and wandering into the shelves of books.

Which at least meant he wasn't leaning here hoping to talk to me.

But I was still going to talk to Tristan and see if there was anything I could do from a legal perspective to get him to stop. It probably didn't qualify as harassment. Not technically. But it would be good to know what options, if any, I did have.

I went behind the counter and slipped my phone out of my pocket. I shot a quick text to Tristan, taking care to downplay how unsettled I was. It wouldn't do to arouse the protective worry of my surrogate brother. Because he'd turn around and tell all the other guys, and then...well, I didn't want to think about what would happen then.

I couldn't afford to hire a second employee to hang out all day so I wasn't alone. I couldn't afford a whole bunch of security cameras—although maybe I needed to look at that more seriously. It had to be cheaper than a salary and benefits. And I didn't want to close down the bookstore and find yet another career to pursue.

I could go back to social work.

Ugh. Just thinking that had my insides knotting. It was good work. Important work. But I'd been close to burning out when I finally listened to my friends and switched to running the bookstore. I loved it here. I loved being surrounded by books and interacting with customers.

I glanced over to see Reuben settling on the couch with a small pile of books beside him and sighed. I guess that should be *most* customers.

The bell jingled and a young mom pushing a double stroller came in.

I smiled. The tow-headed kids were either twins or close enough in age that they might as well be.

"Good morning. How can I help you?"

"Hi." The mom blew out a breath, sending the tendrils of hair that had escaped her messy bun flying. "Is it okay if we look at the kids' books? Their hands are clean and I'll watch them."

"Of course." I gestured to the shelf where the kids' books were all at a kid-accessible height. There was even a small, kid-sized table with two chairs there. I didn't have the room for a true kid play and read space, but Whitney and Beckett said this worked well enough. "Let me drag a chair over for you."

"Oh, you don't have to do that." She shook her head. "I'll just sit on the floor. I'm used to it. Thanks."

I watched as she maneuvered the stroller closer, then parked it sort of out of the way before releasing the kids from their seats. They squealed—but it wasn't overly loud—and bee-lined for the books. Before long, they were at the table with a pile of books teetering between them. Mom alternated kids on her lap, reading a page or two, before their attention span waned and they were up and swapping out the book for something else.

I left her to it and, determined to avoid the area where Reuben was staked out, started on my daily rounds of checking the shelves to fix all the little errors that happened when browsers put books back.

I made notes in my phone about gaps in the sections. I'd get more from the back to fill in. It was a good problem to have and it actually made me feel a little better about the store's bottom line in general. Maybe I'd be able to make this work after all.

I worked steadily, while keeping an eye on Reuben and the mom. After about a half hour, Reuben finally stood. He collected the pile of books. I hurried over to the register. I didn't actually expect him to purchase any of them, but stranger things had happened.

"This one is good." Reuben dropped it on the counter in front of me. "I need to finish it, so I guess it's your lucky day."

I smiled and logged in to the register so I could scan his book. "Just the one?"

"No. It's a series. I'll get them all since you have them." He pushed the small stack toward me.

I made quick work of scanning the books and told him the total.

He grumbled a little as he worked a credit card out of his wallet and shoved it into the reader.

I slid the books into a bag, collected the receipt, and added it before offering him his purchases. "Thanks so much. Have a great day."

He scowled at me before giving a curt nod and striding from the store.

I blew out a breath.

"Does he hassle you?"

I started and glanced over at the mom. I hadn't seen her get up and approach. "I don't think it goes all the way to hassling. Yet. I texted my lawyer about him this morning though."

"Oh, good. My stepdaughter works at the café after school. She said he's not allowed in there unless he can prove he's meeting someone."

My eyebrows lifted. "You're sure it's the same guy?"

"Pretty sure. She pointed him out one afternoon when I was there. Sometimes, if she's feeling generous, she'll get her brothers a cookie with her discount."

"That's nice of her." I wasn't sure whether it was or not, honestly, but it seemed like the thing to say. Blended families had to be a challenge, but it sounded like this mom was doing her best to make it work. At least from a two-second conversation, it did.

"Anyway. Keep in mind that the other merchants on the street are all wary of him. They'll have your back if you need to ban him from the store."

"Thanks." I hadn't thought of talking to the other store owners. I just assumed Reuben was a problem for me, not one for the retail spaces in general. "I will. Find any books you need to take home?"

She laughed. "You know I did. Books are a weakness. Some women have a shoe budget. I have a book allowance."

I grinned. "Why do you think I run a bookstore?"

"I should have thought of that. Maybe when these two hit school age, you'll need a helping hand. I'm a reliable worker. Oh —hold that thought." She hurried back to where her kids had started climbing on the little chairs and jumping off all while laughing madly. She grabbed one in midair and swung him into the stroller, then reached for the other. When she'd wrangled them into their seatbelts, she sorted through the pile of books on the table, scooped up the few off the floor, and carried a large stack to the counter. "I'll put the others back on the shelf."

"Don't worry about it. I'll get it."

"I don't mind." She smiled and went back to quickly finish tidying up. Then she pushed the stroller with her as she returned to the register. "I'm Kim, by the way. I have a feeling I'm going to be here a lot. Especially since you don't seem to mind the minions."

"I don't mind them at all. And you're certainly welcome whenever." I scanned the books and tried not to let my face reflect the happy pitter-pat of my heart with each one I rang up. Even if she didn't buy this much every time she came in, she'd be a welcome regular. "Do you have a favorite genre for you?"

"Me?" She sighed and looked over her shoulder, almost longingly, then turned back to me. "It's been so long since I had two minutes to myself, I'm not sure what I like to read anymore. Romance, maybe? Although it'd be good if it was something I wouldn't be mortified to have my daughter pick up."

I grinned. "You should come on Saturday. We'll have a local Christian romance author in for a book signing. I have a couple of her books now, but I'll have them all then. And you could get them signed."

Kim studied me a moment. "Are they in a series?"

I nodded.

She closed her eyes and visibly had a mental argument with herself. "Maybe you could grab the first in series and add it to that pile? I don't know if I'll ever actually find time to read it, but it sounds pretty close to perfect if I can."

I grinned. "Be right back."

I dashed around the counter and over to the appropriate

shelf. Of course, now I had to hope that the first book in a series was actually one that we had in stock. I ran my finger over the spines until I landed on a number one and tugged it off the shelf. Back at the register, I scanned it and told Kim the total.

"Well, it's not as bad as it could be." Kim sighed and put her credit card into the reader. "I tell myself we're building verbal skills and a love of the written word. Sometimes my husband buys it. Sometimes he just rolls his eyes."

"Well, you're not wrong. That's what you're doing. And you can always pass them on to friends later when the kids outgrow them. Or save them for your next one."

Kim held up both hands. "Oh no. No, no, no. There are no next ones. Twins cured me of my baby fever permanently. But passing them on is a good idea. Better than donating them to the thrift store where I'm pretty sure they just get tossed."

"There you go." I tore the receipt off and tucked it in the bag with the books. "Enjoy. I hope to see you again. And think about coming to meet Heather this weekend. You can bring that one and get it signed."

"I'll see what I can do." Kim hoisted her book bag in a farewell wave and, with the know-how that only moms seemed to possess, navigated the double stroller through the doorway without any accidents or catastrophes.

I checked the time. The morning had flown, which explained why my stomach was rumbling. I'd grab my lunch from the back room and eat it up here before heading back into the shelves to straighten things and restock.

And if my mind drifted to kissing Cody, well, it didn't hurt anyone, and it was a nice way to pass the time.

# 17

## CODY

"Where are we going?"

I glanced over at Megan and grinned. "It's a surprise."

"Ugh. I hate surprises. Didn't you know that? I really feel like you should know that." Megan looked out the window of the passenger seat of my car, her brow furrowed. "Is that the airport?"

Busted. I'd toyed with asking her to wear a blindfold, but I hadn't actually believed she would. Plus, there was the whole thing where it was borderline creepy to ask your girlfriend—or any woman—to wear a blindfold. I imagined we would have been getting strange looks from the other people on the road. Maybe we would even have been pulled over. It was a can of worms I hadn't wanted to get near, let alone open.

"It is the airport. Are we flying somewhere? Really?" She turned to look at me, her face alight. "What a fun surprise. I take it all back. I love surprises."

I laughed. "Well, good. I'm glad you're not going to be mad at me the whole time."

Megan reached over and briefly touched my leg. "Never. I can't imagine a situation where I would be mad at you."

I didn't believe that. Everyone had moments when they got angry, annoyed, frustrated, or whatever word you wanted to use for it with their partner in life. It came from being two distinct individuals. "I would actually worry more if that was true. You need to be able to speak your mind. As do I. And I don't think we're always going to see eye to eye on everything. But we'll work it out. Together. And if you'd decided that you always hated surprises and always would, then I would stop surprising you."

"Aw." She patted her heart and fluttered her eyelashes.

It shouldn't turn my insides to goo. I knew she was playing around, but even still. "Do you want to know where we're going?"

"Nah. Not now. More surprise feels like a good thing. And bonus, we can get home as late as we want, because I'm off tomorrow. Although I feel a little bad about you potentially having a late night and then an early morning."

Was now the time to let her know I'd taken tomorrow off? Or should I wait and let her figure it out? Since I wasn't completely sure what her reaction was going to be, I decided to let it ride. If she got upset? Well, it was easy enough to change plans. No one else needed the plane—I'd checked on that with the guys, even though I left off the part about me taking Megan along.

I parked and texted the pilot that we'd arrived, then pushed open my door and popped the trunk.

"What's in the trunk?" Megan got out of the car and shut her door before wandering over to peek in. "Why are there garment bags in here?"

I reached in and lifted them out. "Do you want to know, or do you want to be surprised?"

She frowned at me, looked at the bags, then frowned at me again. "How am I supposed to choose?"

I shrugged and closed the lid of the trunk, then clicked the lock button on my key fob. "It's up to you. You'll find out eventually, so it's really just a question of when you want to know."

She slipped her hand into mine, and we started walking toward the airport. I appreciated that we could use a smaller airport for our private plane, rather than needing to navigate the larger ones. Not that we couldn't use the big airports when needed, but everything took longer when we did.

We went through security and made our way out to the plane.

"Everything's ready when you are." The pilot greeted us as we stepped on board.

"Thanks. Just let us get settled." I hung the garment bags inside the little closet by the door, then gestured for Megan to choose a seat.

She chose the couch and patted the space beside her.

I chuckled and sat. There were still seatbelts. I hooked mine up while she did the same. "All set."

"Roger that." The pilot gave a mock salute then disappeared into the cockpit. His voice came over the speakers a moment later. "Flight time should be about an hour and twenty minutes."

"Hmm." Megan took my hand and rubbed little circles on the top with her thumb. "What's an hour and twenty minutes from DC? Florida, maybe?"

She glanced at me and lifted her eyebrows in query.

"Cold." I gave a mock shudder. "Brr."

Megan laughed. "Okay. Not Florida. Tennessee, maybe? Although I don't know what we'd do in Tennessee. Don't answer that. Um. Hmm. Cape Cod?"

"Warmer." But now I was going to have to find a reason to fly her to Tennessee. We could go to Graceland and get barbecue in Memphis, if nothing else. That would be a fun excursion.

"Oh, well duh. New York?" She bounced in her seat a little. "Are we going to New York City for the afternoon?"

"We are." I leaned over and kissed her as the plane started its taxi to the runway. I heard the engine noise change and knew we were about to take off. I probably should have ended the kiss, but instead I let the gravitational forces push us closer together.

Megan didn't seem to mind.

When we reached our cruising altitude, I put in a DVD of one of the older TV shows she'd mentioned enjoying. "We should have time for two episodes. I've never watched this."

"Seriously?" She clapped her hands. "It's the best. You're going to love it. We need popcorn."

"Okay." I went to the little galley kitchen in the rear of the plane and stuck a bag in the microwave. I'd been surprised to learn it was fine to have this in the kitchen but it had, in fact, come standard. The plane purchase was one of Scott's good ideas, and he'd definitely taken the lead in figuring out what we needed. Tristan, of course, handled the legal paperwork.

Sometimes, I wondered what I contributed to our friend group, but they kept me around so I must not be completely dead weight.

When the popcorn finished popping, I dumped it into a bowl and carried it back out to the couch.

"This is the best ever. I'm trying to feel a little guilt about jetting to New York for the afternoon, but I can't quite work up to it." Megan reached into the bowl for a handful of popcorn.

I smiled and hit Play.

The flight passed quickly and before I knew it, I was shaking the pilot's hand, gathering the garment bags, and heading out to find our limo driver with Megan clinging to my arm.

It wasn't hard to locate the uniformed driver. He was right

where the company had told me he'd be. And if I'd missed him, Megan's elbow in my ribs would have alerted me.

"He has your name on a sign!" Megan was practically squealing. "I didn't think they really did that."

"How else would you find your guy?" I guess in today's world there could be an app or texts or something where you verified your ride like Uber, but limos were a little fancier than ride shares. I extended my hand. "Hi. I'm Cody."

"Nice to meet you. I'm right out front. Would you like me to carry your bags?" The driver gestured toward the hanging bags.

"I've got them. Thanks."

He nodded and we followed him out of the airport to the curb where his black stretch limo was parked.

Megan stopped, her mouth open, and turned to me. "You got a limo? A *real* limo?"

"It seemed like it'd be fun. I've never actually ridden in one before. We talked about it at prom—me and some of the others I went with—but even sharing the cost, it was more than we wanted to spend. And they had a six-hour minimum and all kinds of requirements that were hard for us as high school students to roll with."

Megan laughed. "I love it! I've never been in one, either, and I've always wanted to." She leaned up and kissed my cheek. "This is the best day ever. Thank you."

"You're welcome." Now I handed the bags to the driver so he could tuck them in the trunk. Then I waited while Megan climbed into the back and I followed. The driver closed the door with a quiet *thunk*. I'd given our first destination when I booked the car, so that surprise should remain intact on the drive from the airstrip.

Megan was exploring the limo with a look of a giddy child. "This is so cool."

I chuckled. "It is. I'm not going to lie. I think I might like having a driver for some things even at home."

"You can afford it, if you wanted to." Megan turned to look at me. "I don't always understand why you guys don't spend more of your money."

It was a reasonable question. "I think most of it is that we don't want the money to become our defining characteristic. We lived without it, you know? We'd be fine if it all went away tomorrow. And we want to make sure we're honoring God with the money when we do use it."

"That's basically what Austin told me." Megan bit her lower lip. "I'm not sure I'd be able to stop myself from going overboard occasionally, though."

I gestured to the limo. "You mean like flying your girlfriend to New York and renting a limo."

She grinned. "Yeah. Like that. It's good, though, right? This is okay?"

"I think so." I couldn't deny there was a tiny niggle of concern in the back of my mind about the gang finding out. It seemed inevitable, at this point. Part of me, though, was ready for that. I didn't like sneaking around, as if what was between Megan and me was wrong. So maybe there had been an element of that factoring in when I planned this excursion.

Looking out the window as we made our way through the streets of New York, I was grateful I hadn't decided to rent a car. I was fairly certain everyone driving was certifiable. It made the DC traffic look like child's play. And the pedestrians? They were fearless. More so than the office workers in Northwest DC who considered crosswalks and crossing lights suggestions for the tourists.

Finally, the limo slid to a stop at the curb in front of the Plaza. Flags hung over an awning protecting three doors in the tall stone building. The driver came around to open the door. I stepped out and offered Megan my hand. She beamed as she stepped out on the black and white checkered entry.

Her voice was an awed whisper. "This is the Plaza."

"It is."

Our bags were whisked away. The driver reminded me that he was at our disposal and I had his contact information. I think I made the right responses, but I was distracted watching Megan take it all in. Any doubt about the idea disappeared. This was something she'd remember.

It was something I'd remember.

Hopefully, it'd be something we could tell our kids about some day.

While Megan wandered around the lobby, I checked in and got our room key. I found her seated near the elevators.

"Ready to go up?"

She stood, blinking. "Up? Like to a room up?"

"Well, we'll need to change. Eventually. But we could go explore some first if you wanted. Either on foot or I can get the car back." I checked the time. I had tickets for a Broadway show, but curtain wasn't until seven. We should get there before that, obviously, but since it was only just three thirty, we had time.

Megan crossed her arms. "Maybe you should go ahead and tell me the rest of the plan."

"Broadway. Late dinner after the show." Here was the sticky part. I took a deep breath. "Tomorrow, I planned to go to Ellis Island and the Statue of Liberty. And then if there was time, maybe a driving tour so we could see more of Central Park and places like Rockefeller Center before heading home."

"Tomorrow." Megan looked away. "So we'd stay here. At the Plaza?"

I waited for her to look back at me, then nodded. "That's what I was thinking. There should be two beds."

"But just one room?"

"They stay pretty full. And I planned this last minute." I licked my lips. "We can go home after dinner, if you'd rather. We can just use the room to change. I'm not trying to do anything nefarious here, Megan. I just wanted to give you something special."

"Okay. You're right. I'm overreacting." She blew out a breath. "You know everyone's going to find out. And they're going to think the worst."

"I only care about that if you do. We're adults. I love you. And I trust you not to take advantage of me."

Megan snickered. "I think that was my line."

"Snooze you lose." I reached for her hand and tugged her into my arms. "If you want to go home right now, we can do that, too. I wasn't trying to make you uncomfortable."

"No. This is amazing. I'm sorry—I just had a moment."

I kissed the tip of her nose. "It's understandable. Maybe I shouldn't have done this as a surprise. But I really didn't want you to say no."

"And I probably would have. And that would have been my loss." She glanced over at the elevators before stepping back. "Let's go walk around. When do we need to be back here to change?"

"Maybe ninety minutes?"

Megan grinned. "Then let's go see New York."

# 18

## MEGAN

I'd been floating all week since we got back from New York late Monday evening. Even Reuben's annoying habit of showing up, sitting and reading for a half hour, and leaving didn't bring me down. Honestly, if he kept buying books like he'd been doing? I'd reserve him a spot on the couch. My bottom line was going up, and I couldn't give all the credit to the author signings.

But they didn't hurt.

Friday evening was still a slow time, though, and I was looking forward to the girls getting here. I wished I could tell them all about Cody's surprise, but we'd decided—well, I'd pushed for it more than anything—to wait and see if they brought it up.

Cody thought we should just tell them. Maybe he was right. But now it felt like it was this whole big thing, and I didn't know how to come clean. Even if they weren't angry that we were dating, they were going to be mad that we'd kept it a secret.

I bit my lip. Was it going to get worse the longer we waited, or had we maybe reached a point where it was going to be awful, no matter what, so there was nothing to lose by waiting?

"There you are." Kayla came through the door, the bell's cheerful jingling a counterpoint to the storm cloud on her face. "What do you think you're doing?"

"Uh." I looked around, checking that there weren't any customers. "Running a business?"

She squinted her eyes, and her scowl deepened. "Don't."

"What?"

"Okay. You're going to play dumb. Fine. I'll ask outright. Are you sleeping with Cody?"

I leaned back like she'd slapped me. "What? No. I'm not sleeping with anyone."

Kayla looked somewhat mollified. "So Austin misunderstood what was going on when he saw that Cody took the plane overnight, and also we stopped by to see you, but you weren't there?"

"I could have just been ignoring the doorbell." I didn't know why I countered with that, but the words were out before I thought them through.

"Which is why Austin used his key. He was worried about you." Kayla cocked her head to the side. "What's going on?"

I groaned. "Cody and I went to New York. It was amazing. We saw a show, ate in a Michelin starred restaurant—in the back at the chef's table where we could see the kitchen in action. We stayed at the Plaza and had a private tour of Ellis Island and the Statue of Liberty before driving around to see all the other sights."

Kayla crossed her arms. "You said you weren't sleeping with him."

I squirmed. "Well, we did sleep in the same room, it's true. And actually, I have fallen asleep once when we were watching a movie. So I have slept with him, I guess, if you're going to be technical."

"You know what I mean."

"I do. I'm wondering when it became your business." I mirrored her posture. I was starting to get annoyed with her attitude. "Did you forget that I'm an adult?"

"Did you forget your brother feels responsible for you?"

"Did I ask him to?" I threw my hands in the air. "And if he's so upset, why isn't he here giving me the third degree instead of sending you?"

"Because we decided we'd divide and conquer."

"Oh, for crying out loud." I grabbed my phone and texted a warning to Cody. "Is it any wonder we didn't tell everyone when we started dating?"

"Do you think it's possible that if you'd been up front about it, maybe people wouldn't be upset?"

I glared at Kayla. Maybe—just maybe—she had a point. On the flip side? When Cody and I had talked about it, we'd had valid reasons for believing that they'd do exactly this.

"I guess we'll never know. But let me just encourage you to do a little soul searching—and to invite Austin to join you in it—to see what your response really would have been."

Kayla seemed to deflate. She scrubbed her hands over her face. "Okay. Maybe that's a point. For the record, I think sneaking around was dumb."

"Noted." I sighed. "Are we okay?"

"Not yet. But we'll get there."

"Is Austin going to kill Cody?"

I could close—or leave Kayla here; she knew how to use the register—and run over there. I wasn't sure how the guys would respond to me showing up, but maybe it would keep them from physical violence. Not that I could actually picture Austin throwing a punch, but Wes might.

"No. And he'll probably keep the other guys off him. But the two of you were stupid. If you were going to keep a secret, you shouldn't have gone on an overnight trip together using the plane that everyone shares." Kayla studied my face. "You're okay?"

"I love him. He's...everything."

I couldn't—wouldn't—lie and say that there hadn't been a good deal of temptation when we'd been at the Plaza. The whole avoiding situations that made it easy to sin hadn't been part of that weekend trip, but nothing had happened.

I was mostly glad.

There was a small part of me that wondered if it would really be so bad. I loved Cody. He loved me. I was reasonably certain we were heading toward marriage. Cody had said a few things here and there that pointed in that direction. So did it really matter if the government had a piece of paper beforehand?

Kayla's expression softened. "I'm glad you found each other. We should order dinner. To celebrate."

"I'm game. Celebrating is better than berating." I took a deep breath. "I'm sorry that we kept our relationship secret. I actually kind of thought you'd figured it out."

"Suspected." Kayla held up a finger. "Which is not the same as knowing. But I didn't push and, when I think it through, you didn't lie. Though you skirted the line a few times."

"We said we wouldn't lie about it. That was something we agreed on. I think...I think Cody knew the trip would force the issue."

Kayla snorted. "Understatement. I've been working hard since Wednesday to get Austin to wait until today to confront Cody. I was hoping he'd cool off. Not sure if that happened or not."

I winced and sent up a quick prayer for Cody's safety. I didn't imagine the guys were going to be as quick to forgive as Kayla seemed to be.

"What food should we order?" Kayla pulled her phone out of her purse. "And should we wait for Jenna?"

"Let's wait. Do you know for sure she's coming?"

Kayla nodded. "Yeah. She texted me earlier. I guess she and Noah went to see that house together this afternoon so she's running a little behind."

"When does Whitney get back? Any idea?"

"Nope. I'm not sure she knows. I guess they're enjoying being in the islands and having his family there. Her folks had to head back to Kansas." Kayla sighed. "Let's go sit. I promise not to bite."

I chuckled and grabbed my phone before joining her in the seating area.

"The Halloween decorations look good."

"Thanks." I'd spent most of the week getting them put out during down time. I was a week behind when I normally decorated, but I hadn't wanted them to distract from the author signing at the start of the month. The author who was coming at the end of the month wrote paranormal thrillers, so he didn't mind having spiderwebs and streamers. "Did I tell you about the book trick-or-treat I'm doing next week until the end of the month?"

"No. You're not giving away books, are you?"

"Ha. No. It's kind of the book blind date idea, but for Halloween. Or, I guess, October. I'm wrapping titles that I love— or that customers have submitted—in plain paper and then writing a two-sentence description on them. For the 'treat' books, I'm including the genre. For the 'trick' books, I'm going to try and make it hard to even guess the genre from the story description I give." I shrugged.

"What if people don't like the book?" Kayla frowned. "You can't exactly take returns. Don't you still have to destroy books that get returned?"

"Most people won't return a book. It's not worth the hassle of coming back to the store with their receipt to do it. But yes, for the big publishers that's how returns are handled. The indie titles I can resell if they aren't damaged, since I buy them outright."

"I wish you didn't have to destroy the others."

I nodded. It was a poorly kept secret of the book business. Or maybe it was well-known and some people didn't care. Because for all I said that most people didn't return books, I still had more returns every month than I would have preferred. "I wonder..."

Kayla looked at me. "What do you wonder?"

"It might not work. But I wonder...what if I made a Little Free Library and put it out front? If people showed me the books they're putting in it, I could do like a punch card and when you filled the card, you got a ten or twenty percent discount on your next purchase. Maybe, then, instead of returning the book, they'd donate it."

"I'd do that in a heartbeat. Would you only let people put books they bought from you in the library?" Kayla tapped her fingers together. "How would that work?"

"I don't think I'd want to curate it that closely. I don't need another full-time job." I laughed, but I was serious. I just was brainstorming to find a way to cut down on returns and incentivize people to come back in and buy more. Honestly, if people had to come in to show me their donations and get a card punched, some number of them would buy *something*. I didn't have a ton of people come in, browse, and leave empty handed. It was getting them in the door that took work.

"Okay. So people what, bring their books inside and you punch their card, then they take those books back out and put them in the library box? Are you worried about missing someone carrying an unpaid title out as if they were donating it but actually they're stealing it?"

"Well, I wasn't." I shook my head. Maybe this was a dumb

idea. "Obviously, I need to think it through a little more. I'd love to say I could do an honor system, but..."

"Yeah. Not around here."

I looked over as the bell jingled above the door. Jenna came in, smiling more brightly than was usual for her.

"You guys. That house is amazing." She rubbed her hands together and dropped onto the couch beside Kayla. "I really hope he buys it."

"Because you think it'd be a great fit for him, or because you want a chance to remodel it?"

Kayla never had been one to mince her words, but her bluntness tonight made me a little uncomfortable.

"Wow. Someone's cranky. Are we ordering food?" Jenna at looked me.

"That's the plan. We were waiting for you. She's upset with me, not you. Although I thought she was over it." I shot Kayla a pointed look.

Kayla held up her hands. "Sorry. You're right. Both of you. I'm sorry."

"Food?" Jenna patted Kayla's arm. "That always helps."

Kayla snickered. "I might be hangry. What's close and fast?"

"Want to get Mexican? I'm pretty sure the Cantina would deliver over here." I could go for something spicy and crunchy. And really, tacos were never wrong.

"Works for me. I have their app." Jenna tapped on her phone. "Why's Kayla mad at you?"

"Cody and I are dating."

Jenna looked up. "Yeah? Congrats. He's hot. Seems nice. Has obviously been smitten with you at least since I came on the scene."

"What? I mean yeah, that's what he said, but I never saw it." I shook my head. "How did you?"

Jenna shrugged. She tapped at her phone, then handed it to

me. "Choose what you want and add it to the order, then give the phone to Kayla. You can just shoot me some cash whenever."

I frowned as I scrolled the menu looking for what I wanted. I considered myself a pretty observant person, and I hadn't picked up on Cody's interest even when I'd been hoping for it. Well, whatever. We were together now, so it didn't matter.

I added my meal and passed the phone to Kayla. "What does Noah think about the house? Cody's stuck on how big it is."

Jenna nodded. "I can see that. That's one of Noah's worries, too. It's a lot. But even if he bought it, we finished the reno, and he sold it he'd come out ahead. They're asking almost six mil now, and they'll probably get close to that, unfinished. I'd say when it's all complete? Noah could resell for twice that. And since he could pay cash, it's not like he has to worry about interest and fees. It's a lot lower risk for him. Or, he decides he loves it and moves in. Either way, he wins. And I win, too, I guess. Assuming he lets me do the reno."

That was an interesting way to look at it. It wasn't as if Noah didn't have options for living space, either. He could buy something else. He could probably move in with Cody in Cody's townhouse. Or he could go back to a longer-term lease on his apartment instead of being month-to-month like he was now.

"Here." Kayla gave Jenna her phone back. "You have a money app preference?"

"Nope. I use them all. You've got my email address. It'll work for whichever."

Right. I should send her my portion too. If I waited, I'd forget. I pulled up the only one I had installed and sent her enough to cover my food plus some of the tip and delivery fees. I didn't love how much extra those added to an order, but I also didn't want to run out and get it myself. Convenience had a cost.

"Would Noah be able to live there after you got some of the rooms done?" Kayla set her phone aside.

"Up to him. Living in a reno is an experience. It's doable. I'm not sure he'd like it." Jenna put her phone away. "Food's gonna be about a half hour."

Kayla and Jenna continued chatting about the townhouse, renovation ideas, and Jenna's hope that Noah would get excited about the idea. I listened with half an ear, but I couldn't stop myself from worrying about Cody.

How were the guys handling things?

Austin...well, he was honestly the least of my worries. I could handle my brother, if it came to that. But the rest of the guys? They saw me as their baby sister, but they didn't actually have the experience of me *being* their sister to know my wrath if they damaged my relationship with Cody.

And all of this was ridiculous. I was a grown woman and completely capable of making my own choices.

And I chose Cody.

# 19

## CODY

I'd never wondered what it would be like to have the majority of the guys some degree of annoyed with me. I honestly hadn't ever expected to be in the situation. Of all of them, Austin was the most okay with things. I guess that shouldn't have surprised me, since he'd essentially given me permission in the spring.

He just wished I'd gone about it differently.

Maybe, in hindsight, I did, too. At this point, I didn't feel like I could let anyone know that, though. It was a moot point, anyway. Megan and I had done what had seemed reasonable at the time. For reasons that were still solid. Ish.

I blew out a breath and stared at the boxes of invitations to the gala that were taking up the empty space of my office. They were stuffed and sealed, thanks to several evenings with Megan's help. We might have gotten them handled faster if we were just friends, but I couldn't regret that, either.

Hearing a knock on my door, I looked over and lifted my eyebrows. "Noah? What can I help you with?"

"I was thinking I could help you."

I blinked. That wasn't something I expected him to offer. "With...?"

He shrugged and tucked his hands in his pockets. "I don't know. The invitations? Anything else you need help with?"

"I need to prep the invitations for the bulk mail. That involves sorting them by zip code into different trays. It's going to be tedious." Which was why I'd been avoiding it all day.

"Yeah, all right. Let's do it."

"Why?"

It wasn't that I didn't want help. Or need it. But while Noah hadn't been ready to take things outside and beat the stuffing out of me like Wes, he definitely hadn't been excited to find out about my trip to New York City with Megan.

"Because you're my best friend, man, and I might not like how you went about things, but I also kind of get it. And it's been obvious to me for a long time that you and Megan should get together. Or at least explore the water some." Noah looked over at the pile of boxes that held the invitations and his eyes seemed to bug out. "Uh."

"Yeah. I know. You don't have to help if you've changed your mind. I appreciate the offer and the spirit behind it." I didn't bother to sigh. The reality was that the gala was my problem to deal with. If there was anyone else at the office who could've been put in charge of it, I was reasonably certain they would have been chosen in the first place.

"No. No it's fine. I offered." He frowned at the pile. "Why don't I go see if the conference room is available."

"That's a good idea." I smiled and pushed back from my desk. "I'll get these somewhat organized."

If I'd known what I was doing, I would have kept them in zip code order when Megan and I were stuffing them. The labels had printed out that way. I just hadn't had enough knowledge to understand why until it was too late. I was hopeful that there might be groups of them still in the right order, since Megan and I had each taken a page of labels to work on. I guessed we'd find out.

Noah poked his head back in the doorway. "We're good. I asked Alicia to block it off for the rest of the afternoon for us. She said that shouldn't be a problem."

"Nice." I stood and moved around my desk to the stack of boxes, then bent and hefted two. "Grab a box or two and let's go."

I carried my boxes down the hall to the conference room and set them on the edge of the table. Noah came in behind me with three boxes in his arms. "Showoff."

He snickered. "If it's any consolation, I won't do it again. Why are they so heavy?"

"Tell me about it. Let's get the rest."

"There's only one more box?" Noah followed me back to my office.

I gestured to the stack of empty mail trays that I'd picked up at the post office after I finished reading up on how to do a bulk mailing. It honestly felt like there ought to be someone at the office to take it over from me at this point. They sent out a monthly newsletter—that was the primary reason we had a bulk-mail permit—so why they couldn't handle mailing the gala invites was beyond me.

But I'd been soundly put in my place when I'd asked.

So yeah. Yay me.

At least the lady at the post office had been friendly and explained the process to me. And hey, bonus, I had to drop them off at a different place at the PO, so I wouldn't be annoying anyone in the drive-through drop-off line like I had with the save-the-date cards.

I set out the zip code trays and then consulted the printouts I'd made. "Okay, I have the zips listed out. Each tray gets invites for a single zip code, so I'll slide the paper with the zip under the front of the tray. We flip through the invites and put them in the appropriate tray so, hopefully, I can take these all to the post office tonight before the bulk-mail drop closes. Otherwise, I guess I'll do it first thing tomorrow."

"Sounds easy enough." Noah reached into a box, pulled out a handful of envelopes, and started flipping through them. "So. How was NYC?"

I grabbed my own handful of invitations and fought not to hunch my shoulders. "It was really nice. Have you ever seen a show actually on Broadway? I figured it wouldn't be much different than the Kennedy Center—but man, it is."

Noah looked over, his eyes full of laughter. "Yeah? You becoming a thespian?"

"No. Probably not. It was, of course, a musical. But Megan sure ate it up. And watching her enjoy herself was nearly better than the show itself."

"Wow. You're completely gone over her, aren't you?"

I nodded. I didn't see the point in denying it. "Have been for a while. Which was stupid, since I didn't think she would give me the time of day."

Noah dropped the envelopes into the appropriate trays and grabbed more from the box. "So Broadway. Dinner? Where'd you eat? If you say you got a hotdog off a street vendor, I'm going to kick you."

"No. I wouldn't do that." Although we had done just that for lunch on Monday. Maybe it was best not to mention that part. Megan had insisted it was part of the experience. I'd been planning to take her to the deli that *When Harry Met Sally* made famous. Megan was a sucker for the older romcoms, and I thought she'd get a kick out of it.

"Good. So?"

I named the place.

Noah let out a low whistle. "How'd you get reservations last minute there?"

"It's the first time the publicity about Austin this spring has worked in my favor. The woman who answered the phone must have a thing for the super-rich, because I mentioned my name and she verified that I was from Virginia and suddenly the chef's table was available."

"Chef's table? Seriously?" Noah shook his head. "We got named in what, two of the articles? Passing mention, at that. She must be a serious newshound."

I dropped my sorted piles into the correct trays. "I thought about that some. I kind of think it might be part of her job. Sure, she has to know the big-name celebrities and influential people, right, but what if I was the kind of person who would make a big stink about being denied service? You know the news would eat that up."

Noah held his hands up like he was framing a headline. "Billionaire turned away from Michelin-starred restaurant. Will he sue?"

"Exactly." I pointed at him before reaching for more invitations. "She doesn't know that I would have just called the next place on my list. I'm not in the habit of trying the whole 'do you know who I am' thing. But I don't mind that she made it happen. The food was beyond."

Noah grinned. "And yet there were no doggie bags for your friends. Not even a bagel came back with you."

I snorted. I had brought back some bagels. They were happily wrapped and stored in my freezer. "I can probably swing a bagel if you're desperate."

He frowned at me. "You brought bagels home from New York and didn't immediately share?"

"There was the whole 'we aren't telling everyone we're dating' thing."

Noah flicked away my excuse. "Bzzt. You had to know the trip would make it clear."

I hadn't *known*. Suspected? Yes. Hoped? Well. Also yes. Sneaking around was awful. I'd spent the better part of the last what, ten years, trying to hide my crush—hide and talk myself out of—and I was ready for the whole thing to be out in the open.

"Uh-huh. You did. Sneaky." He cocked his head to the side. "What's Megan think about that?"

"She's good with it." We'd talked over the weekend. A lot. I guess the girls ganged up on her the same way the guys did me on Friday. Although they hadn't video called Whitney in the way Wes had dragged Scott into the drama at poker.

Scott hadn't cared. Of course, he'd kind of already known. Maybe Whitney would be cool with it, too, since she hadn't seemed averse to the idea when I ran into them getting ice cream.

"That's good. I don't want things to get weird between the two of you now that the cat's out of the bag. Sometimes that whole secret love thing is all that keeps a relationship going, you know?"

"No. I don't know." Geesh. Did I have to worry about that now? I scowled at Noah and dumped sorted invites into trays. "I don't think it's like that with us. It's not like we spent our time together giggling about how we were pulling a fast one on the rest of you."

"Good." He nodded and got more invitations. "Then you're probably fine."

It was time to change the subject. "Did you decide if you were buying that massive project?"

"Smooth segue."

"I wasn't trying to be smooth. I was trying to change the subject." I shot him a toothy, fake grin. "So?"

"Fine. Fine." Noah blew out a breath. "I think I am, yeah."

"Because?" I just couldn't fathom having a place that big. But maybe he was excited about it? Six bedrooms, though. Just...why?

"Is it wrong for me to say that I want to do it for Jenna?" Noah glanced over at the conference room door. It was mostly open. He scooted around and closed it. "She was so excited about the project. She has all these ideas—and they're much better than the designs and drawings the current owners are including in the sale."

"I guess I didn't realize you had a thing for Jenna." I slapped the invitations in my hand against my leg. "It's pretty decent as an opening shot for a courtship."

Noah shook his head. "It's not like that."

"No?" I flipped through the invitations and added them to the trays. I reached into the box and found it empty. One down, four to go. And it wasn't actually taking forever like I'd been worried it would.

"No. We were friends in high school, right? Kept in sporadic touch through college. I took her to a few dinners and dances— definitely in the vein of she didn't have anyone else to take her, would I be willing." Noah shrugged. "I'm her backup date."

"You're her backup date."

"That's what I said."

"I was just wondering if you heard yourself." I shook my head. "Backup dates are for prom. Maybe college. But then? It ends."

"Well, I haven't taken her anywhere lately. So yeah, it ended."

"And you still are considering spending close to six mil on a house so she has a renovation project she's excited about?"

"I guess when you put it that way, it sounds a little weird. But not outside the realm of reasonable." Noah dropped invitations in the trays. "I liked it better when I was grilling you about your love life. Tell me about the Plaza. Who actually stays in a place like that?"

I laughed. That had been my initial question when I first considered the whole trip. But after browsing the website with all the glitz and glam? It had been obvious. "Billionaires in New York."

# 20

## MEGAN

"Happy Halloween." I smiled and waved to the mom with her three kids—all in costume already, even though it was just after three in the afternoon—as they left the bookstore. The kids had gotten a handful of candy out of my stash. Mom had loved the trick or treat with a book idea and ended up buying herself a trick and a treat.

In fact, the wrapped books were disappearing faster than I'd expected them to. I should probably go in the back and grab the pile I'd put together this morning before I opened and replenish the shelves.

I was just heading to the back room when the bell over the door jingled. I turned and my heart sank. "Hello, Reuben."

"Trick or treat!" He grinned at me and pulled down the white mask that covered three-quarters of his face before swirling a black cape lined with red around and hiding it behind his arm.

"Dracula?" I knew it was the wrong answer, but I just didn't want to jump into whatever strange fantasy he'd concocted with me as the Christine to his Phantom.

He pushed the mask back up to the top of his head. "Pfft. You call yourself a bookseller?"

"Dracula is a book. One that's remained popular through the years despite some of the tragic film versions that have nothing to do with the actual storyline Stoker penned." I offered a tight smile.

Reuben crossed his arms. "You're telling me Dracula is more popular than *The Phantom of the Opera*?"

"Book-wise? Absolutely. Most people don't even realize the musical was based on a book by Gaston Leroux." I'd read the book when Phantom had returned to Broadway briefly to celebrate the twenty-fifth anniversary. It was another instance of the book not really having a lot to do with the actual stage production. And, in my opinion, one of the few times the movie —or in this case, play—was better. Probably because of the music.

"Are you obtuse on purpose, or are you really just dumb?"

I lifted my eyebrows. It was the only response he was going to get to his question. "Can I help you find something? I believe we have copies of both books in stock."

He shook his head and turned to eye the table where the trick-or-treat books were. He flicked the wrapping paper. "This is clever. Find it on Pinterest?"

"It's been popular with the shoppers today. Sometimes people want a surprise." That certainly seemed to be the case, as the trick books were considerably more popular than the treats. "I'm sure there's something in there that you'd enjoy."

Reuben snorted. "Doubtful." He looked around. "Where's the candy?"

"I have some in the back for the kids who come around later. Why?"

"I'm in costume. I said the appropriate words. I expect a reward." He tipped his head to the side and took a step toward me. "If you don't want to give me candy, I'm sure we can come up with something else that's sweet for you to give."

For the first time with Reuben, I was nervous. I swallowed and forced myself not to take a step back. "I suppose since you insist on acting like a child, candy is appropriate."

His eyes flashed with anger but he seemed to work to rein it back. His face settled into a stony glare.

I scooted around him back to the register and reached underneath to withdraw the plastic pumpkin that held my candy. I reached in, closed my hand around the first piece of candy I touched, and drew it out. Then I tossed it, underhand, toward him.

Reuben fumbled the catch and the chocolate dropped on the floor. He scowled. "I'm not eating that."

"It's wrapped, it's fine. And it's all you're getting."

"Stingy. I guess it makes sense, since I'm sure your little store here is struggling."

It wasn't. Not anymore. My online orders were up. As were my in-person sales. I couldn't say for sure, but I was fairly certain both C. J. and Heather were encouraging their friends to come and shop.

I offered a tight smile. "Can I help you with anything else?"

"No. I'll just look around some."

I nodded. So much for scooting to the back for more of the wrapped books. I didn't leave the front counter, usually, when Reuben was in the store. If I did, it was only to straighten shelves. It just felt like I needed to be able to keep an eye on him.

The bell jingled as the door opened and I shot a grateful glance in that direction. I felt everything lift when I saw it was Cody. "Hey there, stranger."

Cody chuckled. "I'm not sure I count as a stranger when we had dinner together last night."

I grinned and, after a quick glance to be sure Reuben wasn't staring, rose to my tiptoes to give Cody a quick kiss. "Stranger to the store, then. You're off work early today."

"Mr. Ballentine stopped by to let me know the invitations looked great—I guess he received his already—and he was positive he hadn't seen me doing all the work for them during the workday. So I explained how you and I had done the stuffing and so forth in the evenings, and he said I should leave early to make up a little of the time." Cody shrugged. "I wasn't going to argue."

"That was nice of him. Have the replies started to come in?"

He nodded. "Dribs and drabs so far, but I guess that's not unreasonable. I mailed them a week ago. If you figure two days, maybe three, for them to be delivered, it works. Most people probably have to think a day or two—or more—before they commit and send in their card. I guess we'll start getting more in another week or two. Or right before the deadline."

I laughed. "Probably that last one. I thought about sending mine in, but I keep forgetting. Right now, it's pinned to the corkboard in the kitchen."

"You're coming, right?"

"Of course. Wouldn't miss it. Especially now that I know how good the food's going to be."

Cody grinned. "My plan is coming together."

He paused and looked around the store. His gaze landed on Reuben, and I stiffened. I didn't want a big confrontation. Or a small one. Mostly, Reuben was harmless.

Although...could I still say that after the candy thing? There'd been an implied threat—maybe not even implied—that had caused my stomach to knot.

"That's the guy?" Cody glanced over his shoulder at Reuben again before holding my gaze.

I forgot how well Cody could read me. I nodded once.

"Nice costume. Dracula?"

I couldn't stop the laugh, but my hand flew up to cover my mouth. The last thing I needed was for Reuben to look up from his book and see Cody and me laughing at him. "Phantom of the Opera."

Cody pursed his lips. "Dracula would be better. Then you don't have to leave a mask perched on the top of your head."

"Are you dressing up this year? We didn't really talk about it. I'm sorry I have to work."

"It's not a big deal. I'm not a fan of costumes. I figure Halloween is a way for kids to grub candy. If you're not escorting kids around, but you still dress up? I don't get that." Cody tucked his hands in his pockets. "While my parents weren't on the super strict side of it being a holiday believers shouldn't celebrate, it was also very clearly relegated to a fun way for young kids to get candy. And by the time I turned eleven, it was expected that I'd be done with it. Which I was."

I could see that. I didn't usually jump on the train of Halloween as a gateway drug to witchcraft or demon worship, but I also didn't discount that for some people that was exactly what it was. Because it was a holiday that could easily take a turn away from harmless fun and candy into the darker side of occult practices. If people didn't approach it with prayer and discernment? Well, they could end up in a world of hurt.

"I had a few older teens in right after the high schools let out looking for books on Wicca that, in my opinion, they had no business seeking out. They seemed annoyed that I didn't stock them and wouldn't order for them. To me it's no different than the men—generally—who come in looking for certain kinds of magazines. I have a choice on what I carry. They have a choice to find it elsewhere."

"Do you get pushback on that?"

I waggled a hand back and forth. "Sometimes. Not usually

too much. It's not like it's hard to find someplace else to get their fix."

Cody frowned. "That's sad."

"It is." I cleared my throat. I wouldn't mind a change of subject. "How long can you stay?"

"As long as you want."

I smiled as everything in me warmed.

"You want some ice cream?" Cody glanced back over to where Reuben was sitting with his usual pile of books. "Does he actually buy stuff, or just sit and read like you're a library?"

"He buys things. Please don't worry about it. I have it under control."

Cody gave me a long, measuring look before he nodded slowly. "All right. Ice cream?"

It might be the last day of October, but it was sunny and clear and we were expected to hit the upper seventies. Of course, I didn't know for myself. I kept the bookstore the same comfortable seventy-three degrees year-round. On the other hand? When was ice cream bad?

"Sure."

"Flavor?"

"Surprise me."

He flashed a grin, leaned in for another quick kiss, and headed toward the door. He glanced over his shoulder as he opened it. "Be right back."

A tiny, contented sigh escaped as I watched Cody through the front windows.

"How cozy." Reuben's voice was full of snark and poison as he set three books down on the counter with more force than required.

I reached for the books. "Did you find everything you need?"

He grunted.

I took it as a yes and scanned the books before putting them into a bag and adding a couple more pieces of candy. I told Reuben the total and waited for him to push his credit card into the appropriate slot. When he finally did, I finished the transaction and offered him the bag of books with a smile. "Thanks. Have a good day."

"Yeah. Okay. Whatever." Bag in hand, Reuben stormed to the door and out, heading in the opposite direction of Cody.

I blew out a breath and hurried to the back room to get the restock of the trick-or-treat books.

No one came in while Cody and I ate our ice cream, but shortly after we finished, a steady stream of parents and their dressed-up kiddos began. I was happy to participate in the trick or treating in downtown that families did. It was a good way to entice people through the doors—remind them that they had a bookstore within easy reach.

Cody was a big help. He refilled the candy bowl, helped answer questions and steer people toward the genres they were interested in. I hadn't realized he knew even the basic layout of the shop—but he got it right more than he got it wrong.

Around six, there was a lull.

I glanced at him. "If you want a job, you're hired."

He laughed. "This is fun. I see why you do it. You want dinner?"

"I really do." The ice cream had worn off and now my stomach was rumbling. Quietly, for now, but I knew it wouldn't stay that way.

"Preference?"

"Mia's?" It was walkable, and who didn't love Italian food? Plus, it'd be just as tasty cold if there was a sudden influx of customers that kept me from getting to it in a timely manner. Maybe that wasn't super likely, but it paid to plan ahead.

"Done. Back in a few."

This time, Cody's kiss was far from perfunctory. He wiggled

his eyebrows at me when he pulled away and started toward the door, whistling. He held it for the costumed family that was headed for the bookstore.

At least I wasn't going to be bored while I waited for dinner.

"Well, well. What did I miss?" Whitney's voice came from behind the plastic She-Hulk mask. She flipped it up and pointed a finger at me. "Leave town for a month and suddenly your friend is exchanging steamy kisses with another friend?"

"Whit." Scott flipped up his Red Hulk mask and nudged her in the side with his elbow. He looked at me. "Don't mind her; she doesn't read her texts."

Whitney frowned. "I got a text about this?"

Scott shook his head. "Fill her in. I've got Beck."

Beckett, dressed in the more recognizable Incredible Hulk costume, zipped toward the kid section. Scott followed behind.

"So? Fill me in." Whitney batted her eyelashes. "Obviously you and Cody have stopped mooning over each other. How's it going?"

I scoffed. "Neither of us ever mooned. I deny that. Heartily."

"Sure. Okay. There was no mooning. Or longing looks when no one was supposed to be looking." Whitney leaned against the counter. "And I never drooled over Scott when I was working as his nanny and supposed to be keeping it platonic."

I flicked her arm. "Hey."

"Deets, girl. We've been in the islands—which was amazing and heartily recommended if you ever need to get your life back together."

I studied Whitney. She was tanner than she'd been when she left. But more than that, there was an air of relaxation and calm around her that had been missing for too long. "It looks like it agreed with you."

"It really did. And having the parents—both sets—with us? Icing on the cake. Mom and Dad had to leave a little earlier than they would have liked because Wendy is still struggling and needed them, but I can't blame them for that." Whitney blew out a breath. "And Scott and I decided that we're going to try for a baby in earnest."

"Wow. Congrats." I cocked my head to the side. "You're not worried?"

"I am. I can't deny that. But we spent a lot of time praying together and we both really feel like this is the right next step. So, we'll see what God has for us and face it together."

I nodded slowly. That's how a marriage was supposed to work. My parents were like that. Austin and Kayla looked like they were working the same way. And Cody and me? We hadn't done much praying together. Just quick blessings for the meal, that sort of thing.

I prayed about and for him. And for our relationship. But I did it on my own. I should talk to Cody about it.

My stomach twisted.

I really didn't want to. I wasn't someone who talked about spiritual things easily. It was private. Personal. And I'd had too many people in my life remind me that just because I believed something it didn't mean everyone else did. Or that they had to.

Which, okay, sure. That was true. But I probably shouldn't be as hesitant about speaking up about my faith—or about things that had to do with faith—when I was among friends who all believed the same thing anyway.

"Can I ask you a question?" I glanced over to where Scott and Beckett were playing, happily oblivious, and leaned in, lowering my voice.

Whitney's eyebrows lifted and she leaned close. "Not only can you, but you have to now. I'm curious."

I managed a slight smile. "When you and Scott were living together and dating, did you ever question the whole 'supposed to save sex for marriage' thing? I mean, it's a piece of paper, right? It gives you a tax break. Marriage used to be just two people saying out loud that they were married and going about as man and wife, right?"

Whitney frowned. "I'm going to try and stick to answers, but I have so many questions that I would rather ask you. Yes, it was a challenge at times. And that's one of the reasons we did marry as soon as we realized it was where we were headed. But the rest of what you said? It sounds like justification. If you want to go back in time, having sex was all it took to be married. So, should we just apply that to the world now? Anytime people sleep together, they're married? Then, I guess, for people who feel like there's no big issue sleeping around, what do we say? Are they polygamists? Because the Bible's pretty clear that God created marriage for *one* man and *one* woman. Not multiples."

"But—"

Whitney held up a finger. "Not quite finished. I'm not sure what I think about the fact that the government is involved in marriage now. But that's beside the point. For believers, marriage is a covenant between two people and God. And sex is what seals that covenant. So while it may just be a piece of paper for the IRS, it's a lot more than that spiritually."

I sighed. I didn't have to necessarily like her words, but I'd think about them. It wasn't as if it was new information. A few tweaks in there. I hadn't thought about the covenant aspect, even though it had lurked in the back of my mind, having been mentioned somewhere or other.

Whitney rested her hand over mine. "Are you sleeping with Cody?"

I shook my head.

"But you want to."

Since Whitney hadn't phrased it as a question, I wasn't sure I needed to answer her, but she just kept looking at me, eyebrows raised.

Finally, I managed a slight shrug. "The idea has entered my mind."

Whitney chuckled. "I bet. I know how it is. I'm not going to lecture more, but I'll pray for you to listen to the Holy Spirit."

Which was as good as a lecture. I knew what was right. I knew what the Bible said and what everyone always taught. And I knew the other side of things, from high school, when I'd decided it didn't matter what the Bible said or everyone taught. I could try to justify that it was a different situation. The guy in high school wasn't someone I would have ever considered marrying. Sex just seemed necessary. Everyone else was doing it, and I hadn't wanted to go to prom alone. We'd spent six months together, sneaking sex in uncomfortable places, and when I was late, he'd dropped me faster than I could blink. So I'd ended up at prom solo anyway. And I'd confessed all of that and promised God that I was going to listen to His Word going forward.

Yet here I was, looking for loopholes.

I needed to talk to Cody. Make sure we were on the same page as far as keeping things where they needed to be in our relationship.

Yay.

Not.

"Mama!" Beckett ran over with two books clutched to his chest. "They have bunnies!"

Whitney took the books and flipped over the cover on the top one. She grinned at the cheerful illustrations then flipped to the other book. "Aww. Yeah, we'll have to take these."

"Sucker." I winked and rang up the books. "Should I let you know when we get the third in the series in?"

Scott laughed. "Yeah. Go ahead and set a copy aside for us at that point. You know we love books."

Whitney used her card in the reader and reached for the bag

with the books. "Thanks. And that other stuff? You ever need to talk? You know where I am."

"Yeah. Thanks. There's more candy in there, too."

"Just what we need." Scott shook his head even as Beckett cheered.

I waved as they exited the shop. When the door closed, I blew out a breath. I wasn't looking forward to either of the conversations I needed to have with Cody.

But maybe being in love wasn't all sunshine and steamy kisses.

# 21

## CODY

Mia's had been slammed. Did everyone want Italian for their Halloween meal? I thought I'd glimpsed Wes sitting at a table in the bar, but I wasn't positive. And since he didn't call out or wave me over—if it was actually him—I wasn't going to push it. He was still ticked about me and Megan dating.

I'd deal with it—with him—at some point. But tonight was not it. Especially not in a crowded restaurant.

So, instead, I'd hovered near the hostess stand waiting on our to-go order and trying not to be in the way of all the families and groups hoping for a table until I could finally collect the bag and head back toward the bookstore.

Lots of people—groups of teens, or families with younger kids—were strolling both sides of the sidewalk and popping into the businesses so they could collect candy. I liked that about Old Town. So much of the DC area felt like this swarming, anonymous mass. But Old Town was like a small town right in the heart of it.

I pulled open the bookstore door, smiling as the bell jingled, and glanced around. There were a lot of people milling around in here, too. I caught Megan's eye and nodded toward the back room, hoping she caught my unspoken question. She gave a small shake of her head and gestured toward the checkout counter.

Okay.

Maybe that made sense. It wasn't like she could disappear into the back with a store full of customers.

I carried the bag over and tucked it onto one of the shelves under the counter. A harried mother with two skeletons clinging to her pants came up.

"Thank goodness. I need to check out before I spend all my grocery money in here." She grinned and set a large pile of books on the counter. "I don't know how I managed to go this long without realizing there was a bookstore, but now I kind of wish I could forget."

I cast a frantic look around for Megan before offering the woman a smile. "Well, we're glad for your business."

I eyed the register. It couldn't be that hard, could it? I'd watched Megan do it at least a hundred times. I'd give it a shot. I scanned the first book, barely avoiding pumping my fist in victory when it rang up and showed on the screen. I reached for the next. "Did you find everything you were looking for?"

The woman laughed. "More than. And I see you have local independent authors coming twice a month. I'll be back for the next one. I've met her at church, would you believe, and keep meaning to read her books."

"Then this is the perfect opportunity." I finished scanning the books and studied the keypad before hitting what I hoped would figure the tax and total for me. It looked like it did.

The woman fed her card into the machine and I put the books in a bag while it processed. When she removed her card, I searched for the right button to print a receipt, ripped it off, and added it to the bag.

"Did your kids get can—"

She held up her hand. "So much. No more, please."

I chuckled and offered her the bag. "Thanks. We'll see you later."

I had a steady stream of customers after that. Had Megan ever had a Tuesday night as busy as this one? Megan stopped by to check on me twice, but she seemed content that I was doing things properly and went back out among the books to help people find what they needed. I also caught sight of her cleaning up and reshelving after one little girl dressed as a princess had an impressive tantrum and scooped at least thirty books off the shelf in anger before her distracted mother got a hold of her.

They, of course, left without buying anything.

Finally, the crowd thinned.

Megan came back to the register and leaned against me. "Phew."

"Tell me about it. But also, yay?"

"Definitely yay. Tonight is going to end October's numbers on a good note. Sorry about dinner."

"Pfft." I waved that off. "Don't worry about it. That's one of the best things about Italian food. It's good at any temperature."

"You are correct. But I also have a microwave in back if needed."

"I'm good." I leaned forward to kiss her forehead. "What did Scott and Whitney have to say?"

"You knew it was them?"

"Only when I didn't see them in the crowd. Then I realized that the Hulk family must have been them. I wonder if they're going to keep the comic character theme going forever."

Megan shrugged. "I figure Beckett drives that train. He's been big into Hulk lately, so it's not surprising that they went in that direction."

I waited, expecting her to have something interesting to say about their visit. But she just reached under the counter for the food and opened the bag.

I cleared my throat. "I guess they didn't stay long?"

"Who? Oh. Scott and Whitney?" Megan shook her head. "Maybe fifteen minutes. They had a good time and are happy to be home."

I studied her. "Is something wrong?"

"What? No. Of course not."

I might not be the sharpest tack in the box, but I knew that when a woman protested like that, she meant the opposite. What I didn't know was what to do about it.

"Was Mia's busy?"

I took the container labeled "Parm" and flipped it open. Yum. My mouth watered. "Very. I might have seen Wes, but I wasn't sure."

"You didn't go verify?"

"Nah. It didn't seem like the place for him to yell at me again. And I kind of figure that's what's going to happen. I'm going to have to swing by his place and talk to him."

Megan rested her hand on my arm. "Do you want me to come with you?"

"No. It'll be okay. He just has to adjust his brain, you know? Of all the guys, he didn't even suspect I was interested, so I guess he was the most shocked. Everyone else either knew or had at least considered it." Which basically meant I was terrible at the "secret" part of having a secret crush, but whatever. At the end of the day, it worked out.

"All right. If you change your mind, let me know. And let me know when you go so I can pray for you."

My eyebrows lifted. "You'd do that?"

"Of course. I already pray for you. And for us. And, well, for everyone in the group but in a different way. I love you, Cody."

Her words made me stand a little straighter. If there hadn't been a few customers still browsing, I would have pulled her into my arms. But there were, so I settled for squeezing her hand. "I love you, too. I'll definitely let you know. Prayer seems like a really good idea for that situation. Well, every situation. You know what I mean."

Her laugh seemed strained. "I do. Maybe we can talk about that sometime?"

"About praying? Sure." I looked out into the bookstore then back at her. "Sometime other than now?"

"Well. I guess...ugh." She ran a hand through her hair then crossed her arms. "Probably."

"Okay." What was that? Normally, I could come up with ideas, some kind of speculation. But this? I had nothing. "Is it okay if I eat?"

"Yeah, of course. You can go in the back if you want a table. But I don't mind if you hang here."

I pulled the little stool she kept behind the checkout desk away from the wall and sat, balancing my takeout container carefully on my lap. "I like the view here."

Her cheeks pinked up and it was all I could do not to stand up and pull her into my arms again. But I really didn't get the feeling she'd welcome that. And it wasn't just because of the customers in her store.

Something was up. I just wished I knew what it could be.

"Mom?" I pushed open the front door of my parents' house and called out. "Everything okay?"

"In the kitchen, hon."

I let out a breath at her response. She'd sounded frantic when she called me as I was wrapping up at work, so I'd ditched my plan to head to the bookstore and hang out with Megan—

maybe get to the bottom of the prayer thing, or whatever else was wrong—and come here instead.

I made sure the door latched after I closed it, toed off my shoes, and padded through my childhood home to the kitchen. It was different than when I'd lived at home. Once I'd finished college, Mom and Dad had taken out an equity loan and completely redone the kitchen and breakfast area. And when I'd made all that money last year, I'd convinced my dad—and gosh had it taken some convincing—to let me pay it off.

"There's my baby." Mom wiped her hands on the towel slung over her shoulder and came around the island to wrap me in a hug.

I returned the embrace, smiling at the gentle scent of vanilla that clung to her hair. "What are you making?"

"Oh." Mom stepped back and glanced at the counters. "I got it in my head to make a traditional British Christmas pudding. They have to steep—I think that's the term—for several weeks before you serve them. But now I'm not sure it was such a good idea."

"Hmm." I pulled out a stool at the island and sat. "New recipes are your thinking experiments. What's going on?"

Mom flashed a smile that didn't reach her eyes. "You know me too well."

"You also sounded like you were about to cry when you called."

She looked away.

"Mom?"

"Let me get you some cookies. I made them yesterday. Your favorite." Mom bustled to the counter and opened one of her many Victorian tins. She folded back the wax paper and I spotted the tell-tale cracked surface of snickerdoodles peeking out.

I watched as she piled cookies on a plate and then got down

a glass and filled it with milk. I smiled. It was like coming home from practice in high school, although then I probably would have begged for one of her sandwiches to go with it.

"Here you go. Dig in."

I took a cookie and bit in. Cinnamon and sugar crunched over the creamy cookie—in my brain, I knew she used actual lard to make them delicious, but I didn't concentrate on that. "Mm. Perfection. Just like you. Where's Dad?"

Mom's eyes filled and she turned away. She went to the cookie tin and closed it up before setting it in its spot and fussing over the alignment.

"Mom. What's wrong with Dad?"

She turned, her arms crossed, and leaned against the counter. "I don't think I can do this. I thought I could. But I don't..."

I waited.

She shook her head.

"Should I call him?" I reached for my phone. "I'm going to call him."

Mom didn't say anything, so I opened my phone and tapped Dad's contact. It rang once before he answered.

"Did she tell you?"

"Dad? What's going on? Are you sick?"

Dad's blustery sigh crackled in my ear. "So that's a no. She couldn't even do that right, could she. Typical."

I frowned. That wasn't like Dad at all. Sure, every now and then he could get harsh when someone wasn't meeting his expectations. I'd been on the wrong side of that as a teenager, even though I worked hard to avoid it. But it wasn't usual.

"You didn't answer my question."

"Is your mother there? Put me on speaker."

I hesitated. I glanced at Mom. She was standing in the same place, like she was frozen in time. But her eyes had closed and a single tear was dripping down her cheek. "I don't think that's a good idea. Obviously the two of you have something to tell me. Why don't you just go ahead. Since Mom's having a hard time with it."

Dad's snort of derision morphed my frown into a scowl. "Fine. I figured she could soften the blow and tell it her way. But apparently not. I'm divorcing your mother. I've found someone else, and I think the responsible thing to do is end things first before starting up something new. So I've moved out and started the paperwork. Once our legal separation is filed, I'd be happy to introduce you to my girlfriend."

I pulled the phone away from my ear and looked at it, confused. "I'm sorry, what?"

"Don't be dense, Cody. You heard me. You understood what I said."

"But Dad—"

"Oh, please. Just stop. You're grown and out of the house, and the reality is that your mother and I haven't been happy for years."

"I was happy." Mom's voice was a whisper.

I hadn't realized she could hear him, but I should have. He was using his blustery no-nonsense voice, and it carried.

I swallowed. "I don't know how to respond to this. What about therapy? Couples counseling?"

"No. I'm not interested. I've made my decision and it's final. We agreed that she'd tell you, but she didn't. Big surprise. When you're over your shock, and you want to meet Jasmine, let me know."

"Wait. Dad. Before you hang up. How old is she?"

Dad sighed. "Why? Gonna throw midlife crisis at me like your mother did?"

"Thinking about it."

"It doesn't matter. You can think what you want." The line went dead.

I set my phone gingerly on the counter. "Oh, Mom."

"I'm sorry. You should have heard it from me."

I shook my head. "No. I think it's better to hear it from the horse's a—"

"Cody." Her voice was sharp. "He's still your father."

"You'd defend him?"

She spread her hands. "No. That's not what I'm doing. Not really. But you know how Jesus tells us to love our enemies?"

I sighed. That was a point. Maybe not one I wanted to embrace just now, but still a point. And more, it was so much my mother. She had to be shattered into microscopic pieces, but she was still able to say that? To think it? To live it? "I'm not there yet."

"Try."

I pushed away from the counter and stood, then crossed the kitchen to wrap my mom in my arms. "I don't understand."

Her voice was muffled against my chest as she held onto me. "I don't, either. But we had thirty-six good years together, and I'm not going to forget them simply because of this. I refuse to be bitter."

I closed my eyes and rested my cheek on the top of her head. Was it as easy as refusing to do it? I could already feel the tendrils of bitterness worming into my heart. How *dare* he? And Jasmine? She sounded like an eighteen-year-old stripper. Oh, man. What if she was? And he got upset at the term "midlife crisis"? You shouldn't *be* a cliché if you didn't want to get compared to one.

I sighed. "How about we order pizza, and I can spend the night?"

"You don't have to do that, honey. You have your own life. I just thought it would be better—easier—to tell you in person."

I eased back and looked at my mom's face. There were some little lines that showed the passing years, but I'd always thought she was beautiful. I still did.

Dad was an idiot.

I kissed her forehead. "I'm staying. Don't argue."

Her smile flashed and I thought I saw a hint of relief in her eyes for just a moment. "All right. I think there are some pajamas in your room still. If not, your father didn't take all his things. Go change into something more comfortable than a suit, and I'll call in the pizza."

"Don't forget the spicy sausage. If Dad's not here, at least he won't ruin our pizza with his ulcer."

Mom chuckled. Maybe it sounded like it turned into a sob at the end, but she nodded and shooed at me to go.

I climbed the stairs and went to my old bedroom and looked around. This room had always been familiar. Comforting.

Now I could only wonder how long it had hidden lies.

# 22

# MEGAN

"I brought pizza." Jenna held up two large boxes as she came through the bookstore door. "It's Friday night and we don't eat pizza nearly as often as we should."

I wrinkled my nose. "I'm not convinced there's a 'should' involved when it comes to pizza."

Jenna gawked. "Seriously? How are we friends?"

"Well, see, you're friends with Noah and he recommended you to Austin, and—"

"Okay, okay," Jenna laughed and lifted a hand. "Stop. I get it. And still. Pizza. It's practically an American pastime."

"That's baseball." I sighed. "Honestly. You should read more."

Jenna grinned and headed toward the seating area. When she got there, she stopped. "What did you do?"

"Oh. I rearranged." I headed over and propped my hands on my hips. "What do you think?"

"I'm not sure."

I tried to see it through her eyes. I'd put a low table in front of the couch, making it easier for someone to carry a pile of books over and look through them. I'd taken the armchairs and made two little two-person groupings out of them. The café had let me take two small round tables they'd been planning to throw away. They wobbled, but that had been easy enough to fix. All in all, the space worked better for smaller groups. And let's be real, most of what I got were smaller groups. "We can drag a chair over on Fridays. But it's less intimidating this way."

Jenna set the pizzas on the table in front of the couch, then sat. "If you say so."

"I do." I smiled and put action to my words by scooting one of the chairs closer before plopping into it. "See?"

"Who do you think we're expecting tonight?"

"Whitney's back in town. I'm not sure if she'll bring Beckett or leave him with Scott. As far as I know, Kayla will be here. So the usual?"

"I probably went overboard on the pizza. But that's fine. I like it cold." Jenna leaned back and tipped her head on the back of the couch so she was staring at the ceiling. "Did you hear Noah's going to buy the house?"

"I hadn't. That's good, right?"

"It is. Of course, I just got a big client at work, and now I'm not sure I'm going to have the time to get started right away. Because of course I won't." Jenna blew out a breath. "And it's not like I'm going to turn away a paying client for a personal project."

"Well, Noah's paying you, right?"

She shrugged. "I'll charge him when something costs me money, sure. But I hadn't planned to charge for the design work or anything like that. I know he's only buying it because I pushed him. And it'll be a fun project for me. It doesn't seem fair to make him pay for that."

I pressed my lips together. I wanted to tell her she should charge him market rate—look at how Austin had pushed until she'd relented on that with the learning center—but I also really, really didn't want to get involved.

"What?"

I lifted my eyebrows. "What, what?"

"You think loud. Just spit it out." Jenna glanced over as the bell on the door jingled.

"Hey. Look who I found!" Kayla held the door for Whitney, and the two of them joined us. "I like this. Where'd the tables come from?"

"The café was throwing them out." I glanced at Whitney as she sat next to Jenna on the couch. "You okay? You look pale."

"Just getting back into the home from vacation swing of things. Turns out, Beckett is a lot easier to manage when there are five other adults around to help out. Scott has been going out to Robinson Enterprises to consult on a classified project, so it's just me and Beck all day and I've gotten used to having backup." Whitney shrugged. "I'll adjust. For now, I'm glad Scott decreed that Beckett could join them for man time."

I grinned. Man time. How cute was that? Did Cody and the rest of the guys call it that when Beck was around? I got a little mental flash of Cody with a toddler that looked suspiciously like him on his hip. He'd be such a good dad. Maybe it was rushing things a little—Cody and I had said we loved each other, and we'd talked marriage and family a little. Probably not enough to justify that daydream—but it didn't hurt to dream, did it?

No. Of course it didn't.

"How's the learning center working out, Kayla?" Jenna flipped open a pizza box lid and wiggled a slice free.

"It's good. You were right about the extra outlets in the labs. We use them all. Sometimes, I even wish I had one or two more. But that's what power strips are for." Kayla eyed the pizza. "Is that for all of us?"

"Do I look like someone who routinely eats two whole pizzas

by herself?" Jenna tipped her head to the side and stared at Kayla.

Kayla's shoulders crept closer to her ears. "No."

Jenna narrowed her eyes. "You're sitting there trying to decide how often 'routinely' is, aren't you?"

"No! I swear!" Kayla held her hands up.

"Eat the pizza. At this point? I insist." Jenna pushed the boxes closer to Kayla.

Kayla snatched a piece out of the box without looking at it and took a huge bite.

I smothered a grin and reached for one of my own. Of course I had to put it right back down because the bell over the door jingled. "I'm coming back for that. No one eat it."

I wiped greasy fingertips on the sides of my pants—grateful I'd worn dark jeans today instead of something dressier—and hurried over to greet the customer.

The evening passed quickly. I did manage to eat three slices of pizza—at least one slice too many—in between customers. We laughed. Whitney showed us photos of their time in the Caymans and the beach house they were considering. They hadn't pulled the trigger yet because they still weren't sure what they'd do with it when it was vacant. I guess it would be a challenge to choose between keeping it vacant so you could randomly head down for a long weekend whenever you wanted or rent it out and keep it from just sitting there.

Finances weren't a concern. Obviously. But I appreciated that none of the guys really went overboard throwing money around.

The girls left around nine. I spent the last hour before closing tidying up the shelves so they were ready for tomorrow. I didn't plan to get here super early. Even with closing on Monday, the schedule was starting to get to me.

Sales were up. Maybe it was time to think about hiring someone to cover some hours. I'd have to play with numbers and see if I could make it work. I'd like to be able to make it a full-time position with benefits. But I wasn't sure sales were up that much.

I locked up and made the short walk home. My cell rang as I was closing the front door of my townhouse. My heart leapt and I hurried to dig it out of my pocket. Cody had been acting a little odd this week. Maybe this was him, finally calling to tell me what was going on. Or he could come over and tell me. I wasn't picky.

Actually, I'd like that better. Even with it being late.

Before I traveled down that road too far, I glanced at the screen and deflated. I answered. "Hey, Austin."

"Wow. Way to greet your brother. Your *amazing* brother. Who loves you. And is, of course, your favorite."

I chuckled in spite of myself. "My brother who clearly wants something."

"Hey. That doesn't have to be true."

"All right. It doesn't have to be. But it is. What's up? It's late and it's been a long day."

Austin paused. "Are you okay? Kayla said you had a good time tonight and that the store had steady business."

I closed my eyes and breathed in, reminding myself that it was good that I had a brother who cared. "I'm fine. Just tired."

I dropped my bag by the door and hooked my keys on pegs hung for that purpose before checking that I'd turned the lock.

"Maybe I'll come talk to you at the store tomorrow instead. In person might be better, anyway."

"I have an author coming in the afternoon—at two—so if you do, come in the morning." I'd rather he just spit it out. I also didn't want to argue with him. Maybe there was still time to give

Cody a call and see if I could get him to talk to me. I heard Kayla in the background, but didn't catch her words. "Or you can just tell me the gist and come talk tomorrow anyway."

"We need to talk about the townhouse."

I headed into the kitchen and pulled out a chair. "Okay. What about it?"

"Our lease is up in January. The landlord is nagging about whether or not we're going to renew."

"It's only November. Barely November."

"Sure. But if he has to rent it, he needs lead time. It's not unreasonable."

Maybe not. I'd never really lived on my own in something not owned by a family member. I mean, at the start, we'd paid Grandma rent, but if we'd needed to flex on the deadline a little, it wasn't like she got fussy about it. "Okay?"

"Well, here's the thing. What would you think about switching with us?"

I'd hate it. That was the immediate answer that sprang to my lips. Thankfully, I was able to clamp my mouth shut before they got blurted out. Was he really asking me to go from a townhouse within walking distance of my store to a one-bedroom apartment that would force me to drive?

"You're quiet."

"I'm thinking." And I was. I was thinking about how much I hated the idea. How we'd talked about this in the late spring when he and Kayla decided to get married and at that point, I would've been fine with it. Ish. But they'd been so sure they were okay in the apartment and it was closer to the learning center and blah blah blah. And even then, the other idea had been that we'd all three of us live here. I couldn't help noticing that wasn't an option Austin was floating. "Why the change?"

"Apartment living is not exactly joyous."

I scoffed. Understatement of the year. He'd been positive

he'd be able to handle it though. And now he'd made it what, six months? "Way to sell me on the idea. Sure. I'd love to move into a non-joyous living situation. Thanks so much. Hard pass."

"Megan—"

"Stop. If the two of you want to move in here, I'm still cool with that. I like cats. I don't see the problem. You both get up earlier than me, so if anyone's schedule is going to be inconvenient for the other, it's not you two who'll have the problem." Maybe there were downsides. I wasn't sure I wanted to live with newlyweds. Maybe they didn't want to live with me, either. But I was a lot less willing to give up my home than I had been when we first talked about it.

Austin sighed. "I guess we could look for someplace to buy. I just figured with you and Cody together, you'd probably be moving out soon anyway, and then I wouldn't have to own two houses."

"You realize Cody and I have been dating two months, right? We're not at the get married portion of the program." I paused. Should I ask? "In fact, did he seem off at poker tonight?"

"Maybe a little quieter than usual. I figured he was trying to keep a low profile so Wes didn't start."

I winced. The girls had gotten over the drama. "Was it bad?"

"Nah. I feel like Wes and Cody must have had a talk, because Wes only cracked two jokes, one of which he immediately took back because it was basically bros before hos and he didn't want to call you a ho."

I snickered. "I appreciate that."

Laughter lined the edges of Austin's voice. "Wes then went on a rant about how that was a case in point for why the two of you shouldn't be together and I said that if it kept us from making misogynistic jokes that we'd never found funny before, then I didn't see the issue."

"Go big bro."

"Thanks. Anyway, after that it was fine. But Cody was quiet. Why?"

Should I tell him? I sighed. "He's been off this week. We had a good time Tuesday handing out candy at the store. He was supposed to come help on Wednesday, but bailed and went to see his mom, and since then? It's one- or two-word responses when I text."

"Oof. You want me to pester him?"

"No." I growled. "I don't need people solving my problems for me. I'm a big girl. I just thought I'd ask. Forget I said anything."

"Okay. Sorry. Just trying to help."

"Yeah, well, when I want help, I'll ask." I blew out a breath. "Look. Let me think about the living situation a little, okay? If the two of you want more space, it doesn't make sense for you to buy another place when you already own this one. I can figure something out. Can you give me to the end of the year though?"

"Yeah. Of course. Or longer. We can make it work with the three of us for a little while. I just don't feel like it'd be ideal for anyone."

My chuckle ended in a sigh. He was probably right. But I sure didn't want to live in that apartment complex across town. "I'll see what I can do. Love you."

"Back atcha. Sorry to cause problems."

"That's what big brothers do." I smirked and hit End before he could reply. I sagged in my chair and stared, unseeing, at the kitchen. How had I gone from possibly hiring an associate to figuring out what kind of rent I could afford on my own place in such a short period of time?

Of course, I still really needed the help at the store.

Which meant I was going to have to find a way to handle both.

This weekend, Cody and I were going to have a talk. I needed to know what was up with him.

And I needed his help solving my dilemmas.

Basically, I just needed him. Hopefully, he knew how much.

# 23

# CODY

I pulled into my garage and started the door closing before I'd even cut the engine. Tired didn't even seem close to the word I'd use to describe how I felt. But I didn't know what else to go with. Weary? Exhausted?

Heartsick?

I blew out a breath and got out of the car, hooking the strap of my messenger bag with two fingers and dragging it along with me. Last week had started out so well. Then Mom called and it was like everything else was swallowed by the noise of catastrophe rushing by.

How could my dad do this?

I pushed open the door into the house and went inside. I dropped my bag on the little table I'd found to hold all the junk that came in from the car and kicked my shoes under it, then I padded upstairs.

Of course, I knew how Dad did it. He stopped thinking with his brain and started thinking with something a lot lower. Mom had chided me for it when I'd expressed that opinion, but it didn't mean I was wrong.

It also meant Dad was completely out of touch with his faith.

That was, perhaps, even more distressing.

I'd always looked up to him as an example of what a Godly man should be. Sure, there were times when he might be harsher or stricter than I wanted—but those times were also usually when I really needed someone to kick some sense into me. Teenage boys weren't exactly known for good decision-making all the time, and I'd been a pretty typical teen. Mostly good and levelheaded. But sometimes completely out in left field. Between Dad and the youth pastor, I'd gotten back on track with life. And with God.

But if Dad could fall away so dramatically? Where did that leave my prospects? Was I some kind of ticking time bomb waiting for a trigger to turn me from loving, devoted, Godly husband into someone who had the audacity to expect his son to embrace a woman named Jasmine?

A woman whose age I still didn't know.

I snorted and pulled open the fridge. If she was older than me, I was going to be shocked.

Why was there no food? Oh, I had ingredients. Things I'd obviously purchased when life made sense and I was doing my best to maintain some semblance of healthy eating. I wasn't a gourmet, but I didn't starve. And I'd never poisoned anyone. Mom had made sure I could make staples that went beyond the microwave and reheating something frozen. She'd even taught me a basic alfredo, although more often than not it broke when I made it. I'd have to get her to show me again. If nothing else, it would be reason to spend time over there.

I shut the fridge and moved into the living room, phone in hand. I'd order Chinese, eat out of the carton, and call it a day.

I'd just pulled up the app when the knocking started. I winced. It had to be Megan. I'd been dodging her—mostly successfully—for the bulk of the week. I'd responded when she texted, but that was it. Sunday, I'd gone to church with Mom and hung out with her all day with the barest explanation that there was stuff going on and Mom needed me.

Mom had been adamant that she didn't.

I'd tried to spend the night again, but she'd sent me home, reminded me to pray, and told me she'd be fine.

She might be, but I wasn't.

I briefly debated ignoring the knocking and pretending I wasn't home, but that seemed low and immature even for me. I sighed, dropped my phone on the couch, and forced myself to stand and shuffle to the door.

I peeked to confirm it was Megan and pushed my lips into what I hoped passed as a smile as I opened the door. "Hi."

Megan crossed her arms and lifted her eyebrows. "Hi back. What's going on?"

I could have played dumb. Thought about it for like two seconds, then stepped back. "Why don't you come in? I was just going to order Chinese. You want?"

Megan stared at me for a moment, then nodded. "Sure. Why not."

I went back to the couch and retrieved my phone. "China Palace is the only place that delivers here, that okay?"

She wrinkled her nose. "I guess. They're not the best."

"No. But they deliver."

"A definite factor in their favor." Megan pushed the door shut and came over to the couch. She sat on the complete opposite end from me. "I'll go kung pao."

My mouth watered. That was a favorite of mine, as well. "Eggroll?"

"Yeah, why not. Do they have a fried rice option? I can't remember."

I scrolled through the sides and found it. "Seem to. Do that instead of the regular?"

"If you don't mind."

I shrugged. Rice was rice. Throwing in some peas and scrambled egg just made it tastier. I finished up the order and checked out before setting my phone aside. "Probably forty minutes."

"Sounds about right. Which is plenty of time for you to tell me why you disappeared. What's going on?" A line formed between Megan's eyebrows and she twisted her fingers in her lap. "Is this about Wes giving you crap for dating me?"

I let out a bark of laughter. I wish. "No. I squared things with Wes. He doesn't love it, but he'll get over it."

"Then what? Did I do something?"

I raked a hand through my hair. "It's not you—"

"If you say 'it's me,' I'm going to hit you. I'll feel bad about it, but I'm still going to." Megan swallowed. "Are you dumping me?"

"I—" Was I? My stomach knotted. I didn't want to. At the same time, I couldn't quite get the point that I saw a reason to continue with her. If my dad could throw away a lifetime like it was nothing, what chance did I have to make something that would actually last?

"Cody?"

I shook my head. I didn't want to be the one who ended things. "I'm not. No. But maybe you should walk away."

"Why would I do that?" Megan scooted closer and rested her hand on my leg. "What happened?"

I cleared my throat. I wasn't sure I was going to be able to get the words past the lump in my throat, but I had to try. "My mom called on Wednesday and asked me to come over so she could let me know that Dad left her for another woman."

Megan blinked. "I'm sorry, what?"

I couldn't say it again. I shot her an imploring look. Tears scalded the back of my eyes, but I focused on breathing and willing them away. Mom said it was okay to cry about something like this, but I wasn't convinced. At this point, I wasn't going to be a baby in front of Megan. I might have said she should walk away, but I didn't want her to do it because I was a weeping wuss.

"That makes no sense. Your parents are the epitome of hashtag relationship goals."

My lips twitched. "Were."

"I don't believe this. You talked to your dad?"

"Yeah." I slumped back into the couch. "He said when the legal separation paperwork is finalized, he'll introduce me to Jasmine."

"Her name is *not* Jasmine."

"Oh, it is."

"Does she wear gypsy pants and fly around on a carpet with your dad or something?"

I laughed. "Who knows. I didn't ask. I did ask if she was older than me and he didn't respond. So there's that."

"Your poor mother." Megan's words were quiet. "I don't understand why you wouldn't tell me, though. You can't think I'd take your dad's side in this?"

I shrugged.

Megan slapped my leg.

It didn't hurt, but it startled. "Hey."

"Hey nothing. How big of an idiot are you, exactly?"

"How am I an idiot? I didn't do anything!" I glared at her. "You don't get to come in here and tell me I'm not handling the destruction of everything I believed about marriage the right way. I needed space and time to process. I still do."

Megan drew a long breath in through her nose. "Well. Pardon me for impinging on your space and processing. When you're ready to talk like an adult, you be sure to let me know."

"Megan." I watched her stand and stride to the door. "Come on. Don't be like that."

She turned. "Me? I'm the one who's not supposed to be like

that? You need to take a long, hard look in the mirror, buddy. Pulling away and basically ghosting is not how grownups handle their feelings. I can't stand by you and try to help—or at least support you—if I don't know what you need."

I knew she was right. I should have said something to that effect. I probably should have gotten up and taken her hand or something. Instead, what came out of my mouth was, "I need my parents to be happily married, and it's not like you can do anything to make that the case."

Her face fell. Her whole body seemed to shrink and fade into something a lot more fragile than I'd ever considered Megan could be. "No. You're right. I guess I have nothing to offer you. I'll be praying for you, Cody. And your folks. You know how to reach me when you're ready."

She turned, wrenched open the door, and stepped outside. The door closed with a click that felt all the more final for its silence.

I closed my eyes and let my head drop back on the couch. Now what?

"So nice of you to join us." Wes sent me a poisonous glare as he scooted to make an empty seat on the row where we usually sat at church.

"Yeah. Thanks." I didn't have the energy to get upset. He wasn't wrong to be annoyed. On some level, I was annoyed with myself. I just couldn't quite get to the place where I could do something about it.

"Why aren't you over by Megan?" Wes wasn't letting up. "Did you hose her already?"

"Why is that your business?" Why hadn't I waited in the foyer until the singing started and then slipped in the back row?

I'd thought—wrongly, it seemed—that being with my friends might do something about the thick, heavy, black fog that seemed to coat me wherever I went.

"Megan is all of our business. Which is why you should never have started something up with her if you were going to treat her like this."

I shook my head. I could defend myself, but why? Better to let Megan—and everyone—down now than in thirty-five years when nobody expected it. Might as well let Wes get his shots in and then crow about how right he was.

I sighed. This was a bad idea. I stood up and edged out of the row.

"Where are you going? They're about to start."

Wes's hiss followed me as I made my way to the foyer.

I didn't stop. I just kept walking out of the church, past the confused glances of the greeters who had welcomed me just moments before, and out to my car. But where was I supposed to go?

Mom had made it clear that as much as she appreciated my support and love, she had to learn how to manage on her own and that this was hers to walk through. I suspected she was trying to keep from saying something bad about Dad or influencing my future relationship with him in a negative manner.

I snorted.

Like there was going to be a future relationship.

I started the car, backed out of my spot, and headed toward the main roads. I wouldn't go see Mom, but I didn't want to go home. I'd spent entirely too much time cooped up in those walls lately. After Megan's visit on Monday, I'd limited myself to work —where my office door stayed firmly closed and I only talked to people when they came looking for me—and home. Work and home. Work and home. It was already more of a rut than a routine, but what was I supposed to do?

Megan didn't want to see me until I was out of my funk. Mom didn't need me. Mom also didn't seem to realize how much I needed her. I might be an adult, but no one seemed to understand that Dad's choice had shaken my foundations.

I was wobbling. And I was fairly certain it wouldn't take much more before I crashed completely.

The green sign on the side of the road caught my eye, and I eased over so I could exit. A few turns and I was pulling into the parking lot at Gravelly Point Park. Like a miracle, someone was in the process of pulling out of a spot. I zipped a little to ensure I was in line and snagged it as they left. A car turning into the row blared its horn at me as it passed, the driver adding in some sign language to express their displeasure.

I just finished parking and cut the engine. That was the one good thing about the fog—other people's emotions couldn't penetrate it. It just trapped mine inside and amplified them.

I wormed through the cars and made my way to the grassy field, looking for a spot away from the happy couples and families who'd decided to brave the slight chill and spend their Sunday morning watching the planes use the Potomac River as a guide to the runways of Reagan National.

I found a spot, sat, then laid back, pillowing my head on my arms, and stared at the sky. It was cloudy today. The breeze off the water was chilly enough to remind me it was November. The distant whine of engines grew louder. And louder. And louder. Then the belly of a plane, landing gear lowered, soared over me, almost appearing close enough to touch if I wanted to reach up and jump. Scant minutes later, another plane soared overhead, this one with its landing gear retracting as it took off and headed to points unknown.

Maybe that was what I ought to do.

Would a change of scene get me away from the fog? Would it

do something to thaw the thick walls of ice that seemed to encase me?

Mom would call it running away. But what was so bad about that, really?

I'd lain there for close to ninety minutes as countless planes flew in and out in the skies above, when someone bounced a sneaker off my hip before sitting.

"Hey!" I turned and focused on the interloper, grimacing when I saw it was Wes. "Why are you here?"

"Because I'm the one who guessed where you'd be. Noah, Scott, Austin, and Tristan all went to different spots. Hang on while I text them that I found you."

I scowled and pushed to a sitting position. My phone didn't chime with a notification, so I turned and glared at him. "So now you all have a group chat that doesn't include me? Nice."

"Get over yourself, man. Did you really want to be included in our discussion of where to find you in the middle of your sulk fest? Which, by the way, is not a good look." Wes plopped on the ground beside me. "Also? It's cold. Why are you sitting out in the cold?"

"It's nice. It's probably in the sixties. Get a grip." I was going to ignore everything else he'd said, because it was ridiculous. And mean. "I'm not sulking."

Okay, fine. I didn't ignore all of it.

Wes snorted. "Keep telling yourself that."

I shifted slightly so he wasn't directly in my line of sight. Why did it have to be Wes? Why couldn't Noah or Tristan have found me? Or even Austin. Or Scott. Really, anyone who wasn't Wes.

Wes's sneaker connected with my leg. "Spit it out so we can move on."

"Seriously?" I turned to look at him. "That's your tactic? Just go away. You found me. I'm fine. Mission accomplished."

"Not how it works. You know that."

I sighed. The problem was, he was right. We were friends, and we helped each other. Of course, in the past, I'd believed that was when the person in question actually *wanted* to be helped. But whatever. He meant well. "It's not going to matter."

"Okay. Then it won't matter. Spill anyway."

I frowned and turned to study my friend. "When did you get this annoying?"

One corner of Wes's mouth poked up. "Who says it's new?"

I laughed in spite of myself. "I guess that's a point."

Wes just lifted his eyebrows.

I pressed two fingers between my closed eyes. Wes, clearly, wasn't going away until I told him what the problem was. Maybe I ought to spit it out. But seriously, what was the point?

"Did I mention this wasn't going to change anything?"

"You did. I believe I responded that I didn't care. Hurry it up. I could freeze."

"You'd be the first person in the history of the world who froze in sixty-degree weather."

Wes pulled out his phone and tapped the screen. "It's only fifty-four."

"Oh. Well in that case." I rolled my eyes. "Do we need to go find a coffee shop?"

"If I thought you'd actually show up and tell me what your problem was, I'd be all over that. But right now? I think you'd better talk while I have you here." Wes put his phone away. "So talk."

"My dad left my mom." I had to force the words out. There was a part of me—a reasonably large part—that was annoyed that I was having so much trouble with this. It wasn't like I lived at home. I kept waiting for that part of me to be the one in charge.

"Oof. That's rough. I'm sorry."

I looked at Wes and tipped my head to the side. "No judgment for it pushing me off the rails?"

Wes shook his head. "Nope. My folks are divorced, remember. They split up when I was seventeen. Just before high school graduation. They said they'd held it together as long as they could, and since my exams were over, they figured I'd be fine."

"Were you?"

"Not even remotely. You really don't remember me the first semester of college?"

I tried to think back to freshman year and our group of friends, but didn't land on Wes until after Christmas break. "I don't, no. Did you hang with us right away?"

"Not really. Scott kept trying, but you didn't party, and party was all I was looking for."

That got a glimmer of memory. "Oh wow. That was you. I remember me and Austin having a chat with Scott and trying to get him to stop bringing his loser stoner friend around."

Wes nodded, pointing at his chest. "AKA me."

"How did Scott know you?"

"I was roomies with a friend of *his* roommate. Those two hated me. They talked a lot of crap. I guess Scott felt bad for me and tried to help out." Wes shrugged. "I wasn't interested at first. But you all grew on me. And since being the group's stoner friend didn't look like it was going to fly, I got it figured out."

I could tell there was more to the story, but I also didn't figure it was my place to pry. Not right now. "And your folks?"

Wes blew out a breath. "They're...tricky. I love them, but they make it hard. Mom went off the rails even worse than I did. She's in AA now and seems to be determined to stay sober. Dad has a whole new family, and I don't really know where I fit in it. We're cordial, but I try not to overstay, you know?"

"I don't. But I guess I'll find out."

Wes patted my shoulder. "So your dad walked. Why?"

"Her name's Jasmine."

"Eessh. Ouch."

"Right?" I looked at him and made a face. "She sounds like a teenager. I'm sure there are middle-aged women named Jasmine out there; it's not like the name is new. But he wouldn't tell me how old she is, so yeah."

"How's your mom?"

"Better than me." It was the plain truth. Mom continued to amaze me with her response. "She's so—"

"Resigned?"

I shook my head. "No. Peaceful."

"Huh." Wes stared out at the Potomac for a moment. "Have you asked her why?"

I hadn't. I was too busy being angry and feeling sorry for myself. I could admit that, even if I didn't like to. "I guess I should."

Wes nodded. "So. Your parents are splitting up. I get the tail-spin. Why are you ghosting Megan?"

"I'm not ghosting her." I bit my lip. Okay, I was. Sort of. "I'm not trying to."

He laughed. "Do you hear yourself? Look. I can admit to not handling the news of the two of you being together well. And I'm sorry."

"We squared that up. I get where you were coming from."

"Since I've had time to think about it, I can't help but realize the two of you are really good together. So you need to not screw it up. And right now? You're screwing it up."

I swallowed. "She and Austin have this perfect family, though, and it's just..."

"Pfft. Stop. Their grandmother practically raised them. You notice how rarely they ever talk about their parents? But Grandma? All the time. No one has a perfect family. Not a single person. Even Jesus didn't."

I lifted my eyebrows.

"Come on. His siblings basically tried to have him committed because they were embarrassed he was there healing and teaching people." Wes shrugged. "I'm just saying. Everyone has stuff. Family is hard. But you don't get to stop loving them just because they mess up."

"I still love my dad. I just don't like him very much right now." I frowned. "It's not so much that I didn't think she'd understand. I told her the other night and she was great and I pushed her away."

"Because?"

Could I say that part out loud? "It's going to sound stupid."

"Maybe—just throwing this out as an idea—if it sounds stupid, that's because it is stupid."

"You're not exactly the poster child for committed relationships, you know."

Wes nodded. "It's true. But we're not talking about me. And also, I went to enough therapy in college that my lack of a long-term, committed relationship is more about not having found the right woman yet and not at all about the fact that my parents split up. You're not your dad."

"Right now. But I never thought my dad would do this. Ever. Like how did nobody see this coming? What happens if I marry Megan and in thirty years or forty years, I have some strange mental break and hose her and our kids because I'm an idiot?"

"What if you get hit by a car crossing the street?"

I shot Wes a quizzical look. "What?"

"I'm just saying. It's absolutely as valid a what-if question as any of the ones you're asking. We can't know the future. We can't plan for bizarre hypotheticals fifty years from now. You're hurting Megan *now*. Stop worrying about maybe hurting her down the road and fix what you're doing today." Wes pushed himself to his feet, dusted off his jeans, and stretched out a hand. "Come on. I'm freezing. Let's find coffee."

I took his hand and stood. "You don't think I'm going to ditch you now?"

"Not when I tell you I'm buying."

I laughed. "Oh. Yeah. 'Cause money's such a problem for me."

"Har. Har. Moneybags. Fine, you can buy."

I shook my head, grinning and feeling lighter than I had in more than a week. "Oh, no. You asked me out. Dating rules say you pay."

Wes snickered. "You're such a jerk."

"Takes one to know one."

Wes shook his head. "And a child."

"What if we got lunch instead of coffee? I'm starved. I've been eating Chinese leftovers all week."

Wes looked at me like I'd lost my mind. "Why would you do that?"

"Long story. Not important. Food?"

"Yeah, man. Food is good. I'll follow you."

I headed to my car and waited for Wes to pull up behind me. I exited the parking lot, heading into Crystal City and a pizza place that was there in the mall. Maybe while we ate, Wes could help me figure out how to make things up with Megan.

I wasn't sure a simple apology was going to be enough.

I'd said I loved her. It was time to prove it.

# 24

# MEGAN

Monday morning, I dragged myself out of bed, through a shower, and into the store. It didn't seem to matter that today was my day off, there was always work to do. And working had to be better than obsessing about whatever was going on with Cody.

I closed the door to the office so, hopefully, no one would notice I was in here. Usually, people read the sign and moved on, but sometimes Reuben was persistent.

I groaned.

Reuben had to be a problem for another day, because I had enough problems on my plate right now. Maybe—just maybe—Cody had managed to get the point across to Reuben. I was praying that was the case.

*Sufficient unto the day are the problems thereof.*

Grandma always said that. And she was right. So. First things first. I booted up the computer and logged in to the store email.

Four replies to my job posting? If even one of them was a good fit, it would be a huge help. I'd ultimately decided, against my better judgment but after a long call with Grandma, to look for multiple part-time workers and pray that the candidates didn't even want benefits. Maybe older ladies whose kids were out of the house and they wanted something to do to fill their time?

I clicked on the first response and scanned the body of the email before opening the attached résumé. Hmm. She'd be a great fit. And she didn't mind taking a Saturday now and then. I didn't mind Saturdays, either, but it sure would be nice not to have every single one dedicated to the store.

I switched to the next one. This was a high school junior looking for after school or weekends. Worth investigating, although I wasn't sure about a teenager being here alone. There were times I didn't love being in the store on my own. Still, I could give them a call and see where it went from there.

The other two also had potential. And by the time I'd finished reading the email and printing résumés, I was juggling my thoughts trying to see if it would be possible to hire all of them. It would be nice not to have anyone here on their own. Would the business support it? I'd take another look at the books.

Maybe talk to Austin.

Austin.

I checked the time. None of the candidates were available for me to call until the afternoon, so I might as well start tackling my next big hurdle: a place to live.

I'd discarded any thoughts of the apartment complex Noah lived in. I understood a little more why he and Cody had been roomies before they'd made their billions. There was no way I could afford even a studio in that place. No matter how much I liked the amenities.

The same was true of the waterfront places that weren't condos.

Which meant I needed to look for a basement apartment in someone's townhouse or venture out of Old Town proper, closer to the high school where Austin and Kayla had worked, and see what rent was like there.

I didn't want to have to drive every day. It might not be far in miles, but it was going to be a half hour, at the least, between traffic and stoplights.

Maybe I should tell Austin that he needed to buy a place for him and Kayla. I could talk to Grandma about it. She'd probably take my side. But did I want to go tattling? Because that was what it would be.

I leaned back in my chair and closed my eyes. Sometimes being an adult was the worst.

I heard the front door rattle, then knocking. I waited for whoever was there to get the idea and go away.

My phone rang.

I glanced down and in spite of everything, my heart leapt. Cody.

"Hello?"

"Hey. It's Cody. Are you at the bookstore?"

"Yeah."

"Can you let me in?"

I blew out a breath. I didn't really want to. As much as I didn't love the weird limbo we were in right now, I didn't want him to officially end things between us. But I'd answered the phone and he was waiting for me to speak. "I'll be right there."

I ended the call and dropped my phone on the desk. I looked at my sweatpants and long-sleeved T-shirt from college and wanted to crawl in a hole. But we were closed today. No one was supposed to come by.

Whatever. It wasn't as if he hadn't seen me ratty before.

I headed toward the front door, ominous music thrumming in my brain, and flipped the locks. "Hey."

Cody's eyebrows lifted. "Hi. Are you doing inventory or something?"

I shook my head and relocked the door. "Let's go to the office. I don't want anyone to think we're open."

"Sure." Cody tucked his hands in the pockets of his khakis. "I should have called first, right?"

"No, it's fine. I put up an ad for some part-time help. Between the holidays coming up—yay, retail—and the fact that I can't keep doing this all on my own, it was time. So I wanted to check the store email. And I figured I'd do some apartment hunting here where maybe it wouldn't be as hard."

Cody sat across the desk from me and cocked his head to the side. "Apartment hunting?"

"Yeah. Austin and Kayla want the townhouse. Her lease is ending at the end of December."

He frowned. "So they're kicking you out?"

I shrugged. "It's not exactly like that. But also kind of. Yes."

"That seems dumb. Austin can afford to buy a place."

"He offered." Half-heartedly. And it had been obvious he would have been disappointed in me if I took him up on it. So I hadn't.

"Uh-huh. Did he do it in that 'no really, it's fine' way that makes you realize you can't actually say no?"

I couldn't help it—I laughed. "I didn't know he did that with his friends, too."

"Oh, yeah. He doesn't pull it out often, but man. It's effective." Cody reached out like he was going to take my hand, then pulled back and clasped his hands in his lap.

My vision blurred and I looked away. I wasn't going to cry. Not now. I could hold it in until he left. Probably. "If you're here to officially break up with me, could you just do it fast? I thought I could play it cool and just be friends, but..."

"Oh, baby." This time, Cody's hand did cover mine. "I don't want to break up with you. I came to say I was sorry and ask if you'd forgive me."

I swallowed the lump in my throat and looked over at him. "Really?"

He nodded. "This thing with my parents...I don't know how to handle it."

"That's reasonable."

"Is it? I'm not a kid." He squeezed my hand before letting go and leaning back in his chair. "I know my mom's disappointed in me."

"I doubt that." I shook my head. I couldn't imagine any parent being disappointed in Cody. For any reason. He was such a good, solid guy. "Has she said that? Those exact words?"

"Well, no. But she keeps telling me not to be too hard on Dad." Cody scoffed. "As if it was possible to find a level of harsh that was too much after what he did."

I flipped my hand over and wove my fingers through his. I understood what he was saying, but I was also pretty sure it wasn't the right response. "Have you been praying about it?"

Cody gave me a long look. Finally, he shook his head. "Not like you mean."

"Is there more than one way to mean that?"

He shrugged. "I've been praying for some smiting. I won't lie."

I snickered. "You know what? That's actually reasonable. I think it's okay to talk to God about stuff like that. But you also have to listen. And you have to be open to hearing Him remind you that it's not our job to decide who gets smited. Smote? Smitten? You know what I'm saying."

"I do. I don't really like it." He closed his eyes and sighed. "I just don't understand. My whole life, I've considered my parents pretty much the epitome of hashtag relationship goals, you know?"

I smiled. "I do know. You're stealing my phrase."

He squeezed my hand, but his lips twitched up, and a tiny bit of the humor I was used to seeing in his eyes came back. "When did Austin drop this 'I want the house back' bombshell on you?"

"Last Friday." I watched as he worked through the timing. He'd been avoiding me that week. That continued through the weekend. Then, with all that still on my mind, I'd gone to see him Monday night.

"Ouch."

"It hasn't been the best two weeks of my life. No."

"I'm sorry."

"It's okay. I think you're allowed to get thrown for a loop when something big like that happens." I shrugged. I'd been thrown to a degree with the house thing. "But you don't get to shut out your friends. Or the woman who loves you."

Cody closed his eyes. "I know. All I can say is I'm sorry. Does it help to mention Wes gave me a swift kick in the butt yesterday after church?"

"Knowing Wes? Yeah. Actually." I smiled. "Especially if that's what brought you around here today. Although...you didn't take off work to come see me, did you? You could have waited until tonight."

"I did. And no, I couldn't have. You're important to me, and I needed to let you know that." He glanced around the office. "Is there any way I can help out around here? Since I'm off and everything?"

I had a lot that I'd planned to do today, but suddenly I had no desire to do any of it. I shook my head and reached for my computer mouse. "Nope. In fact, let me close everything up here. Then, if you don't mind if I run home and change first, maybe we could do something together."

"That sounds perfect."

I grinned and shut down the computer. I really shouldn't walk away from my responsibilities like this. I needed to hire people for the store. I needed to get busy finding a place to live. I had follow-up with our next author that needed to happen, because there'd been a snag with her books, and I wasn't going to be able to get it untangled without help.

But I couldn't convince myself that any of that mattered right now. I wanted to do whatever it took to get things back where they'd been with Cody. All my work would still be there tomorrow.

I collected my keys and double-checked that I wasn't forgetting anything, then stood. "All right, I'm ready. You want to meet me at my house?"

Cody took my hand and pulled me into his arms. He rested his cheek against the top of my head and just held me. I might have wished for a kiss, but there was something about this hug that filled up the restless corners of my soul and calmed them in ways nothing ever had before. We stood like that for several minutes, and I felt him relax.

Finally, he said, "I've got my car. I'll drive you home."

# 25

## CODY

In the week and a half since I bailed on work so I could try to make things right with Megan, I'd been going overboard trying to get us back to where we'd been before my world fell apart and I reacted badly.

That was how I looked at it.

Everything fell apart. I still wasn't sure how I was supposed to be reacting, but I was getting through each day. One day at a time.

Mom said that was the best I could hope for.

Now, I looked around my house and bit my lip. The gang— and Mom—were coming for Thanksgiving. They should start arriving soon. Thankfully, Mom was bringing the turkey. Since I was hosting, it was technically supposed to be my job to make it, but I was banking on the fact that arranging for it would count. Bonus? This was homemade, not from a grocery store.

I strode into the kitchen and stepped out onto the deck. I'd told Mom to come around the back and park under the deck. There was no point in her fighting for street parking and then trying to lug a twenty-pound turkey down to the front door.

A flash of sun bouncing off glass caught my eye and I turned.

Mom's car crawled down the alleyway between the town homes. I waved at her, pointed down, and then hurried back inside. I went down to the garage and hit the button to open the door. I was walking out as Mom navigated under the deck and stopped her car.

She cut the engine and pushed open her door, a wide grin on her face. "Happy Thanksgiving! I'm so glad you invited me. This is much better than the other offers I had."

"You had other offers?" I tugged the handle on the side door so it would slide open. You had to love a minivan with the fancy doors. I couldn't quite believe Mom was content to drive the kidmobile so long after I was gone and on my own, but she kept telling me it worked, so it was silly to change to something new. Maybe now that more in her life was changing, she'd be willing to take another stab at a new car.

"Of course I did. I have friends." She pointed to the pot holders on the seat. "Make sure you use those, it's hot. Can I go in and turn on the oven? I'd like to keep it in there so it stays warm."

"Sure. Of course." I knew Mom had friends. She and Dad had always been out on Fridays and Saturdays with other couples from church or Dad's office. They'd had a rich social life. It was part of those relationship goals—I'd never considered them "just parents." They'd always been a couple in their own right. I sighed and put on the glove style oven mitts before picking up the covered roasting pan. I bumped the door-close button with one fingertip as I maneuvered the giant dish out of the van and headed inside.

By the time I got upstairs and into the kitchen, the aroma of the turkey had my mouth watering. "This smells amazing."

"Thanks, honey. I do love cooking a Thanksgiving turkey." She pulled open the oven door. "Just slide it on in, okay?"

"Can do." And I did.

When I'd stepped clear, Mom shut the oven door.

I pulled off the oven mitts and tossed them on the counter. "So. Who were your other options?"

"Oh, well, let's see. The pastor invited me to join them. The Murphys are in town this year and they said they'd love to have me. Mrs. Harder—do you remember her? Her grandson Gavin married that nice girl who had a baby when she was a teenager. She was hoping I'd join her and the other older ladies who were gathering at her place."

I laughed. "I don't know how you'd choose if I hadn't invited you."

"You're right. It was a good reason to give everyone so no one thought I was sulking at home. Your father—" Her gaze cut over to mine and she lifted an eyebrow. "It's okay if I talk about him, right?"

I considered saying no. I didn't actually want to hear it. But maybe it would help Mom somehow. "I guess."

She patted my hand. "He left several messages trying to figure out where I was going. I think he might have had a few invitations himself."

I bristled. "Why would anyone invite him?"

Mom sighed. "You need to forgive your father."

"Have you?"

Her lips twitched. "Let's just say I'm working on it."

"How, Mom?" I crossed my arms. "I just don't understand how to start."

"The very first thing you need to do is remember how much Jesus forgave you."

I shrunk a little at her pointed look. I might be willing to say that, in the grand scheme of things, I lived a pretty good life. I tried to be good. To do good. But I also understood that no amount of good behavior could erase the stain of sin in God's eyes. That needed Jesus's blood. His sacrifice for me on the cross. It was only because Jesus died and was raised that I was able to be forgiven and appear "good" in God's eyes.

"So. In light of that, I have to forgive. Right now? I'm still basically telling God—and myself—that I forgive your father. And then asking for Him to help me forgive and let go. I don't have to do it every five minutes anymore though, so I'm calling it progress."

I pushed off the counter, crossed to my mom, and pulled her into a hug. "That's great progress. And I think I can do that. I don't really want to forgive Dad, but I do understand that I need to."

Mom's arms tightened around me. "I'm not going to push you to do anything more than that. Yet. It's a good start. And today, of all days, we have a lot to be thankful for."

I stepped back. "I guess we do."

Mom looked around the kitchen. "I thought you were going to get some help with decorating."

"I was. Megan and I talked about it. A lot, actually. But then life got busy with the fundraiser at work, and she and I started dating, and then I didn't want to spend our time together looking at furniture. I have a folder full of emails with links from her—I just haven't done anything with them yet."

Mom frowned. "You need to follow through. It'll help her know you're serious about her. You are, aren't you?"

I wasn't sure how to answer that. I wanted to say yes, absolutely I was. But there was still this small part of me that wondered if holding back wasn't a smarter idea. Because what if...

"I see your wheels turning. You're asking yourself how you know you won't get thirty-seven years in the future and have her walk away, aren't you?" Mom shook her head. "You can't know it. You just have to believe. And trust. And do everything in your power to make sure that you keep your marriage vibrant and alive."

I tipped my head to the side. "Don't try to tell me you're taking on *any* responsibility for this."

"No. Not really." Mom shrugged. "It's hard not to look backward and analyze. Or over-analyze. And there are things I could have done differently."

"None of that excuses cheating."

"You're absolutely right. If your father was dissatisfied, he should have talked to me. We could have worked on things together. And it probably would have been work. He took the easy way out. But the fact remains that there were things I didn't like, and I stayed quiet, too."

I wanted to put my fingers in my ears and hum. Loudly. I didn't like the last little shards of the picture-perfect relationship I'd attributed to my parents being knocked onto the ground and shattered.

Mom's smile was slight. "Now you're disappointed with me. Marriage is work, Cody. Every day. And a choice. Every day. And the minute you stop doing the work or making the choice, there are cracks. If you ignore the cracks, they become chasms when you aren't paying attention. Love is wonderful when it's fresh and new and everything feels easy. And it's a different kind of wonderful when it's been around the block a few times and is covered in battle scars. It's always worth fighting for. But never think it isn't a fight."

The doorbell rang.

I'm not sure what I would have said in response, but I was grateful that I had a reason to turn and walk into the living room. I didn't think love was some romance movie, music-swelling crescendo all the time. Did I? I'd seen my parents work at their relationship—even having put it on a pedestal, I'd known they worked at it.

I guess I hadn't realized that the work was sometimes hard.

With a sigh, I pulled open the door.

"Happy Thanksgiving!" Kayla, carrying a laundry basket covered with brown fabric decorated in pilgrim hats and fall-colored leaves, stepped in.

"I can get that." I reached for the basket.

"I've got it. Kitchen, right?" She scooted around me and headed toward the kitchen.

Austin chuckled, following close behind with a foil-covered dish in his oven-mitt bedecked hands. "I tried to take it at the car. She's protective of her pies."

I shut the door. "Pies are good. She made them? They're not from the store?"

Austin's eyes rounded. "Oh, no. Those are the result of her blood, sweat, and tears. People better rave or she might just lose it. I've never seen someone remake pie crust that many times because it wasn't just right."

"Wow." I was happy with grabbing a box of crust out of the freezer section and hoping. And that was when I took the pains to dump a can of filling into a crust and bake it. Usually? Well, usually I figured that was why grocery stores had bakery departments. I nodded toward Austin's dish. "What's that?"

"Green bean casserole. Apparently, Thanksgiving doesn't count without it."

I snickered. "Take it on back. If it needs to go in the oven to stay warm, Mom can probably figure something out."

I decided to hang by the door. Megan should be here soon with stuffing and something cranberry. Those were her words, "something cranberry." I was a little nervous about what form that was going to take, but Mom had raised me to be a champ at taking and choking down a small serving for politeness. I'd manage. Tristan and Wes were also coming. Tristan had said he'd bring rolls—probably from a can that he'd whacked on the counter and rolled into crescents. And Wes was supposed to handle sweet potatoes and the stuff we'd need for the post-dinner gingerbread house contest. Jenna said she was going to try to come, but didn't volunteer for food since she might end up not making it.

Scott and Whitney had taken Beckett to Kansas. Whitney's parents thought a family gathering might help cheer up Whit-ney's sister, Wendy. While I'd miss having the whole gang here, I got it. And I was glad they were willing to do what they could to help out. I couldn't imagine what Wendy was going through as she approached the one-year anniversary of losing her husband and daughters.

What would the one-year anniversary of Dad leaving Mom be like?

I didn't get far down that road before the doorbell rang again. All three of them were there. I think I acknowledged Wes and Tristan as they bustled in and headed immediately to the kitchen, but I wasn't sure. Megan captured all of my attention.

Would she always be able to make it seem as if the world stopped?

According to Mom, that would wear off. I couldn't imagine it. I didn't want to imagine it.

"Hi." I reached for the baking dishes she had stacked on top of each other. "Let me grab those."

"Thanks." Megan released them to me and went up on her tiptoes to brush her lips across mine. "Hi, back."

If I hadn't had the dishes, I would have followed up and made the greeting last longer, but given the houseful of guests, it was probably just as well that I didn't. "I think everyone's in the kitchen. You ready for tomorrow?"

Megan groaned and waggled her hand from side to side. "Ish? We're as ready as we're going to be. I checked with some of the other shops on the street and decided to go ahead and open two hours earlier than usual for Black Friday. No one's doing any super early morning doorbusters, thank goodness, but opening at eight is still not high on my list of exciting ways to spend the day after Thanksgiving."

I chuckled and set the dishes on the counter. "The joy of retail."

"You know it." Megan shook her head, then brightened. "But I have three new employees. They're all going to come in and work for part of the day, so it shouldn't be as crazy as it might have been otherwise. At this point, I'm so ready for massive numbers of customers, I'm going to be disappointed if we don't get them."

"Well, I'm praying you do." Kayla beamed at Megan. "And I'm so excited for you having employees again."

"Me, too." Austin nodded to underscore his words. "You were headed toward burnout. Again."

Megan shrugged, but she didn't deny it.

I was also glad, but that joy was tempered somewhat by knowing that from now until the new year was going to be her busy season. Which meant our relationship wasn't her priority, even if it might be mine.

"All the food is ready. And it smells wonderful." Mom looked around at the gathering of my friends and beamed. "Should we eat?"

I could get behind that. "Let's. I thought we could set up a buffet here on the counter and then I have the table set in the dining room."

There were murmurs of assent and before long, everyone had pulled together to set up the serving area so we could all fill our plates.

Mom glanced at me. "Cody, since you're the host, why don't you pray and you can carve the turkey."

My eyebrows lifted. "I'll pray, definitely, but you should carve. You're much better at it."

Everyone chuckled, but I was gratified to see Mom's cheeks pink with pleasure. She nodded.

I held out my hand to Megan and the other to Mom. Before long, we stood in a loose circle, holding hands, and I bowed my head.

"Dear Jesus, thank You. Thank You for this group of friends. For my mom. For the blessings we all have in You. Bless this food to our bodies, and our bodies to Your service. In Your name, amen." I squeezed Megan's hand and added to my prayer in my thoughts. *Thank You for Megan. Help me to know how to show her just how much I love her.*

## 26

## MEGAN

"Great job, guys. Thank you. I couldn't have done it without you." I offered each of my new employees a high five. They laughed, but joined in. I sighed. What I wanted—more than anything else—was to sit down and take off my shoes. "Go home. Get some sleep. I'll see Linda tomorrow morning at nine thirty, right?"

Linda nodded. "Yes, ma'am."

I fought a wince. The girl was a high school junior and she ma'amed and sirred everyone. Which was super polite and seemed to go over well with the customers, but it made me feel old.

"I really am fine with everyone calling me Megan. If it's comfortable for you, of course."

Linda winced. "I'll try. My parents have drilled it into me for years."

I chuckled. "It's a good habit. For the rest of you, I'm still hammering out the schedule and I'll shoot an email by the end of tomorrow letting you know your hours for next week. I don't see any reason you can't get the schedule you all requested. I just need to put it on the grid and make sure it's got the coverage we need. Okay?"

Everyone murmured assent. They said their goodbyes and made their way to the front of the store. I unlocked the door to let them out and relocked it behind them before blowing out a breath. I had a few things that *had* to be done as part of closing the store, but I wasn't going to spend time on any of the "would be nice to do" items.

I was beat.

A knock on the door made me jump. I spun and the spike of adrenaline dissipated as I spotted Cody.

I put one hand over my chest as I unlocked the door to let him in. "Way to freak a girl out."

"Sorry. I'm sorry." Cody was fighting not to laugh. "I didn't mean to. I thought you saw me hurrying down the sidewalk when you let everyone out."

I shook my head and relocked the door.

Cody slipped his arms around me and pulled me close. He lowered his lips to mine and all the thoughts drained out of my head as he kissed me.

"Well, hi." I eased back, but stayed in his loose embrace. "Was your day as good as mine?"

"Probably better, since I was off. I almost came by, but I didn't want to distract you on a hopefully busy day."

"Super busy, but I would have been glad to see you. Come on back, I just have a few things to do so I can head home." I stepped out of his arms and aimed toward the office. I'd already closed out the register, so it really was a matter of putting the cash drawer in the safe and shutting down the office machines.

"Today was good?" He leaned against the door frame.

I felt his eyes on me as I picked up the cash and squatted by the safe. I glanced over my shoulder at him. "Best Black Friday I think we've ever had. I'd have to verify it with Grandma, but honestly, if she had better, I think I would remember. It was amazing. It helped a lot that C. J.—you remember my first author to do an in-person event?"

Cody nodded.

"Well. She's been spreading the word everywhere she goes, apparently. So many people came in today and mentioned that she'd told them about the place. I should give her a commission."

"Or maybe just ask her back for another signing?" Cody grinned.

"Oh, definitely. That's a fantastic idea. But I still might send her flowers as a thank you." I spun the dial on the safe and checked the handle to ensure it was locked, then stood. "What did you do with your day if you weren't working?"

"Lots and lots of dishes."

I laughed. "We offered to help."

"I know. But you clearly didn't catch the look Mom gave me. I won't lie, I thought because she did that she'd stay around after everyone left and help, but nope. She headed out right after you."

"Aw." I faked a sad face for him. Of course, if I'd known his mom was going to leave, I might have stayed around longer.

Something still felt a little off between Cody and me, and I didn't know how to fix it. Or even what it was. But some quiet time snuggled on the couch probably wouldn't hurt it. "She seems like she's doing really well."

"Yeah. I think she is. I don't always understand it, but she said something yesterday that got me thinking. I'm going to work on forgiving my dad."

My eyebrows lifted. "Good for you."

He sighed and ran a hand through his hair. "Yeah. I'm not sure what that means in terms of meeting his new girlfriend, though. If I forgive him, do I have to play happy family like none of this happened?"

I shook my head. "No. I'm pretty sure forgiving someone doesn't mean you have to have a restored relationship. Restoration requires a lot more—repentance, for one."

"Ha. Well good luck on that. Dad still leaves messages explaining how he didn't really do anything wrong." Cody waved his words away. "I didn't mean to get into all of that. I wanted to come celebrate a big day with you. You probably had some kind of dinner, right?"

I didn't love how he shifted the topic away from his parents, but I could also understand not wanting to belabor it. Kind of. "Can I ask a question?"

He looked confused. "Of course."

"Is it that you don't want to talk about your parents at all, or you just don't want to talk about them with me?" I pressed my lips together. Was that too blunt? I was tired and had very little tact left after some of the customer interactions we'd had today. Which probably meant I shouldn't have pushed right now, but I didn't want him to keep doing this. If we were a team—and to me, being in love meant we were—then he needed to be okay talking to me about his feelings.

Even the ugly ones.

His Adam's apple bobbed as he swallowed. "Mostly at all. But also...I guess I'm worried you're going to realize I come from a damaged family and decide I'm not worth the risk."

"Oh, Cody." I shook my head and crossed so I could wrap my arms around him and lay my head on his chest. "You didn't have anything to do with this. Your dad made a choice. It's on him. Even if things between him and your mom were terrible, he had choices of how to handle things that would have been better than the one he made. And none of that is your fault."

My heart broke for him all over again. I hadn't really thought that a grownup would have those same questions or feelings that I'd seen so often with the kids I'd worked with when I'd been a social worker. But why not? His world had shifted. Maybe he didn't have to deal with alternating houses depending on whose week it was, but things in his family had still been broken and were getting rearranged.

He took a deep breath. His heart beat steadily under my cheek, and his arms tightened around me. "You're sure?"

"Of course, I'm sure." I tipped my head back so I could see his face. "I love you. Nothing's going to change that."

He closed his eyes and nodded once. "Okay."

I squeezed him before stepping back. "As to dinner, yes. We ate. I ordered from the café for everyone and we took turns wolfing it down in the back room."

"Yum."

I shrugged. "I can't complain. We were busy, and I needed that more than a leisurely dinner. But."

"But?"

"I bought an ice cream cake for tonight."

"To celebrate?"

I grinned. "That's the beauty of ice cream cake. It can celebrate a record-breaking sales day, or it can console a miserable start to the biggest six weeks in retail."

He laughed. "Is it big enough to share with someone you love?"

"It absolutely is. Are you asking to follow me home?"

"I am."

I reached into the desk drawer for my purse, snagged my keys off the desk, and pointed a finger at him. "Then you're in luck. Maybe you can take a look at my top three apartment contenders and help me figure out which one I should go with."

Cody drew in a breath like he was about to speak, then let it out. His smile was tight. "I can do that."

I'd driven today. I wasn't sure how late I'd end up needing to stay and hadn't felt like walking home in the pitch black if it was late. There were street lights, and it was reasonably safe, but also, if I was moving, I'd wanted to get a feel for how hard it was to park in the morning.

We walked through the store and I flipped off the lights before opening the door so we could leave, and locking it behind us.

I pointed down the street to my car. "I'm down there."

"I know. I'm right behind you."

I squinted down the street. Sure enough. "Nice. That's handy."

"It is." Cody took my hand and we headed to our cars. He opened my door and waited until I was settled before leaning in. "I'll see you at your place in a minute."

He shut my door.

Austin had done the same thing for me on numerous occasions, but boy, when my brother did it, it didn't leave me with the feeling of being cherished like Cody's actions had.

I buckled up, started the car, and eased away from the curb.

Cody followed me home and pulled up behind me in front of my townhouse. Or, I guess, Austin's townhouse.

I frowned.

I really didn't want to move out.

I shook my head and gathered my things before stepping out of my car and making sure it was locked. I opened the front door and let Cody in ahead of me. "Cake's in the freezer, if you want to get it out. I've been dreaming of comfy clothes for the past two hours. You don't mind if I run up and change, do you?"

He shook his head and started toward the kitchen.

I dropped my keys on the table by the door, kicked off my shoes under it, and darted up the stairs to my bedroom. It was a little odd shimmying out of my work clothes knowing Cody was downstairs in the kitchen, but I pushed the thoughts away before I could linger too long and take myself places I didn't need to go. I pulled on sweatpants, a long-sleeved T-shirt, and thick socks before heading downstairs.

Cody looked up from his study of the ice cream cake when I entered the kitchen. "We're just cutting this in half, right?"

I crossed to the island and frowned. Technically, the cake probably served four. It was about four inches across. But tonight was for celebrating. What better way to do that than overindulge in ice cream? "Sure. Why not live life on the edge."

Cody snorted. He turned and drew one of the chef knives out of the knife block and proceeded to slice the cake in half. "Plate or bowl?"

I scooted around behind him and grabbed bowls from the cupboard. "Ice cream equals bowl."

"Sure. But cake equals plate."

I shook my head. "Ice cream trumps cake. Always."

He laughed. "So if you have ice cream served on top of a piece of cake, you—"

"Use a bowl. Duh." I frowned at him. "You'd put it on a plate?"

Cody shrugged and picked up the fork I put next to his bowl. "I don't consider that a failing. Why are you using a fork if you're eating out of a bowl?"

"Seriously?"

"To use your words, duh." He winked. "Bowls require spoons."

"You know where they are. Or, you could live on the edge." I stabbed my fork into the ice cream cake and wiggled off a bite that had some of both parts. "Mmm."

I carried it over to the kitchen table and sat.

Cody followed. He sat beside me instead of across and

scooted his chair so his leg pressed against mine. "Tell me about your apartment contenders."

"Hang on." I pushed back my chair and stood, then hurried into the living room to gather the printed sheets I'd been making notes on. I went back to the kitchen and set them beside Cody's elbow. "Here."

"You printed them?"

I shrugged. "I think better on paper. I know our generation is supposed to be all about the technology, but there are some things paper does better."

He snickered. "You keep telling yourself that."

I gave his arm a light slap before tapping the top sheet of paper. "This is the complex Austin and Kayla are in now. I could probably get their exact apartment if I wanted, but they have some ground floor units available too, and those have a little garden space instead of a balcony."

"You garden?"

"Well, no. But I could." I frowned. I didn't do a lot with the tiny backyard of the townhouse, but that didn't mean I was never going to.

"Uh-huh." Cody tipped his head to the side. "It's safer not to have a ground floor entrance."

"You sound like my brother."

"We both love you." Cody waited until I met his gaze, then held it. "You know that, right?"

His intense eye contact continued to do things to my insides that I wasn't sure how to handle. Especially after he'd proven how quickly he could—and would—shut me out when he was dealing with his own problems.

I bit my lip. "I love both of you, too."

Tiny lines formed between his eyebrows. "The same way?"

Ugh. Was he really going to push this right now? We'd said the "L" word before. And I meant it.

I sighed and looked away. "No. But I'm not sure how smart that is."

"What do you mean?"

"You pushed me away and shut me out." The words tumbled out before I could stop them. I didn't love the slight whine—the younger sister whine—that was there, but I couldn't stop it, either. I paced to the other side of the kitchen, unable to sit still. "I don't want to be your fair-weather girlfriend. If I'm in this—if we're in this—then it's a two-way street. I share my problems, you share yours. You don't shut me down and build walls because you're...I don't know what you thought you were doing. Protecting me?"

Cody's lips thinned and his jaw ticked.

A tiny part of me wanted to take the words back and apologize for making him angry. The other part of me was ready to just have it done. For good. Whatever way that ended up happening.

My stomach clenched. Okay, not whatever way. I really didn't want it to end in him walking away permanently. But if he couldn't treat me like an equal, then that was what would have to happen.

He blew out a breath. "I'm sorry. I really am. And yeah, I guess I thought I was protecting you."

"I've been around divorced people before. It's not that uncommon."

Cody blanched, but he nodded. "I was more trying to protect you from me. Like I said at the store, what if I end up like my dad?"

I snorted. My hand flew up to cover my face as I started to laugh.

He stared at me a moment before shaking his head. "Glad I amuse you."

I held up a finger and struggled to get myself under control.

"You can't protect someone from hypothetical futures. That's not a thing."

He blinked. "I wasn't—that's not..."

I took a deep breath and pushed the last of the giggles away before turning what Kayla called my "teacher look" on him. "Go ahead."

He shook his head. "No. You're right. It's exactly what I was trying to do. Does it help at all if I reminded you that it's because I love you?"

I crossed back to the table and wormed my way onto his lap. I rested my head on his shoulder and wound my arms around his neck, basking in the warmth of his arms when they clamped around me. "It helps a little. But I hope you'll get it through your head that we're a team. I love you. We're in this together. And for clarity's sake, I'm going to remind you that 'together' means we fight back-to-back, you don't push me into a cave and try to handle everything on your own."

"Noted." His arms tightened in a brief squeeze. "It won't happen again."

"If it does, I'm kicking your butt."

He chuckled. "That's fair. Push you into a cave, huh?"

I shrugged. "I might be reading too much fantasy. There are too many instances of heroes pushing women aside while they, as they're all big and manly, try to handle the attacking hordes."

"Well, if it works—"

"That's the thing, it never does. Not until the woman breaks out of her protective prison and comes to stand at his side. *That's* when they win."

"All right. Point taken. Do I need to apologize again?"

"No. You're forgiven."

"Then can I eat this cake before the ice cream is completely melted and it's a disgusting mess?"

I brushed a kiss over his lips and slid off his lap. "I guess we wouldn't want ice cream cake to go to waste."

"Exactly." He put a big bite in his mouth before flipping the top paper over to reveal the second apartment complex. He frowned in concentration as he chewed.

I stirred my cake and ice cream together. It was already nearly inedible as far as I was concerned, but its sacrifice hadn't been in vain.

It felt like Cody and I were truly back on the same page.

Finally.

# 27

# CODY

I'd been trying to figure out how to approach Austin since Friday. Ice cream cake with Megan had fixed a lot of things between us, and I was grateful. But I really didn't like any of the apartment options she was considering. I'd said as much. When I'd asked about the complex where Noah lived and where Scott and I had also lived previously, she'd just shrugged. It had taken a lot of prodding to get her to admit her budget limitations.

And while tackling the living situation problem she was facing probably fell into the category of butting in and trying to save her, I couldn't just walk away.

I parked in the learning center lot and looked around. There were a handful of cars, but not as many as I'd expected for a Wednesday afternoon. I pushed open the door and climbed out, hunching my shoulders against the cold breeze that whipped across the parking area. Winter—or at least fall—was finally making itself known. Maybe I should've grabbed my jacket off the passenger seat, but I shut the car door and hurried toward the main entrance.

I wasn't likely to freeze before I got there.

"Can I help you, sir?"

I smiled at the security guard. "I was hoping to speak to Austin Campbell. I'm a friend. Cody Miller."

"One moment." The guard looked down at the desk. Maybe he was checking an allowed list? Or texting Austin? Who knew. I could speculate all day, though, and have a good time doing it.

He looked up. "He's up in the art room on two. There are stairs or you can use the elevator down the hall. You'll need this."

I took the lanyard the guard offered and looped it around my neck before heading to the stairs. The subtle sneer in the guard's voice when he'd mentioned the elevator had been enough to convince me I'd never use that option in his presence unless I was visibly injured. Not that I was liable to be at the learning center often. Tutoring wasn't my thing—unless it was on the receiving side.

There were signs at the top of the stairs pointing toward various departments and rooms. I scanned for the art room and headed in that direction.

Murmured conversation drifted out into the hallway as I passed classrooms and what were probably offices on my way to a big, open space full of light. I peeked in the door.

"I just think—" The woman speaking broke off and shot me a polite smile. "Can I help you?"

"I was looking for Austin. The security guy said I'd find him here."

Austin glanced over. "Hey, man. Can you give me five? You can sit in my office if you want."

"Okay." I lifted my eyebrows. "Where's that?"

Austin laughed and told me the room number.

I tapped my forehead with two fingers in a mock salute before stepping back into the hall to look above the art room door. It started with a two. So did Austin's office number. So it was probably on this floor.

I retraced my steps to the stairs and studied the signs again before heading in the opposite direction. I only got turned around once before finding an office with Austin's name in big letters on a plaque beside it.

It was strange going in without him there, but the door had been open. So I took a seat at the small round table that filled the corner of Austin's office and let my gaze wander around the room.

I was finishing a sudoku on my phone when Austin came in, and shut the door behind him.

"Sorry. That was more than five. I love having an art program. I think it's fantastic to be able to provide that extracurricular that kids can't always work into their schedules for credit, but I just don't know about having a gallery night at the end of the semester."

I frowned. "Why wouldn't you?"

"Seriously? You're on her side?"

"You're not?" I shook my head. "These kids are working hard and producing something they can show off. Why wouldn't you let them? In fact, you ought to talk to the artists at the Torpedo Factory and see if any of them wanted to have a mini-showing here as part of it. That'd help the kids feel even more legit, and maybe strike up opportunities for mentorship with professional artists, and it could be a community event that would drum up interest and support for the center."

Austin stared at me.

"What?"

"When did you become an event planner?"

I laughed. "This fall. Got thrust on me, but I find I kind of like it. Don't tell Mr. Ballentine, though. I don't actually want to only do fundraisers as my job."

Austin grinned and held up a finger. "One condition."

"Name it."

"You help us with our events."

"Sure. I can do that. Or, well, Megan and I can. I couldn't do any of this without her help."

Austin's gaze narrowed. "Tell me more."

I fought the urge to shift in my seat. "You're good at that."

"Uh-huh. No deflecting. This is my sister."

"You know I love her."

Austin's eyebrows lifted but he didn't speak.

"That's actually kind of why I'm here."

"If you want permission to marry her, you need to talk to my dad. And he'll probably mention how outdated it is to ask and how Megan's her own woman and capable of deciding her future on her own."

I laughed. "I wasn't actually going with permission. But I do plan to just touch base with your dad. I was—"

"Hold up." Austin held up a hand. "You're seriously already thinking marriage? You haven't been dating that long."

"No. But we've known each other for years. Been hanging out for years. I loved her like a sister for years. So maybe the change in that love is newer—probably not as new as you think —but it's not like we just met and this is some kind of weird love-at-first-sight thing."

"All right. You're right." He frowned. "I don't like thinking of my sister like that."

I grinned. "That's probably a good thing."

"Eww." Austin picked a pen up off the table and chucked it at me.

I batted it down. "As I was saying, that's not why I'm here. Or only tangentially." I licked my lips. "I don't think it's right for you to kick her out of the townhouse."

"We're not kicking her out. We just—" Austin glanced over

his shoulder at the door and leaned forward, lowering his voice. "Kayla wants to start trying for a baby. If it works, we're going to need the space and we'd rather not have to move in a big rush."

Big rush? "Don't babies take nine months?"

Austin blew out a breath. "Yeah, but—"

"But your sister is looking at places she can rent for right around a grand. You know what kind of places those are."

He winced. "She can afford more than that."

"She doesn't think so." I rubbed the back of my neck. We'd gone a few rounds over text about her budget. Megan wasn't willing to pay herself more than she already was until the store had shown an increase in profit for a year. It was probably good business sense, but that was in direct conflict with wanting to take care of her. And I still hadn't quite figured out how to reconcile—for her or for me—my desire to provide for and protect her with her need to not feel as if I thought she was incapable of doing both on her own.

"Stubborn." Austin's face scrunched up. "You really want to marry that?"

I chuckled. "I really do. And if there's a way for you and Kayla to back off a little on the moving thing, then I could convince her it's a good plan and she could move into my place and you could have the townhouse and everyone would be happy."

"Just to clarify, the order of operations here is you convince her, you get married, and then she moves into your place. Right?"

Heat crawled up my neck. "Yes. Definitely."

"Just checking." Austin tapped tented fingers against his lips. "Any idea on the time frame we're talking?"

"I thought I might propose after the gala."

"That's—" Austin paused and I could practically hear the math in his head. "Seventeen days."

I nodded.

"And then?"

I held out my hands. "I don't know what kind of wedding she's going to want. Or how fast she'll be able to plan it. I don't imagine we'll get married before the end of the year though."

I didn't really want to elope. Maybe I didn't care about an enormous and fancy to-do, but I wanted Mom to be able to dress up. I wanted to see Megan at the top of the church aisle coming toward me in something white and floaty. I wanted to have that party afterward with our friends and family and good food.

"It's a busy season for the bookstore. This would be a terrible time to elope."

There was that, too. I looked at Austin. "So maybe around Easter? Just after? Sometime in the late spring, early summer?"

"All right. I'll talk to Kayla. I think we can swing a six-month lease with the landlord, especially if he knows we're for sure leaving at the end of it. I get the feeling it's more about uncertainty for him than anything else."

"Question."

Austin's eyebrows lifted.

"Why don't you just pay him for the year whether you stay that long or not? It's not as if that would even make a dent for you." It was one thing not to be extravagant and spend on stupid things. But that wasn't what this was at all. "And if the complex ended up with a little extra cash, maybe that would keep him from having to raise the rent on someone who couldn't afford it."

"That's a point. All right. We'll do that. I'll explain to Kayla—but I'm warning you, you'd better propose at the gala. Kayla won't be able to keep it under wraps forever."

I snickered. "Guess I'd better see about a ring."

I stood.

Austin stood, too, and held out his hand. "Guess you'd better. And I'm serious about you helping with the art thing."

"For sure. Send me an email with details and I'll start thinking about it. Who's hosting poker Friday?"

"Tristan, I think. I'll ask in the group chat."

I made my way to the door of Austin's office and rested my hand on the knob. "Thanks, man."

"Treat her right, or I'll know about it." Austin pointed a finger at me. "I'll put Dad's cell number in that email for you."

I laughed as I opened the door. It probably wasn't a bad idea to let Megan's folks know my intentions. Hopefully, they'd be as okay with it as Austin. If they weren't? Well, Megan was her own woman. I'd let her deal with them.

I got through the halls and down the stairs to the front entrance more easily on the way out. I handed the lanyard to the security guard. "Thanks. Have a good one."

"Yes, sir."

I'd meant to ask about the whole security situation, but, unsurprisingly, had gotten distracted with the more important conversation. I spotted a group of teens heading toward the building, laughing and joking like they did. Each one had a lanyard around their neck.

Huh.

After the big to-do that had cost Austin and Kayla their jobs last year, I was still somewhat surprised that most of the rest of our group managed to stay under the radar enough that we didn't need to drag personal security around all the time. Maybe the guy at the entrance to the learning center was Austin's compromise.

Tristan was pushing for all of us to do more. But...ugh. I just didn't want to be that guy. I liked driving myself. Being my own person. Let alone not wanting to deal with whatever it would do to Megan's bookstore.

No, for now I was pretty happy that I was flying under the radar. I'd do what I could to keep it that way.

Back in my car, I checked the time and considered. I had tentative plans to swing by the bookstore and bring Megan dinner. But there was still time for me to visit a couple of jewelry stores. Especially if I stuck to the more boutique shops locally instead of trying to get across town to the big malls at Tyson's Corner.

If I didn't find what I was looking for? Well, there was always the Internet.

# 28

# MEGAN

"I'm so glad you asked me to come with you." Whitney looked around the dress shop with a glimmer in her eyes I wasn't sure I liked.

"I'm glad Scott didn't mind watching Beckett." This place was definitely not kid friendly. Which, okay, what dress shop was? But it felt like this one was worse than usual with its open cases of necklaces and tiaras. "This feels more like a bridal shop than a place for me to find a cocktail dress."

"Live a little." Whitney gestured to the far side of the room where there were racks of dresses that were not ivory or white. "The website said they specialize in evening wear as well. Probably over there."

Evening wear still seemed more...more than what I wanted. "I just wanted something that was a little jazzier than my current little black dress. I don't think I need to go all the way into evening wear."

Whitney frowned at me. "Did you not read the invitation to this fundraiser? It's black tie optional."

"Emphasis on *optional*. Right?" I blew out a breath and trailed after Whitney. I wasn't sure she even heard me. But if black tie was optional, then surely a cocktail dress would do. Wouldn't it? "I should just wear—"

"If you talk to me about that sad, poly-cotton blend catalog black dress again, I'm going to cry. It's great for funerals. Or maybe something like an industry cocktail party. It's not going to cut it for the Ballentine Christmas gala. Trust me." Whitney started flicking through the hangers on the first rack of long evening gowns. Every now and then, she'd pause on one, look over at me, then pull off a dress and hook it on her wrist.

"You need to check the size, don't you?" And the price? Please someone let me check the price!

"This isn't Macy's. You try it on. They order the right size. You tailor it."

I gulped. "I don't—we don't—have time for that. The gala is next Friday. That's not quite two weeks."

Whitney waved that off. "So we have them rush it. It's doable. I called to ask."

My stomach sank. It might be doable if I was married to a billionaire. But I wasn't. Or if I wanted to ask my billionaire brother or my billionaire boyfriend to finance things. And I didn't. "Maybe Macy's isn't such a bad idea."

"Seriously?" Whitney thrust the three dresses she'd pulled in my direction. "Go see about trying these on."

Since my options were to let the gowns—and I wasn't kidding myself into saying they weren't gowns—fall on the floor and probably be ruined somehow, or take them, I took them. I looked around and spotted a woman who clearly worked in the store and started easing in her direction.

"Did you need a fitting room?" The woman reached for the gowns and I released them into her care with a relieved breath.

"I guess. I'm not sure..."

She offered a sympathetic smile. "First big event?"

"I guess? Prom was a while ago. The invitation said black tie optional, and I really think this black dress I have at home will be fine." I'd finished my sentence even though the woman had started shaking her head when I got to "black dress."

"Not many people opt for cocktail under those circumstances. Let's get you set up and see what we see. When is the event?"

"The fifteenth?" I really hoped she'd gasp in horror and kick us out of her store for having the gall to look at such short notice.

But she just nodded. "I think we should be able to make that happen. Let's have a look."

I shot a glance in Whitney's direction. She was busy at the rack and had what looked like at least two other dresses set aside. Hopefully, they were for her, not me, because I'd caught a glimpse of one of the price tags and there was just no way.

"Here we are." The woman whipped a curtain aside and gestured me into a room of mirrors. "Try the red one first, I think. Step out here when you're in and I'll see what adjustments we need to make."

I managed a weak smile as she hooked the hangers on a bar and stepped out of the dressing room, closing the curtain with an expert flick of her wrist.

I pressed my fists to my eyes, but when I moved them away, I was still in the middle of what had to be the world's worst nightmare. I pinched my leg, close to tears when it hurt. So, fine. I'd try on some dresses and then make my excuses for why I couldn't possibly, and maybe I could order something online that would get here in time.

With a resolute nod, I shed my clothes and wriggled into the red dress. It was a darker red—verging on burgundy—at least. Not something that screamed, "Look at me!" But it was a halter-style with a deep V in the front and a swoop in the back that made it obvious I wouldn't be wearing a bra. I fought the urge to cross my arms over my chest as I looked in the mirror.

The rest of the dress, I kind of loved. It had a sort of deco feel with form-hugging seaming on the bodice, across my hips, and then about mid-thigh it flared out into floating waves. I'd call it almost mermaid-esque, except that brought up mental pictures of Morticia Adams mincing around and this was definitely not that.

I poked my head out of the curtain.

"Ready? Come out and stand on this pedestal." The woman was waiting right there. Hovering, even.

There went my dreams that she'd gotten busy and I could escape. I offered a tight smile and slipped out to do as she said.

"This is practically made for you." She circled me. I felt her fingers briefly at my waist and hip. "Let me get some shoes. I'm not sure you'd even need it hemmed."

"I don't—"

But the woman had already walked off, so my whispered, "need shoes" fell into empty air. I guessed I was getting shoes.

I surreptitiously looked at the price tag hanging on the side under my right arm. Oof. I could swing it. Barely. I'd just have to bring sandwiches or Cup-O-Noodle to work for lunch for a month or so instead of all the café ordering I'd been doing. That would probably be better for my waistline anyway. Even though I most often got salads, there was no way the dressing I drowned them in did anything to help with a lower or healthier calorie count.

"Here we go. These are just made for that dress."

They might as well have been. The color was a near perfect match, and they had the same style of seaming across the toes, with the addition of winking rhinestones in the crisscrossing straps.

I slid my feet into the shoes. "How'd you know my size?"

"I'm very good at what I do." The woman beamed. "You look ravishing. Was that your friend I saw you with?"

I nodded.

The woman held up a finger and disappeared. It wasn't long before she returned with Whitney in tow.

"Oh." Whitney's hand flew up to cover her mouth. "Cody is gonna die. That's the one. It's perfection."

Whitney drew a circle with her finger in the universal command for someone to turn.

I rolled my eyes but did a little twirl, secretly loving the way the bottom of the skirt flared out and spun around my ankles when I did.

"Sold. And it's a perfect fit." Whitney looked at the store associate, who nodded in agreement. "You were worried."

"Shouldn't I try on the others?" The dress might not be stoplight red, but there'd been a navy dress in there that would draw less attention.

"No. Because you don't mess with perfection." Whitney cocked her head to the side. "Unless you're telling me you don't love it?"

I sighed. I did love it. I didn't want to. I wasn't sure about the whole no-bra thing, but I couldn't deny that I looked good. "When am I ever going to wear it again?"

Whitney waved away my objection. "Please."

"I'm serious. I'm not spending this much on something I'm only going to wear once." Because a bookstore owner didn't exactly have black tie optional invitations coming around every other week.

Whitney scooted close and lowered her voice. "Did you forget who Cody is?"

"What does that have to do with anything?"

She grunted. "You could wear this to a Broadway show. Or out to a nice dinner in New York. Or Paris."

"Paris?" I had no plans to go to Paris with Cody. Or without Cody, for that matter. I mean, yeah, I'd love to go there. Hello, bucket list. But I couldn't buy a dress because I dreamed about going somewhere to wear it.

"My point is, he can afford to make it possible for you to wear this as many times as you want."

"Oh." The whole billionaire thing. But I wasn't with him because of that. "I don't care about his money."

"No. I know. So does he. No worries there. But it doesn't mean you don't buy the dress."

I wasn't sure I followed her logic, but the fact was I needed a dress. I liked this one. It fit. I could afford it. Basically. And if I bought it now, I could go home and put on sweats and be done with this whole shopping excursion. "All right."

"Yay!" Whitney clapped her hands together. "Now I just need to find the right one for me and we'll be set. Can I use your changing room?"

"Let me get out of this first." I stepped down off the pedestal, wobbling slightly in the unusually high heels. I'd have to practice in them before next Friday so I didn't make a fool of myself.

I made quick work of getting back into my regular clothes.

The saleslady was standing close, ready to take the dress and shoes from me right as I stepped out. "I'll put these up at the register for you and be right back."

"Sure. Thanks." I tucked my hands in my pockets. "I'll hang here, I guess. You're going to show me your choices, right?"

Whitney grinned. "Of course, I am. Like you could get out of it."

I had the sinking suspicion this was going to take a lot longer than I wanted. Well, it had already taken longer than I wanted, so yeah. But honestly, Whitney seemed like she was looking forward to the whole thing.

Ridiculous.

Was it wrong to pray she found something fast so we could go have lunch together and then do something that wasn't related to buying overpriced, single-wear dresses?

The saleslady brought me over a chair and I passed time between Whitney showing off dresses by browsing some of the bestseller lists on various online e-book retailers. There were so many independent authors out there, I'd love to have more of them in the store. I hadn't run into any, so far, who weren't excited about the prospect of having even one copy of their book on a physical bookstore shelf.

Finally, after what felt like the whole day but was really only a little over an hour, Whitney landed on a navy-blue gown covered in so many sequins and little faux diamonds that she'd probably be visible a half-mile before she actually entered the room. But it looked great on her and she clearly loved it, so it worked.

We stowed our garment bags in the trunk of Whitney's car and agreed on hitting up Mia's for lunch, since we were close.

When we were settled and the server had delivered our drinks, Whitney leaned forward. "So? Tell me how things are with you and Cody."

I reached for my water and busied myself squeezing the lemon and stirring in the juice. "Good."

"Really? That's all I get? Things were weird for a couple of weeks—everyone noticed. Now you're saying it's good. Is it not working out?"

I glanced up, startled. "No. It's good. We fixed things. He was freaking about the situation with his parents."

Whitney nodded. "I can see that. It's a big change, no matter how old you are."

"Yeah. So, it shook him. Badly. But I think he's coping. Ish. He's at least not pushing me away to protect me from some hypothetical future where he divorces me anymore."

Whitney snickered. "That's...such a guy thing."

Was it? I shrugged. "So things are good with us."

"Then what's wrong?"

"I still don't know where to move. Austin and Kayla haven't brought it up, thankfully, but I know they have a deadline to get out of their apartment by the end of the month and none of the options I can find—that I can afford—are places I want to live."

"This area is such a strange mix of ridiculously high rent for nice places and equally ridiculous, but at least semi-affordable, rent in places where women shouldn't live alone."

"Exactly." I paused to take a drink. "I was actually thinking I might see if Jenna wanted a roommate."

"Isn't she going to be basically camping in Noah's remodel?"

I wrinkled my nose. "Is she? I missed that."

"I think that's what I remember her saying. Come January, she's going to bunk there so she can work in her off hours."

So much for that idea. Jenna—and Noah—would probably be fine with me joining her. But living in a construction zone sounded terrible.

"Why don't you tell Austin you need more time?"

"I guess I'm going to have to. I just hate to make him sign another year on their lease when he probably won't need the full year." I pushed my fingers between my eyebrows. "Maybe I should just explain that they can move in and I'll try to stay out of the way until I can find a place that makes sense."

"Why can't he pay for your lease someplace?"

"I'm sure he can, but I don't want that. I can support myself. I don't need a handout from my brother."

"Sorry." Whitney winced.

Maybe I should apologize for the harsh edge to my words, but I was tired of the implication that I needed bailing out. It seemed to come from all sides.

Rather than belabor the topic, I changed it. "We're all going to Wes's shop on Friday afternoon, right?"

I watched Whitney struggle with the change of subject, but she got there. "That's the plan. I still don't believe he has a pool in there and found a way to keep the whole store from being muggy as all get-out."

"He promises he does." I was with Whitney, though. Skeptical. Although I'd looked up a few of the private swimming lessons places Wes had mentioned at one point as his model, and the websites all showed indoor pools that didn't look steamy and miserable in the stands. Maybe technology had improved since they built the rec center—the last indoor pool I'd visited.

"I guess we'll find out Friday." Whitney shook her head. "Did you ever start that Little Free Library?"

"No. I could never quite work out the logistics of it. Instead, I let people know I'd have a small used book section starting in the new year. I buy back used books, they get a punch card for future discounts. Everyone wins." It wasn't exactly as amazing as I initially planned, but it made more sense than anything else I'd come up with. And this way, if I had too many copies of something or a book was in terrible shape, I could say no. Did it pain me to know some books were going to get tossed? Yes. But I couldn't save everything and everyone.

"Smart. Well, I've started a bag for some of the kid books Beckett is outgrowing. I'll be your first customer."

"You don't want to save them for the baby?"

Whitney frowned. "Given how long it's taking? Not really. I'm trying to adjust my mindset to only having Beckett."

I reached out and gently squeezed her hand. "I'm sorry."

"Thanks. Maybe I'll be wrong. I'm certainly praying for that. But I also am trying to be content where we are. Because if this is how God wants it? Then that's how I want things to be."

I got that. I was trying to be in that same space when it came to my own life. Particularly things with Cody. I hadn't lied when I told Whitney things were good. They were. But it felt a little like we were in a holding pattern now—where before the whole situation with his dad, it had seemed like we were on a path toward marriage. A future.

We'd talked about it in the early fall. Now, whenever I tried to nudge the conversation that direction, Cody didn't follow. It could be that I was being too subtle. Or maybe, as much as he loved me and I loved him, this was the place we needed to be for a while.

# 29

# CODY

My cheeks hurt. Three hours of smiling at people as they'd arrived, as they milled around during the cocktail time, and then as we'd chatted at our smaller dinner tables had given my face muscles more of a workout than I'd known was possible.

Now, finally, it was time for the speeches and donation pleas. And then, thank the Lord, it would be over.

Mr. Ballentine stood from his table, looked over at me with a nod, and made his way to the podium I'd had put on a platform at the front of the main seating area.

"Good evening, ladies and gentlemen. Thank you so much for coming tonight to our Christmas gala. I'd like to begin by thanking Cody Miller for putting the whole thing together. He got this project dropped in his lap at the beginning of September, with very little notice, and I have to say I don't think anyone would have known if I hadn't just spilled the beans."

Polite chuckles floated around the room. I fought not to squirm in my seat. As much as I appreciated Mr. Ballentine's approval, I didn't love getting called out in front of such a huge crowd.

"Cody, stand up so we can give you a round of applause."

Megan reached over and squeezed my hand. "Go on. You deserve it."

Her words meant more than any amount of applause. But still, it didn't do to disregard your boss when he asked you to do something, so I stood, did a quick turn and wave as the clapping roared around me, then sat.

"Was that terrible?" Megan had leaned close. Her breath tickled my ear, shooting little sparks of awareness through me.

"Pretty much, yes."

She laughed and took my hand under the table.

I fought to concentrate as Mr. Ballentine droned on. In all fairness to him, there wasn't much that would have captured my attention from Megan in her stunning burgundy gown. I'd kept her in my sights all evening—thankfully, she'd seemed content to stay nearby—and I would have sacrificed every dollar I had for five minutes alone with her.

Austin, seated on my left, nudged my foot.

I glanced over.

He nodded at his sister and waggled his eyebrows before mouthing, "Tonight?"

Nerves did the cancan in my stomach. I gave a slight nod, but I wasn't completely sure I could follow through. I had the ring in my pocket. I'd honestly been surprised it wasn't obvious, but the lines of the tuxedo were generous enough that it didn't show. I hadn't been able to keep it in the box, obviously, and that had caused its own set of problems. Half the night, I'd been trying to find reasons to check that it was still there. The other half I'd been convinced it wasn't and wondered how—or if—I'd be able to find it when the event was over.

Everyone around began to clap again. I'd missed Mr. Ballentine's speech. Oops. It was unlikely that he'd said anything I didn't already know, but hopefully I hadn't looked as distracted as I was.

The next part of the program moved quickly as four different recipients of Ballentine grants took five minutes to explain how they'd used the money and how grateful they were for our organization. Finally, Mr. Ballentine was back with a short—thank goodness—plea to all the donors, reminding them that the organization was wholly donor-supported and blah blah blah.

I glanced around, trying to be subtle. Nearly everyone at the tables I could see without being obvious was reaching for an envelope in the middle of the table or already writing on one. I let out a breath. Maybe this was going to be a success after all.

More than one person had stopped to talk to me about the food, and they'd been enamored to know that Season's Bounty was focused on local, sustainable fare. One more checkmark. Hopefully, Jackson and his wife, Paige, would see a bump in their own business from the event.

Megan squeezed my hand. "Stop worrying."

I turned to look at her. Everything in me relaxed. She was a soothing anchor.

"I know God's got this. I just can't seem to stop double-checking."

"What will you do with yourself, now that this is off your plate?" Her eyes sparkled in the light from the candle on the table and the fairy lights we'd strung between the balconies on the second level.

"Jackson asked if I'd agree to do the summer picnic. I said yes."

Megan laughed. "You've got the event planning bug."

"I guess. Maybe it's just that I know I have the best possible person to help me right here." I brought her hand up and brushed a kiss across her knuckles. "You will help, right?"

"Hmm." She gave me a sly grin. "I might have to check my

calendar. Plus, I'm not sure you can afford my new rates."

I tipped my head to the side. It seemed like as good an opening as any. Maybe it wasn't exactly what I'd had in mind—especially since our group of friends was all right here, pretending not to watch. But maybe, in other ways, that was what made it perfect. They'd been there for everything else—watching and pretending not to see—why break tradition?

I reached into my pocket and pulled out the thick platinum band sporting a trio of diamonds on top. "Will this work as a down payment?"

Megan's eyes widened and her free hand flew to her mouth. "Cody..."

"Megan." I held her gaze and squeezed the hand I held. "I love you. I don't want to live my life without you. You make everything brighter and full of joy. Even the hard things. Will you marry me?"

"Of course, I will. I love you." She flung herself into my arms as our friends started to clap. I glimpsed Kayla wiping her cheeks before Megan caught my face in her hands and kissed me.

"Put the ring on her finger before you drop it, man." Austin nudged my arm with his elbow. "You're making a spectacle of yourselves."

Megan, blushing prettily, eased back into her seat and held out her left hand.

I slid the ring onto her finger, then kissed it.

"Congratulations, Cody. Everyone, our event planner."

I turned and saw Mr. Ballentine grinning behind the microphone, clapping along with everyone in the building.

I stood and tugged Megan to her feet, then I pulled her close and dipped her back to seal our engagement with a proper kiss.

It might not have been what I planned, but from the crowd's roar, everyone seemed to agree it was exactly right.

# EPILOGUE

### Noah

I pushed my chair back and stood, along with the rest of the crew, clapping as Cody dipped Megan in some kind of Hollywood kiss. I chuckled a little and looked over at Jenna so I could give her an exaggerated eye roll. Show off.

She grinned and fanned her face.

"That's one way to end a fundraising dinner." Jenna tucked her hands in the pockets of the sparkly, wide-legged pants that she was wearing. "I bet that squeezes out at least another couple of grand from someone."

"Probably." I turned to study the crowd with her. Most of the guests were in the process of collecting their things and leaving. Some of the other Ballentine employees were moving around the tables and picking up the pledge envelopes before they had a chance to wander off in the wrong hands. I'd dodged that bullet this year, thankfully. Maybe I shouldn't find it awkward, but I always did.

"Cody, you need help with cleanup?"

Cody nodded, still gripping Megan's hand. "If you don't

mind? We have to stack the chairs and tables on the equipment racks. I can go get them rolled into place. If we all help, it shouldn't take too long."

"Yeah, why not?" Austin shrugged and glanced at Kayla. "You mind?"

"Of course not. What about the tablecloths?" Kayla tapped the table in front of her.

Cody looked around. "The caterer is supposed to collect them, but if you wanted to fold them and set them aside, it would make it easier."

"Sure thing. Ladies?" Kayla glanced at Whitney, Megan, and Jenna.

"It's better than stacking chairs." Jenna grinned. "First I need to see that ring."

Whitney squealed and clapped her hands. "Me, too!"

I shook my head. Women.

Cody was right, though, with all of us helping, the cleanup didn't take long. Within thirty—maybe forty—minutes, I was holding the door to my car open for Jenna. When she was in, I went around and climbed behind the wheel.

"Thanks for coming."

"You know I don't mind being a plus-one when you need one. Although, neither Wes nor Tristan had someone, so you probably would've been fine."

It was true. Of course, when I'd asked if they were bringing dates, they'd said they were. Thus Jenna. How was I supposed to know they wouldn't follow through?

"Probably. Still, hopefully it wasn't a horrible evening?"

"Not at all. The food was good. I enjoyed hearing more about the place where you work. In fact, I might reach out and let them know that I'm always happy to work low- or no-cost design work into my schedule if that's ever something they could use."

Jenna shrugged. "And you didn't have to go stag. Everyone won. I might have a thing in late January. I'll let you know."

"Absolutely. I owe you one."

She chuckled. "Are we keeping track now?"

"No. It's a figure of speech." I glanced over to double-check that she'd been joking. Looked like. Good. "You know you can always say no, right?"

"Duh. Of course. I was teasing. I've never minded being your backup."

Something in the way she said that made me glance over, but her face didn't reveal any clues. I was probably tired and imagining things. She said she didn't mind, so I'd take her at her word and be grateful neither of us was clinging to that ridiculous pact we'd made in college. Because thirty-three was just around the corner, but I still wasn't looking to settle down.

READ MORE in The Billionaire's Backup.

# ACKNOWLEDGMENTS

I'm grateful to so many people that I'm not sure where even I should begin. First, I guess, to you. The reader. Without you reading, there's very little point to writing beyond the enjoyment I get from putting words on the page and living, if only for brief snatches of time, in a world of my imagining. But knowing that I get to share that world with you makes the whole experience richer.

Hopefully for both of us.

To my family — your patience with me knows no bounds and I am grateful. So grateful. I will never take for granted the moments you give me to slip away and spend with my imaginary friends. Even if it means dinner is a little late or I forget to swap the laundry and have to run it a second time.

To my author friends, who are basically family at this point. Thank you for putting up with my whining and helping me brainstorm and for generally giving me a kick in the pants when it's been easier to complain about not writing than to actually sit down and put words on the page.

Also to C.J. Brightley and Heather Gray for letting me have them come to my pretend bookstore. Both ladies are wonderful writers and I hope you'll look them up and give their books a try.

And last, but never least, I am grateful to Jesus for giving me stories and making it possible for me to put words on the page in the first place. It's my prayer that you will be challenged, enriched, encouraged, and refreshed from spending time in these books.

# WANT A FREE BOOK?

If you enjoyed this book and would like to read another of my books for free, you can get a free e-book simply by signing up for my newsletter on my website.

# OTHER BOOKS BY ELIZABETH MADDREY

Billionaire Next Door

The Billionaire's Nanny

The Billionaire's Best Friend

The Billionaire's Secret Crush

The Billionaire's Backup

The Billionaire's Teacher

The Billionaire's Wife

Postcards, A Novel

So You Want to Be a Billionaire

So You Want a Second Chance

So You Love to Hate Your Boss

So You Love Your Best Friend's Sister

So You Have My Secret Baby

So You Need a Fake Relationship

So You Forgot You Love Me

Hope Ranch Series

*Hope for Christmas*

*Hope for Tomorrow*

*Hope for Love*

*Hope for Freedom*

*Hope for Family*

*Hope at Last*

Peacock Hill Romance Series

*A Heart Restored*

*A Heart Reclaimed*

*A Heart Realigned*

*A Heart Redirected*

*A Heart Rearranged*

*A Heart Reconsidered*

Arcadia Valley Romance – Baxter Family Bakery Series

*Loaves & Wishes*

*Muffins & Moonbeams*

*Cookies & Candlelight*

*Donuts & Daydreams*

The 'Operation Romance' Series

*Operation Mistletoe*

*Operation Valentine*

*Operation Fireworks*

*Operation Back-to-School*

*Prefer to read a box set? Find the whole series here.*

The 'Taste of Romance' Series

*A Splash of Substance*

*A Pinch of Promise*

*A Dash of Daring*

*A Handful of Hope*

*A Tidbit of Trust*

*Prefer to read a box set? Get the series in two parts! Box 1 and Box 2.*

The 'Grant Us Grace' Series

*Wisdom to Know*

*Courage to Change*

*Serenity to Accept*

*Pathway to Peace*

*Joint Venture*

*Prefer to read a box set? Grab the whole series here.*

The 'Remnants' Series:

*Faith Departed*

*Hope Deferred*

*Love Defined*

Stand alone novellas

*Kinsale Kisses: An Irish Romance*

*Luna Rosa (part of A Tuscan Legacy)*

For the most recent listing of all my books, please visit my website.

# ABOUT THE AUTHOR

USA Today bestselling author Elizabeth Maddrey is a semi-reformed computer geek and homeschooling mother of two who lives in the suburbs of Washington D.C. When she isn't writing, Elizabeth is a voracious consumer of books. She loves to write about Christians who struggle through their lives, dealing with sin and receiving God's grace on their way to their own romantic happily ever after.

facebook.com/ElizabethMaddrey

instagram.com/ElizabethMaddrey

amazon.com/Elizabeth-Maddrey/e/B00A11QGME

bookbub.com/authors/elizabeth-maddrey

www.ingramcontent.com/pod-product-compliance
Lightning Source LLC
Chambersburg PA
CBHW031550240626
47153CB00002B/447